DEADLY

BY

SYLVIA MCDANIEL

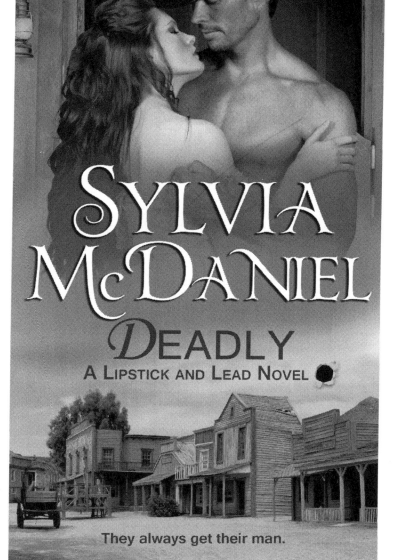

SYLVIA McDANIEL

DEADLY

A LIPSTICK AND LEAD NOVEL

They always get their man.

Chapter One

Meg McKenzie stood in yet another hotel room, another dusty frontier town, on the hunt for yet another wayward criminal. She pulled out her Baby Dragoon revolver from her holster, spun the cylinder, and checked to make sure a bullet graced every chamber. With a gentle tug, she checked the leather case, and then she slid the weapon back into its holster, just a fingertip away.

She wore her gun low on her hips just below the waist of her father's hand-me-down pants. No fancy dress for Meg.

"The McKenzie sisters are about to strike again," her sister Ruby said, as she slid her own gun into the hidden sheath-like case neatly tucked beneath her petticoats. Her saloon dress dipped low in the front, to the edge of her breasts, the straps completely off her shoulder. She flipped her blonde hair back and checked her image one last time in the mirror. "How many men have we brought to justice?"

In the last year, they had learned the bounty hunter trade and continued the legacy of their father. With his death, the girls had been forced to find work in order to save the farm and in a desperate moment chosen their

1

current path. Meg and Ruby chased wanted criminals, and Annabelle maintained their family farm. At least until they returned and could join their sister once again. They'd never intended to make this their lifelong occupation. Just long enough to pay off the mortgage on the farm.

"At least twelve. Seems we've spent more time on the road than we have at home," Meg said, homesickness surging through her like an open wound.

"Just as well with Sheriff Zach still coming out to the house looking for you."

"Zach Gillespie wants a quiet, retiring woman who wears a dress and has tea parties. Do I look like that kind of woman?" Meg shook her head. Her heartache was nearly healed, though she could never look at Zach again without smiling and remembering him naked.

Ruby laughed. "No, but you could if you wanted."

Meg glanced out the window. The glow of the setting sun cast a shadow, but she could still see the dress shop down the street. After she'd spoken to this no-name town's sheriff, she'd spent time in the little dress shop, gazing and fingering the available dresses and the patterns of the latest fashions. Inside these pants, a woman longed to emerge and live like a lady, not the rough bounty hunter façade of a life she lived now.

"I'll never change for any man. As soon as we pay off the farm, then I'm going to begin my life and do things the way I want to," Meg vowed. She had dreams, she had plans, and soon, it would be her time.

Circumstances required she dress like a man. But the girly-girl in her had a hidden vice. Her own little secret pleasure…a rouge pot. Just a tiny bit of color to her lips helped her remember she was a girl. A girl who had the same desires as every other woman.

As the sun continued its descent, cloaking the street in darkness, she knew it would soon be time to carry out their plan.

"Your weapon's ready?" Meg asked one last time. She worried about Ruby and hated leaving her alone with the criminal they were chasing.

"Yes," Ruby said. "And you'll be there with me?"

"Until you give me the signal."

"Remind me how much this guy's worth?"

"Five hundred dollars." This could be their last bounty if things worked out like Meg planned.

Ruby smiled and walked over to the window. "Papa would be so proud of us."

Meg shook her head, knowing their Papa would have been furious at the chances they were taking. "Maybe secretly, but he'd tell us we should have taken jobs in town. He'd have been more concerned about our safety than how quickly we were paying off the farm."

Ruby turned, her mouth twisted with displeasure. "No. I will never become a maid again. Never. This last year has been exciting, and criminals are too stupid to realize a pretty woman is going to pull a gun on them."

Meg nodded. In the last year, Ruby had changed and matured. She'd gone from a love-crazed girl to being driven to catch as many low-life criminals as they could. She enjoyed the chase, the thrill. "Annabelle said we need six hundred dollars more, and the farm will be mortgage free."

"Old man Bates will fall out of his chair when you pay off the note."

Meg smiled. "Annabelle said he wasn't too friendly when she took in the payment on the note this year. He had plans on repossessing the farm. Too bad."

"I miss Annabelle," Ruby said, with a wistful whine in her voice.

"Yeah, me too. But someone had to take care of the farm, and she's good at the bookkeeping."

Meg glanced out the window and watched as men entered the saloon, the doors swinging wide. Now was when her nerves had her stomach rolling, her heart racing, and fear choking her throat. What if something happened to Ruby? How could she live with herself?

"The drinking has begun," Meg said quietly, listening to the music spilling out into the street from the local saloon.

"And will soon end for Simon Trudeau," Ruby said laughing, her eyes shining with excitement.

There was no fear in her gaze, only excited anticipation. Only reckless adventure. And that worried Meg.

"The horses are saddled and ready to go. Give me your satchel, and I'll secure it on your horse. I can't go in with you, or they'll make the connection between us." Meg stared at her youngest sister, fear sitting like a pit in the bottom of her stomach. "You're all set? Your weapons are ready?"

Ruby shrugged. "My knife is in my boot. My gun is in my holster." She smiled. "And my charm is ready to ensnare this poor bastard."

Meg was always stunned at how much Ruby enjoyed the chase. They used her as the bait, and then Meg would pull a gun on some poor unlucky bastard, and Ruby would tie him up. Every time before a catch, her blue eyes would sparkle and shine with excitement. She loved being a bounty hunter. She loved catching criminals, and most of all she loved playing her many roles.

They'd done everything from the distraught woman, pregnant wife, and now a saloon girl. Wherever the unlawful resided, they'd lay a trap and ensnare the wanted.

"Where's your hat?" Ruby asked.

"Right here," Meg said and picked up her black cowboy hat and pulled it down tight.

But for Meg it was just a job. A means to an end. A way to earn a decent living and pay for the farm. Once they had enough money, she would retire and never chase another criminal. But Ruby loved the chase, the entrapment, and the thrill of turning in the longrider.

Music echoed down the street, and Meg knew it was time. "Are you ready?"

Ruby smiled, her lips painted red, her cheeks tinted with the same color. "Let's get this done, so we can go home for a while."

"Let's go."

The two walked out of the hotel room together, but once they reached the street, Ruby walked to the saloon alone.

Meg gave her just enough time to get inside, and then she followed. Time to go to work.

*

Ruby strolled down the street toward the saloon, her head held high, a smile on her lips. In the last year, she was no longer the love-obsessed young woman who only wanted to find herself a husband. Now, she wanted anything, but a man, in her life. They were worthless dogs. She'd made it her mission to put as many of the loathsome jackeroos behind bars.

Where before she'd dreamed of hearts and flowers,

now she dreamed of tricking outlaws into believing they could have her, only to capture them in her net and hogtie them before she and Meg carried them off to the law. She was ridding the world of evil bastards who preyed on women and children and killed innocents. And she loved her new life.

Pushing open the doors to the saloon, she stopped and glanced around. Men congregated at gaming tables, talking or just staring down into their drinks. Her gaze swept the room, looking over the clientele. Some men came for the women. Some men came for a drink, and some came to gamble. Most had women and children at home, who they should have been spending time with.

Some were there for the pleasures the saloon offered before they headed out of town, running from the law once again. Her stomach tightened, as her nerves tingled, when she spotted her prey at the bar, drinking, his head bent low, hat pushed forward over his forehead.

She sauntered over to the bar and took the stool next to Simon Trudeau.

"Hey, cowboy," she said, her lips turned up into a smile, giving him her best come-and-get-it look.

With a flick of his finger, he pushed his black cowboy hat up on his head. Beautiful dark emerald eyes gazed at her like he was starving and she was cream pie. His eyes sauntered over her skimpily attired body, lingering on her breasts before his gaze returned to hers.

This fourflusher would be easy pickings as long as he continued to stare at her breasts.

"Like what you see?" she asked, unable to keep the sarcasm from her voice. A shiver of revulsion shimmied up her spine, the remembrance of that closet with Clay Mullins never far from her memory.

It was a miracle that bastard still lived and breathed.

"Nice," he said, his eyes once again on her face and not her breasts.

"Looking for some company?" she asked.

"I don't pay for women," he said, looking away like he'd seen all he wanted to see, presenting more of a challenge. A challenge she loved. But she'd lay odds he liked sex.

"I don't charge men," she responded, her voice low and sultry. "I bet a big strong, handsome cowboy like you has women begging for attention."

He smiled and reached out, skimming her face with his fingers. She had to force her body not to shiver and maintain her smile, while she let him touch her skin. The urge to vomit was strong, but she knew she couldn't let him see her reaction.

"If you don't charge, what's a pretty girl like you doing here in the saloon?" he asked. "Surely there must be some man waiting for you at home.

She laughed. "If I had a man at home, why would I be here?"

"Exactly," he said.

"Buy me a drink, and I'll tell you about my wicked ways," she promised.

He grinned. "You don't look old enough to have a torrid past."

"You don't look old enough to bed a woman."

He laughed.

"Bartender, two whiskeys," he called out.

She had to build trust before she could get him out the door and into the alley, where Meg would be waiting, once she gave the signal. They had this little scenario down to an art, and most criminals were stupid enough to fall for their trick.

The bartender placed the drinks in front of them, and she lifted her glass and clinked it against his, the sound vibrating. "To strong men who like pretty girls."

Oh, if he knew she was being sarcastic. That she was using her sexuality against him and that before the night was over, his roving eyes and lustful nature would cost him his freedom.

She smiled and leaned close to him, giving him an up close and personal view of her cleavage. "I like whiskey, and men like to buy girls a drink if they show their bosom."

Simon grinned a sexy smile that if she'd wanted a man, would have worked some charm on her, but instead, it only left her wary. He turned on the bar stool until she was in between his legs. "I'll buy you as many drinks as you want, honey."

"Then buy another round," she told him and finished off her drink, setting the glass on the bar.

While he ordered the drinks, she gave Meg their signal. Ruby watched her sister slip out the front to go to their agreed meeting place. Laying her hand on his leg, she rubbed his thigh, knowing most men almost purred when she touched them. "My, oh my, you are certainly a big man. I wonder what the rest of you looks like?"

He grinned and clinked his drink glass against hers. "I'd be more than happy to show you, miss."

"I just bet you would," she said. This was the dangerous part. The part where she had to make certain he would follow her out to the alley, or she'd have lost her opportunity.

She downed her drink, the rough whiskey burning her throat. When he'd sat his drink down, she slid off her stool and kind of fell into his arms.

"Whoa there, sugar. I think the whiskey's done gone to your brain," he said, smiling at her like she was the prey, and he was a hunter, which was exactly what she wanted him to believe.

God, men were simple creatures, who a pretty woman could lead around with just a smile and the hint of a promise. A sexual promise and they would follow you blindly until they were suddenly trapped.

"Oh, no," she slurred happily. "It's gone straight to my legs."

He laughed, placed his finger beneath her chin and tilted her face up to his. She watched as he lowered his mouth to hers. He tasted of whiskey and sin and things she didn't want to experience with him. Revulsion swirled through her stomach, and she had to step back. "My, oh my, you certainly know how to get a girl all excited. I think I need some fresh air."

"Maybe you need me to help you outside," he said his smile wide, his eyes dark with passion.

"Oh, honey, I'd love for you to help me out the door. I might even let you show me what a big strong man you are."

He grinned, and she knew he'd just taken the bait. She had him, and she stepped back out of his arms. No, she wasn't drunk. Hell, she wasn't even tipsy. The bartender here was known for watering the drinks down, but Simon didn't need to know that. She wanted him to believe she was a poor, inebriated, foolish woman who he would soon be fornicating.

Only instead, he'd be tied up, trussed like a turkey, and turned over to the sheriff's office, and they would be five hundred dollars richer.

As she walked toward the door, she noticed a man sitting in the corner, his hat pulled low over his forehead, his head down as she hurried through the saloon with Simon. Something about this cowboy seemed familiar, like she knew him, but she couldn't stop and stare.

She pretended to sway on her feet, and Simon grabbed her by the arm. When they stepped outside, she leaned against him.

"Where to now, buttercup?" he asked.

Buttercup? Really? Inside she cringed and couldn't wait to hogtie this bastard.

"Around the corner and down the alley," she said, steering him in the direction that led to his capture.

When they reached the darkened alley, she pulled him into the shadows. He covered her lips with his own, kissing her, shoving his unwelcome tongue into her mouth. She moaned, not from passion, but from trying to halt the vomit she could feel rising in her throat.

Finally, he pulled back from the kiss. "Gosh, darn it, woman, I gotta have you."

"And so you shall," she said, glancing around the shadows looking for Meg. Where the hell was she? Ruby had their prey ready to abduct, and her sister was nowhere to be seen.

Simon pressed her against the building, and it was all she could do not to scream. This felt so familiar, and she had to resist the urge to fight. His hand grabbed her breast, and she swallowed the nausea she could feel rising inside her. Her fingers twitched with the need to grab her gun. Where the hell was Meg?

He fumbled with his pants, quickly releasing them. They fell to the ground, and he reached beneath her dress. Her scream rose inside her throat, choking her with the need to be released.

The sound of a gun clicking made Simon freeze.

"Remove your hands from my sister, hornswoggle, and slowly step back."

*

Meg's heart pounded in her chest like a runaway stallion. She hadn't been able to find Ruby. Somehow the girl was in the second alley from the saloon and not the first one. She'd known she was running out of time, and she'd been unable to find her baby sister.

God, Ruby took chances and scared Meg at the way she seemed to enjoy chasing criminals. It was almost like she had to prove she was stronger.

"Damn it, Meg, you took your sweet time," Ruby fussed.

"You weren't at the agreed spot," Meg replied, her hand gripping Simon's shirt, the gun pressed against his forehead, her heart pounding, her breathing harsh. She'd run until she'd found Ruby. "One move, buster, and your brains will be splattered on that wall. You're worth the same amount of money, dead or alive."

His mouth had turned into a mean grimace. "I'll kill you for this."

"Get in line with all the others I've turned in," Meg told him. "Get the rope, Ruby. It's laying on the ground."

Ruby picked it up. "Hold your hands out."

He complied. "I will hunt you down. I will make you scream for mercy."

"Hobble your lip. Your pride is just smartin because you got caught with your pants down," Meg said.

Wrapping the rope around his arms, Ruby glanced down. "You know for such a big, strong man, your manly parts are shrinking."

"Shut up," he said. "You wanted it a moment ago."

"No, you thought I wanted that pecker a minute ago. I wanted you all right, but not for a banging up against the wall. Like that's where a woman wants to experience sexual pleasure."

Ruby stood back and admired her rope work. "Not bad."

The sound of a gun hammer clicking had Meg whirling around, dragging Simon by his shirt, putting his body in front of her own. Unease spiraled through her, gripping her heart in its hand and twisting the hardened organ. There stood none other than Sheriff Zach Gillepsie.

"Let him go, Meg," Zach said, his gun pointed at them.

"Why, Sheriff Gillespie," she drawled, "I haven't seen you since that cold, dark night when I left you unshucked, and all tied up," she said, faking cockiness she didn't feel, but refusing to release her prisoner.

"I see you're still tying people up." He glanced down and laughed. "At least he's only missing his pants."

"Meg, what's he talking about?" Ruby asked.

She ignored Ruby, not wanting to answer her sister at this moment.

Zach smiled like it was Christmas and Santa had just delivered him a present. "Drop your gun, Meg, and let him go."

If she let go of her gun, she'd be vulnerable to Zach, and she'd already let him hurt her once. Why make herself vulnerable again?

"Why should I?" she asked, not wanting to let this bounty go. This last criminal would pay off the loan; she would be free to follow her dreams, rather than chase dangerous men.

"Because I'm the sheriff, and I told you to. Now do it."

"But you're not the sheriff in this town."

"Doesn't matter. Drop your gun."

Meg hesitated, but he was the law, and she could get into all kinds of trouble for resisting a lawman. Not to mention he clearly still had a vendetta with her.

"Don't do it, Meg. I have a bad feeling about this," Ruby warned, glancing between her and Zach. "He's our prisoner."

"Shut up, whore," Simon said.

Ruby slapped him in the face. "I'm not a whore. You're just upset because your pants are hanging around your ankles. And your pecker is now the size of a fishing worm."

Simon tried to get to Ruby, and Meg held him tight, pressing her gun against his temple. "Stop."

"Meg, I'm only going to tell you this once more. Drop your gun," Zach warned.

Meg sighed. She couldn't go against the law, even if she wanted to. "You better not double-cross me."

"Or what?"

She stared at him as she laid her gun on the ground. Her tightly strung fingers were slow to release the weapon as her heart pounded inside her chest.

"Now, that's my prisoner you have, and I'm taking him back with me."

"I don't think so," she said. "We caught him, and we should get the bounty money."

Zach ignored her. He still held his gun on her as he reached down and picked up her weapon. "Ruby, toss me your gun."

"I don't have a gun," she said, her voice all sweet and innocent.

"Don't make me reach up under your skirts and find it. I know you have one. All of you McKenzie girls carry guns, and I want yours right here with Meg's."

She growled and turned her back, while she pulled out her gun and tossed it to him.

"Thank you. Now, ladies, you're just damn lucky you helped me today and I'm in such a good mood, or I'd be hauling both of you back to jail with Simon here. Stand back to back."

"Why?" Meg asked, smiling at him because she knew it would get to him. Smiling because she wanted him to think that none of this bothered her, yet she was seething inside. "You're not still mad about me tying you up, are you?"

He grinned. "How could I be mad and wanting revenge when you left me tied up and naked in the middle of Main Street?"

Ruby turned to look at Meg. "You left him naked in the middle of Main Street? You didn't tell us that part."

Meg ignored her. "You know the reasons for me leaving you naked."

All the pain of Zach's betrayal filled her, causing her to hold her head high, her back rigid, as she glared at the man who she'd almost married.

"Back to back, ladies, now! I don't have all night," he said brusquely.

Ruby stood behind Meg. "Tied up and naked. Wow, sister, you do like to extract your revenge."

Zach picked up the rest of the rope left lying on the ground. He slowly untied it from their outlaw, keeping his gun trained on them.

"I don't think I'd do that if I were you."

"Why not?"

"He's wanted for murder."

Zach left the rope around the man's hands.

"Would you please pull my pants up?"

The sheriff looked over at him. "I don't know. These girls like to tease a man and leave him hanging out naked."

"Pull his pants up. We've seen enough of that pecker to last us a lifetime," Ruby said.

Zach deliberately ignored Ruby as he began to wind the rope around the two girls, tying them together.

"What are you doing?" Meg cried, suddenly realizing how he intended to get his revenge. Fuming, she watched as the rope wrapped around their bodies.

"It's called vengeance. You're being served up. You should be glad I'm not leaving you naked and exposed. See, I'm a better person than you because I left your clothes on," he said.

"You were in the bathhouse. What was I supposed to do?" she asked. Then in a meek falsetto she said, "Oh, sheriff, put your clothes on because I'm going to tie you up and leave you in the middle of Main Street after you didn't defend me. After you and your boys trashed me."

Zach stared at her in the darkness then yanked hard on the ropes. "Meg, you have a smart, sassy mouth."

"Thank you, Sheriff," she said, smiling once again at him, knowing there would come a day when she would once again get revenge.

He finished tying them together and stood back to admire his handiwork.

"And just how are we supposed to get out of this?" Meg asked.

He grinned. "The same way I got out of my knots. But then, you left me with a rag in my mouth, so I couldn't call for help."

Ruby turned her head, trying to see Zach and Meg. "Wow, Meg. Remind me not to make you mad ever again."

"You were close enough to a saloon I knew sooner or later someone would find you," Meg said, pulling on the ropes.

"And they did just about the time the saloon closed. There I was naked, wet, cold, and shivering in a wash tub."

Meg shrugged and tried to keep all the hurt she'd buried deep inside at bay. Just the sound of his voice brought it all back. "All you had to do was defend my honor. All you had to do was tell those lowlife bastards that I wear pants because I have no choice. But no, I heard everything you said and you joined in their laughter. You ridiculed me just like they did."

He walked up to Meg and grabbed her chin. Meg's heart raced, and her breath quickened as she stared into his dark brown eyes. For a moment, she felt dizzy like her world was tilting. She licked her lips as her mouth suddenly turned dry. "I was going to marry you," she said. "I wanted you to be my husband."

His mouth descended on hers, and he kissed her, his lips covering her own. Her mouth opened accepting him, and he drank from her like a man starving and needy. They'd never shared such a kiss before, and it left her knees weak, her breathing harsh and her body warming in areas she'd never considered. It was the kiss of a man seducing a woman. It was the kiss of a man in the throes of passion. It was the kiss of a lover branding his woman, and damn him, she refused to feel anything for him anymore.

The outlaw cleared his throat. "I didn't know you had it in you, Sheriff."

Zach raised his mouth from hers. "Shut up, Simon." He gazed into Meg's eyes. "I wanted to marry you. There could have been so much more between us."

"Yes," she whispered, her heart reeling, her body yearning for this man. How could he still make her heart race and her lungs squeeze with want? Why him? "If only you would have defended me."

Her words seemed to break the spell he was under. He stepped back. "Well, I didn't and now look where we're at. You're all roped up like a calf at round-up time. So I'm going to take my outlaw and leave you two to get help somehow."

"Zach, that bounty is mine," she yelled at him.

"I want to thank you for catching my criminal."

"Damn it, Zach," she said, her voice rising as he led his prisoner to a waiting horse.

He reached down and handed the man his pants. "That's all I'm doing for you. It's up to you to get them buttoned up."

"My hands are tied," Simon said.

"Your problem, not mine," Zach commanded. "You wouldn't be in this mess, if you hadn't been thinking with your tallywhacker."

Zach helped the man up on the horse. "Don't get any funny ideas. I'll be right behind you. We're headed to the jail."

"Which jail are we headed to?" Simon asked.

"Mine," Zach replied. "Good night, ladies. I hope someone comes along soon to help you with your tied up situation." He climbed up on his horse, laughing.

"Damn it, Zach. You're going to pay for this," Meg promised.

Chapter Two

The sound of hooves pounding against the earth told Meg that Zach had ridden off, leaving them alone. She wasn't afraid, just madder than a buzzard in a sandstorm. Zach may have won today, but she'd get even. She'd find him and retribution would be hers.

"You left him tied up and naked in the middle of Main Street?" Ruby asked Meg as they stood there in the darkened alley, trussed together back to back.

A cat gave a lonesome meow and knocked over a trash barrel, causing Ruby to jump.

"Yes, I did," Meg admitted. She clenched her fists, anger streaking like fire along her backbone at the memory of overhearing him and his bath buddies laughing at the way she dressed. "He deserved it."

Ruby struggled to reach the knots that had them tied together. "I don't disagree, but Meg he's the sheriff. He could have thrown you in jail."

He had the right to, but he knew he was guilty of hurting her, and anyone would have agreed he hadn't defended her to his buddies at the bathhouse.

"Nah, I don't think so. Everyone in town would have been talking about his naked butt being left in the middle of the street. Now it's just a rumor. There's no proof."

"Still, you took a huge chance," Ruby admonished.

Meg knew she'd taken a risk. Except for a tiny bit of remorse, it had been so worth it to see his eyes above the rag stuffed in his mouth, screaming at her to come back. That memory was like a balm to the pain of his not defending her. "My Irish temper got the best of me."

Ruby laughed. "I know that feeling."

They needed to get out of here before some drunk cowboy stumbled into this darkened alley. Tied up behind a saloon was no place for ladies during the day, let alone at night. If you could call them ladies. One of them wearing pants and the other a saloon dress didn't exactly fit the ideals for a lady by this small town's standards.

"You still have that knife in your boot?" Meg asked.

"I sure do. On three, let's squat together, and I'll pull it out."

"One. Two. Three." Meg knelt at the same time as Ruby, and she felt her sister pulling the knife out of her boot.

"Got it. Give me a moment to slice through Sheriff Gillespie's knots," Ruby said, already cutting the strands of rope.

Why had the sheriff been after Simon? Sure, he was expected to arrest criminals, but what was he doing two-days ride from home in a dust choker town's small saloon. Why had he taken her prisoner from her?

"He's not going to give us our captive back," Meg admitted, wondering why Zach hadn't turned his criminal in to the sheriff here in town instead of traveling all the way back to Zenith with him. Something wasn't right about this situation, but she didn't know what.

"I can't wait to tell Annabelle what you did to the sheriff," Ruby said aloud, not listening to Meg.

"She won't be surprised," Meg responded as the ropes slid to the ground releasing her and Ruby. She shook her arms, letting the blood flow back into her hands. "Let's get the hell out of here."

"We should go after Zach and Simon," Ruby prompted, her blue eyes shining as together they strode out of the darkened alley.

Meg thought about it for a moment. She would love to steal Simon back from Zach and maybe even leave him tied up again. "Zach shouldn't have taken our captive. He doesn't have that much of a head start on us. We could catch them. Maybe even get Simon back."

"I think we should."

"The money from that bounty would help us be done with this life," Meg said.

Ruby shrugged. "I love being a bounty hunter. It's fun and exciting. I don't want this life to end."

"I miss the farm. I miss being at home," Meg said wistfully. She had her own dreams to accomplish and chasing dangerous men wasn't the life she would have chosen.

This money would pay off the loan. And wouldn't it just stick in Zach's craw that they took the man away from him. They walked along the wooden sidewalk, their boots making a *thunk, thunk, thunk* noise. "If we turn him in to another sheriff, then what can Zach say? He can't stop us, and we'll get our cash."

"Let's go," Ruby drawled, reaching her brown gelding and throwing her leg over the saddle. Her skirts spread about her. "I want to see Zach's face when we steal his criminal."

"I just want that bounty," Meg replied, knowing that wasn't entirely true. She liked the idea of getting revenge, especially on Zach.

*

Zach held the reins of Simon's horse, the one he'd brought with him from his mother's farm. Yes, he'd lied to Meg. They weren't heading back to Zenith. They were going to Dyersville, a small east Texas town close to his mother's farm.

Running into the McKenzie girls had been a close call. If they found out he didn't intend to turn over Simon, he could lose his job. But he'd given his word, he would find out the truth, and if Simon was innocent, get the charges dropped. Zach had to prove Simon's innocence, and God help him if he were wrong.

"Are you going to untie my hands?" Simon asked as they rode along.

Zach glanced behind him. Knowing Meg, she and Ruby wouldn't be tied up for long in that alley, and he fully expected her to come after him. Once they'd ridden out of town, he'd changed their direction, and they were now heading directly east, rather than north toward Zenith. He had to keep Meg from following him to Dyersville.

"Why in the hell should I?" Zach said irritated. "You're a criminal. I'm going to treat you like one."

"I didn't kill that man," Simon responded, his voice exasperated, his hat pulled low over his head as he swayed in the saddle.

"The report I read said you shot him in cold blood, right in front of his wife," Zach replied, letting his brown mustang choose the trail as they rode by the light of the full moon.

"Frank is trying to frame me, so he doesn't hang," Simon called out.

That was possible, but still Zach wasn't sure. If he found out Simon had killed this man, he was as good as dead.

"Simon, every criminal says it's someone else's fault."

"So if you think I killed him, why did you come after me?" Simon asked.

Zach sighed, his chest tightening like a cinch on a saddle. "I gave my word that I would find out the truth." He had to prove either Simon's guilt or innocence for once and for all. There could be no doubt. "I'm going to help you, but if I find out you're lying, I'll turn you in myself."

Simon laughed. "Ohhh...the big bad lawman, is threatening me."

"It's not a threat; it's a guarantee," Zach responded.

The mustang meandered along at a steady pace, as they passed pines and oaks towering above them in the darkened sky. Stars twinkled, giving the heavens a glittery appearance.

He feared the outcome of this adventure. Praying he was wrong about the knowledge he'd learn. "So here's the plan. I'm taking you back to Dyersville. You're to stay there and lay low. Maybe even go deeper into the East Texas woods. Just stay hidden until I can get your name cleared."

"Do you really think they'll hang me if I get caught?" Simon asked, his voice sounded unsure, and Zach didn't know if it was because of the idea of dying or something else.

"If you killed that man, you're as good as dead if

you're caught. Tell me your side of the story."

There was a moment of silence, and then Simon released a heavy sigh. "I swear, Zach. I'm innocent. You've got to clear my name."

"So tell me what happened." He couldn't help but wonder if Simon would tell him the truth.

"I was riding with Frank Jones and his brothers. The plan was for us to steal this farmer's sheep to teach him a lesson. While we were rounding up the smelly creatures, the farmer rushed out of his shack and started shooting at us. Frank pulled out his Colt and shot the man."

A surge of anger skittered across Zach's spine, tightening his stomach. Killing was so senseless. To shoot another man only for protecting his property, the shooter had to be heartless. Cold. Callous and cruel.

"So Frank shot an innocent man who was trying to make an honest living, which is more than I can say about the two of you."

Simon laughed. "He was a sheep farmer."

"So what. He was a man working hard to provide for his wife and kids."

"We don't want sheep farmers in Texas," Simon replied, his tone indignant and put out.

"Why do you care? Why do you care if the man was a sheep farmer, a rancher, or even some sodbuster? He was just a man who was trying to make a living for his family. What if someone had shot your pa while he was working the farm? How would you have felt?" Zach said, trying to control the feelings of frustration that threatened to overwhelm him. Right now, he wanted to turn his horse in the direction of the nearest town, turn Simon over to the local sheriff, and be done with this nonsense. But he'd made a promise. And he was a man who kept his word.

"My pa's only interest was drinking and whoring," Simon responded bitterly.

Zach didn't have a comeback. What could he say to a statement filled with such disgust? Yet, the son didn't fall far from the apple tree.

"Seems like a man's life is worth more than somebody shooting him because they don't like the way he's living." Zach gently nudged his horse with his thighs. The mustang crossed a small stream.

"Again, I didn't kill him," Simon stated in the darkness.

Zach wanted to believe Simon would never deliberately shoot another human being. He wanted to believe the best of all men, but unfortunately, as sheriff, he'd seen some of the worst men could do to each other. And this man had been in and out of trouble for most of his life. "Can you prove it?"

"His wife was the only witness. I've been looking for her. Seems she left the farm, and I haven't been able to find out if she's still in town," Simon said.

"Stay hidden in Dyersville until I get back. Let me find the wife, and I'll let you know once I learn the truth. Once your name is cleared, then you're a free man."

Zach's mustang plodded along, and once they cleared the trees, he watched as the full moon rose in the sky. They would travel until midnight then bed down for the night. With Simon tied up, to the casual observer, it appeared Zach was taking him in as his prisoner.

After a long silence, Simon asked, "How long do you think that's going to take?"

"Depends. If I find the wife and she admits that you're not the killer, then it will take a couple of weeks.

But if she says you killed her husband…"

"I understand. You'll turn me in."

"It's my job, Simon. It's who I am. Killing is murder, and it's against the law. I represent the law," Zach replied with a sense of pride. He enjoyed what he did. In his small town, mostly he broke up fights and settled neighbor's disagreements. Occasionally, he closed the whore house to keep the preachers in town happy, but mostly he liked the respect the town gave him. "You could still be wanted for accessory. For not turning in Frank when he killed that sheep farmer."

Simon snorted. "Oh yeah, I'm going to ride in and file a complaint against the most notorious outlaw this side of the Rio Grande."

"Would be better than swinging for Frank."

Hours passed as the two of them rode side by side, not talking as the moon rose to the top of the sky. Finally, exhausted and unable to continue on, Zach pulled his horse to a stop. "I think this is far enough away that they won't locate us. We'll eat a quick bite and get some sleep."

"And if they find us?" Simon asked.

"If you're convicted, you'll hang."

*

"Meg, I'm getting really tired," Ruby called to her. "When are we going to stop and rest for the night?"

They had ridden for hours. Twice, Meg had gotten word from strangers that they'd seen a man on a horse, pulling a man tied up behind him. It could only be Zach and Simon, and they were heading east, not north to Zenith. The confirmations were enough to keep Meg's blood pumping with excitement as they hurried to catch Zach. The thrill of taking Simon back from Zach fueled her on, even when her body reminded her it was time to rest.

"I know, but that old man said he saw Zach and Simon headed in this direction," Meg speculated. "I know Zach Gillepsie. He's trying to lose us. If we keep going, we're bound to catch up with them."

"I think he's done a good job of covering his tracks. Hell, I don't know where we are," Ruby admitted, her mouth opening with a yawn. "Some sleep would be great."

Meg stopped at the top of the hill and looked out into the darkness. The full moon shed light on the valley beneath them. She threw her leg over her gelding and slid down. She walked to the side of the hill and gazed into the darkness.

Zach was out there somewhere, and every time she thought of catching him, her breath quickened and her heart beat an irregular rhythm. In the last year, she'd imagined days of her and Zach together, living as man and wife. But those were not the dreams of a scorned young woman. Those were the dreams of a woman who had wanted to marry Zach. Now those dreams only made her chest ache with pain.

A flicker of a campfire had her glancing a second time at the movement. Then she saw them clearly, two men, sleeping around a dying campfire. No longer could she restrain her excitement, and she started laughing softly. "Look there. Isn't that Zach and Simon? He was even cocky enough to build a fire, thinking he'd gotten away."

Ruby dropped to the ground from her horse. "Oh, my God, you're a genius. How did you find them?"

"Think like a man. A man who is trying to outwit

us." She gazed toward the small, almost died out, campfire. "Now I think it might be time to play a trick on Sheriff Gillespie."

"What kind of trick?"

"Do you still have that rattler's tail?"

"It's in my saddlebags. Why?" Ruby asked, her brows drawn together suspiciously.

"Because I think Texas's deadliest snake is going to pay the sheriff a visit."

They climbed back up on their horses and rode as quietly as possible until they were about one hundred yards from Zach's campsite.

Silently creeping into some bushes that surrounded the two men, they watched the camp. Both men breathed evenly, sounding like they were asleep.

Meg couldn't contain her smile as she slipped Zach's gun out of his holster. Unbelievable, he slept right through the taking of his shootin' iron. A part of her gazed at his full lips slightly parted in slumber and longed to kiss him once again. But that was impossible. Yet, the idea left her lungs squeezing and her gasping quietly for breath.

She slid a loose slipknot around Zach's right arm and right boot. Then she gave a thumbs-up signal to Ruby.

Let the party begin.

Ruby covered Simon's mouth and placed a gun at his temple.

He awoke with a start. At the sound of her gun clicking, she jerked him up by his shirt. Slowly, he rose from his saddle bed. Once on his feet, she quickly moved him toward his waiting horse.

When they reached the edge of the clearing, Zach rolled over, and Meg tightened the slip knots. His eyes came open. As soon as he saw Meg, he reached for his gun.

She smiled and dangled it out of his reach. "Sorry, cowboy, I have your gun."

"Damn it, Meg," Zach said sleepily. "Don't you believe in rest?"

"Zach, you're airin' your lungs in front of a lady! That's not nice, and no, I don't rest when I'm catching a bounty."

He glanced over at the empty bedroll where Simon had been laying. "Where's Simon?"

"Safely tucked away." She smiled as she watched the realization that he was tied up and his prey was gone slowly reach his brown eyes. His eyes were shooting bullets at her smile.

"I knew better than to stop," he said angrily.

Ruby rattled the rattlesnake tail and his eyes widened. "Freeze, Meg, there's a snake somewhere close by."

How sweet that he was concerned about her getting snake bit. But not sweet enough for her to tell him the truth.

"Yeah, about that snake. He's inside your blanket." She rolled the small stick she'd pushed into the blanket. In the dark, she watched the blanket shift, and Zach seemed to shrink. "So I'd suggest you don't move. He's between me and you. I think I'm okay, but I wouldn't recommend you make any sudden shifts."

"Damn it, Meg."

"There you go cursing again. That's not nice," she cajoled as she slowly backed away from Zach. "We'll take good care of Simon and make certain he gets turned in."

"Meg, you can't go off and leave me tied up, no gun,

with a rattlesnake in my bedroll. That's not right," Zach cried, staring at her, his brown eyes wide.

After the last year of her heart healing from the damage he'd inflicted, it was hard for her to suddenly feel all soft and full of pity for him. And she knew for certain that the only snake close by, was in Zach's pants.

"You know, Zach, the last year has made me a strong woman. Whatever womanly softness I possessed has pretty much been dried up by the trail and the hunt for bad men. I've kind of lost faith in the human race, and well, I can do a lot of things I'd never been able to do before. And leaving you behind…tied up with a snake in your blanket. That's your problem."

Zach fought the urge to jump up and move as quickly as possible from the blanket, but the rope ties restrained him. He'd witnessed a snake attack a man before, the bite dangerous, the venom lethal.

A rattle echoed again in the darkness, Zach was almost sure he saw the snake slither in his blanket. He hated snakes! He didn't move. He didn't breathe; he didn't even twitch.

"See you, Zach. Best of luck to you."

She scooped up Simon's saddle for his horse and carried it away with her.

"Meg, don't leave me."

"Too-da-loo," she called and walked away from the camp.

Zach barely breathed, fearful that deadly strike would come any second. His ears strained to hear the rattle again, and his eyes were fixed on the blanket waiting for it to move.

God, when he caught up with her, there would be hell

to pay. If he weren't so frightened, he'd be untying these ropes and following her. But a rattlesnake bite could be deadly. So, he focused on the blanket, waiting for it to move.

Thirty minutes passed with him not moving, just listening for the deadly rattle of that rattlesnake. Finally, he'd had enough. Swallowing his fear, he slowly raised his left arm. No sound, nothing. He quickly untied his right arm.

Glancing at his blanket, he listened. Nothing.

Slowly, he reached close to his blanket and untied his left foot. There was no sound. Sweat trickled down his forehead as he inched back away from his blankets. When he was certain he was far enough away, he jumped up from the ground. He found a piece of firewood and beat the blanket with the stick.

No sound. Nothing. Fearing what he would find, he lifted the blanket off the ground with his stick.

There was no snake. She'd fooled him once again.

A blast of red-hot heat zipped up his spine, causing him to clench his fists. He all but stomped over to his mustang, and there was his gun. She'd at least left him his weapon.

"Damn it, Meg. You'll pay for this!" Once again she'd gotten to him, and now she had Simon.

*

"What's going on between you and the sheriff?" Simon asked when she finally slowed their horses after leaving Zach.

"None of your business," Meg replied, trying to stay awake and knowing if she calculated her timing just right, she'd beat Zach back to town. Oh, she knew he would follow her. Part of her even wanted him to try to catch up and best them again, but she wouldn't let him.

"Why's the sheriff so interested in you?" Meg asked.

Simon laughed. "None of your business."

"I guess we're at a stalemate with neither one of us talking," she responded, not really wanting to speak with Simon. The less she knew about her prisoners, the better. She didn't want to hear their sob stories and why she should let them loose. She'd learned not to listen to their tales of woe and sorrow.

Everyone had a story. Everyone had an excuse. But Meg had little sympathy.

Beneath the stars, they steadily rode back the way they'd come. Hours passed, and exhaustion tormented Meg. Her butt was numb, her eyes felt gritty, and all she wanted to do was find a nice soft bed, kick off her boots, and sleep.

Now as a faint hint of light rose in the eastern sky, they were closing in on the town. Back where they'd started from. Meg hoped to reach the town at daybreak, and then she could turn in Simon and collect their pay. By the time Zach caught up with them, she hoped they would be lying on a soft mattress in a local hotel.

The sun was just beginning to peak over the edge of the horizon, and she could almost feel the taste of victory. Just a little longer until they could claim their bounty.

"Meg, what's that up in the road ahead?" Ruby asked.

Meg strained her tired eyes at the long rope stretched across the road. "I don't know. Be on the lookout."

She slowed her horse and gazed at the bushes ahead of them. There was no sign of life. Nothing moved. Even the birds were silent. Normally, just as the sun rose, the birds were chirping and singing to one another. Silence hung heavy on the air, like just before a storm when the air didn't move, and the stillness could foreshadow death.

"Something's wrong," Meg said quietly, her heart pounding in her chest, her eyes searching everywhere. Zach was here. She could feel him. She could sense his presence.

Simon started to whistle.

"Shut up, or I'll put a bullet in you," Meg replied, swiveling in her saddle toward Simon. He grinned wickedly and continued to whistle. A whirring noise alerted Meg as a blanket dropped down from above, covering her. She shoved the blanket off, reaching for her gun.

A rope whistled through the air, and Meg watched as her sister was lassoed right where she sat atop her horse. The rope effectively pinned her arms to her sides.

Zach dropped to the ground right in front of her, sliding his gun from its holster and pointing the barrel at her.

"Zach Gillespie," Meg cried out.

"Good morning, sweet Meg. So happy to see you again. Don't expect any quarter from me this time. There was no snake."

They were so close to Creed. So close she could almost imagine handing over Simon and riding away. Frustration roared through her chest, causing her to gasp, pushing away all fear.

Meg laughed. "So you would have preferred a real snake in your blanket? I can arrange that next time if you'd like," she promised, knowing she would never deliver. She hated snakes. But when you fear something, she'd learned to face it by acting tough. Never letting her fear show.

"Hardly. But I'm not going to fall for your tricks again."

"How did you get ahead of me? I left you tied up with a snake in your blanket," she asked.

He smiled. "I took a shortcut. Helps to know the farmers in this area," he said with a grin that she wanted to swipe off his face.

She couldn't let him witness her vexation because then he would win. She glanced at her hands.

"Don't think about grabbing your gun. I'm tired and frustrated, and I'm just itching to lay my hands on you the way a man should never touch a lady."

She smiled. Somehow the idea of him being embittered left a warm spot in the center of her belly. How would he touch her? They'd shared a few brief kisses when there had been the idea of a wedding and a ring between them. Now, all that was left were disappointed memories.

"Do tell. What would you do, sheriff? Tie me up? Oh, let's see you've already done that. Kiss me? You've already done that. Hit me? That's still open, but just be forewarned, I pack a mean punch."

He pointed his gun right at her chest. "Toss me your gun."

Meg pulled the gun out of her holster and flipped it to him. He picked it up and slid it into his leather case.

"Now get off your horse, nice and easy."

She slid down her gelding until her feet touched the ground. "Now what, sheriff? Are you going to take my prisoner away again? What's your interest in this man?"

"Same as any other criminal. He's wanted."

There was something in Zach's dark brown eyes that flickered when he lied. He slid his gaze to Simon and then back to Meg. She turned to glance at Simon. She'd seen his face before. Maybe it was the wanted poster, maybe she'd seen him in town, but there was something about his face that seemed familiar.

"Since tying you up didn't do me much good, I think I'll try something new. Take off your shirt."

For a moment, her ears rang with the sound of his words. He didn't just tell her to remove her shirt did he?

She stared at him in disbelief. "What did you just say?"

"I said remove your shirt."

"No." Meg crossed her arms and glared at him.

What his intentions were, she had no idea, but she was not about to be naked in front of this man. He had the wrong woman if he thought she would completely disrobe in front of him.

He cocked his gun. "I'm tired of playing games with you, Meg. Take off your shirt."

"May I remind you that there are other people here? Unlike you, I don't flaunt myself naked before half the town."

"I don't care," Zach demanded in a voice that no longer held any warmth.

Meg glanced around at the smirking Simon and her sister who both still sat on their horses. Oh hell, what would they see? Her chemise and that was it.

"You now have three seconds before I help you."

"You? Alone? Who's going to help you?" she asked.

"One. Two. Three," he commanded.

She stood there, glaring at him. "Just tie us up and be on your way. I'm too tired to fight you."

"No, take the shirt off," he growled.

"Is this the only way you can get women to undress for you, sheriff? Hold a gun on her and threaten?"

He took a step toward her, and she stepped back, not wanting to feel his hands on her. She didn't want him near her. She wanted to escape this attraction she felt toward him. The sooner he left, the better.

"Oh, all right," she said. "I hope you enjoy the view."

With a yank, she pulled her shirt out of her trousers. Her hands trembled as she unbuttoned her shirt and slid it off her body. Her cheeks flushed as embarrassment traveled down her body, riling her Irish temper like a sleeping lion. She threw the garment at him. "Happy?"

His lips turned up in a smile, but his eyes had darkened to a deep brown as his gaze swept over her, lingering on her chemise that barely covered her breasts. Heat traveled through her, but she refused to acknowledge the desire and only focused on the anger his actions had awakened.

"Not yet. Take off your pants," he commanded, his voice husky.

"No. The shirt was enough. I'm not removing anything else," she shouted, exasperated beyond belief.

He would have to shoot her before she would strip down naked on this road.

"Simon, can you crawl off your horse and come help Miss McKenzie?"

She glared at Zach. That criminal would feel the brunt of her fist if he dared touch her.

"Sorry, she tied me to the saddle horn," Simon called.

"Meg, go untie Simon, so he can help undress you."

"Not no, but hell no. I'm not doing it. No man is touching me, do you understand?"

He laughed. "Then take off your pants."

"Why should I?"

"Because I'm just about to put a bullet in your sister, Ruby," Zach announced, staring at her.

"You wouldn't dare," Meg said, her voice rising. No, he wouldn't hurt Ruby. He was a good guy, even if Meg had obviously pushed him to his limits.

He cocked his pistol. "I'm really tired of chasing you, Meg. You've got to the count of five. One, Two. Three."

"Oh, all right. But why are you doing this?" she asked, unbuttoning her pants. Then she slid them down her long legs.

"If your clothes go into town with me, then I'm hoping you don't follow me any longer. If I leave you naked on the trail, then maybe you won't come after me."

"You wouldn't," she said, staring at him, knowing he'd have to fight her to get anything else removed.

Zach smiled that cocky grin that she wanted to swipe off his handsome face. "Did you leave me naked on Main Street?"

"But that wasn't where just anyone would find you. Only the men from the saloon."

He grinned. "You're right. It wasn't. I'll leave you in your drawers. At least you'll be covered up."

Walking over to Ruby, he lifted her skirt and easily pulled her Baby Dragoon from her hidden holster.

"Hey," she cried.

"I apologize, Miss McKenzie, but I have to protect myself and my prisoner from you girls."

He loosened the noose around her arms. "Now, I will need you to remove your dress."

"You're just getting your eyes full. Zach Gillespie.

37

You're a pervert," Ruby said.

Simon laughed out loud, sending an eerie shiver through Meg.

"Come on down from your horse, Ruby."

Ruby swung her leg over and slid to the ground. She peeled the saloon dress off, revealing her chemise and drawers beneath the skirt. "I never really cared for that dress much any ways."

He grinned at her in pantaloons and chemise.

"Zach, I will find a way to make you pay," Meg vowed. In her mind, she went over all the ways she could kill him. God, she wanted to put a bullet in him.

"That's what you said last time, and I let you off easy. I let you keep your clothes, but this time I'm leaving you in your underwear. If you come after me again, I will leave you as nude as the day you were born. Just like you did me."

So, this was how he planned on getting his revenge. "You deserved that and more."

"You think I deserved to be punished for my lack of defending you, and I think you're making a big deal out of nothing."

Meg could almost hear the explosions going off in her head as her hands clenched and her body went rigid. He thought she was making a big deal out of nothing?

"Oh, come on, Sheriff. If you heard me telling everyone your pecker was the size of a toothpick, would you be upset?"

"No, because I know it's a lie." He smiled at her. "You know it's a lie."

Warmth rushed through her body, filling her from her toes to her forehead, crackling like lightning. The man was impossible. "But not everyone in town would know it's a lie."

Simon cleared his throat. "Excuse me, while this conversation is quite interesting, even entertaining... Can we go, Sheriff?"

"What is it with you and this prisoner? Why are you after him?"

"I'm after all wanted men."

"Even those who aren't in your jurisdiction? Who's back home taking care of the town, Sheriff? Who's looking out for the good folk in Zenith?"

Zach frowned. "This is a special case. And we're headed back to Zenith right now."

"You're going east and Zenith is north. Are you lost?" Meg asked staring at him, watching his reaction.

"You caught me. I got turned around. Now we'll go north," Zach responded with a smirk. "Remember, ladies, if you come after me again..."

"Yeah, yeah, yeah," Meg said as a sliver of fear spiraled through her, sending shivers through her midsection. She knew he was serious. And while she didn't want to be tied up, she wanted to get to Zach. And she was willing to risk it all. "The next time I catch you, Sheriff, I'll leave you in the middle of town, with no bath tub to cower in. Think of that on your journey back to Zenith."

"Can we please stop with the threats and get going?" Simon asked, interrupting them again.

Meg started laughing, the sound almost hysterical. "I've never seen a prisoner so excited to be going to his own hanging. Your prisoner is mighty familiar with you, Zach."

"Simon, not another word," Zach shouted.

"I'm finding this little exchange very interesting,"

Ruby said. "If we were in the school yard, I'd think they liked each other." She glanced over at Simon.

Meg turned to glare at Ruby. "He doesn't like women who wear pants."

"Oh, that's right," Ruby said. "His manhood is challenged by a woman in pants."

Zach shook his head. "Keep talking. You'll both be naked soon."

"What now, cowboy?" Meg asked, wishing he would just leave. "I think we've slung enough threats, and you've given enough ultimatums."

A frown creased his forehead. "Don't follow me, Meg. I'll bring your clothes out to the farm next week. Don't let me see you before then."

"I don't take orders from you. What about our guns?"

He pulled her gun out of his holster and took the bullets out. He did the same with Ruby's revolver and handed them back to Meg. "Okay, ladies, you know the drill. Turn around, and I'll tie you together again."

"Damn you, Zach,"

"Watch your language, Meg." He tied them up then blew Meg a kiss. "See you in Zenith."

"See you in hell!"

Chapter Three

In the pre-dawn light, Meg, stood in the middle of the road, tied to Ruby, as their horses munched on the grass along the edge of the road. God, she'd been so stupid to let Zach catch them. But she thought she'd had enough of a head start on him she could beat him to town. Now, she stared at the backend of his horse carrying him down the dusty road. Mentally, she was throwing daggers at those broad shoulders, wishing just one would halt him in his tracks.

"Meg, I'm tired, I'm dirty, and I just want to find the nearest hotel and sleep," Ruby whined.

Something wasn't right. Zach wasn't telling her the truth. She'd find him and soon learn the real reason he was taking this man back to Zenith. Though why he rode east when he was suppose to be going north, she had no idea. And if he thought a simple threat of undressing her was going to stop her, he was dumber than a claim jumper.

"He's taken our prisoner. We have to go after him." Meg gritted her teeth, clenching her fists until her nails dug into her hand, sending sharp pains through her palm. She wanted to ride after them and take Simon back. She wanted to make Zach pay for the way he'd left them behind. Tied up, in their pantaloons, no access to weapons, they would be unable to defend themselves from any traveler who happened along the road.

"Do you still have that knife?" Meg asked, hoping Ruby had put it back in her boot.

"Yes, on the count of three," Ruby replied, her voice tired. "One. Two. Three."

They squatted down until she could reach her boot and pull the knife free. Slowly they rose back to standing height. Meg tried to wait patiently for Ruby to cut the ropes, but she wanted to get on the road to catch Zach.

"This is getting to be a habit. Next time, we take all of his rope with us when we leave," Meg said, thinking when they caught up to Zach, she would make certain he couldn't follow them.

"Let's go to a hotel and rest," Ruby pleaded. "We can head to Zenith tomorrow. Then after we get home, you can go to the jail to make sure he turned Simon in."

Rest sounded wonderful, but she couldn't leave Simon with Zach. She couldn't just give up on their quarry. She wanted that bounty, if only to keep Zach from having him. She wanted to pay off their small farm. She wanted that money to start her dress shop.

"No," Meg said sharply. "We're going to catch Zach and Simon. He's not been gone long. It's daylight and should be easy to find them."

"And get tied up naked?" Ruby asked. "You're my logical sister, but you're so tired you're not thinking straight."

The memory of Zach laughing at Meg in the bathhouse made her stomach churn with a side of revenge. Sure, she'd gotten to him once, but now they were playing a game of hide and seek, and she had every intention of winning. "We're going to get our prisoner back, and we won't be tied up naked. We're going to win."

The ropes slid off their arms as Ruby cut through them. "I need to rest, Meg." She sat down on the ground. "I've not slept in what feels like days. I'm tired."

For Ruby to be whining, she must be exhausted. Meg was tired, but the thrill of the hunt, spurred her on. The excitement of knowing she was going to win, if she had to die trying.

"Do you want me to leave you and go on alone?" Meg asked. "I could leave you in town."

"We do this together, not alone." Ruby gazed at her, her blue eyes flashing determination. "This thing between you and the sheriff... You're getting a little obsessed."

Meg laughed then held out her hand to her sister, yanking her up from the ground. "I'm not obsessed. But it *is* personal. I'm not losing this bounty. I'm going to take Simon back."

This was the second time Zach had left them tied up, and now the recapture of Simon had become her objective. She was going to win, by golly, or die trying.

As they walked to their horses, Ruby gazed at Meg, her blue eyes shadowed with concern. "When you let it get personal, is when you get hurt. You need to let this one go, Meg."

"No," she responded, not even pausing to think. With Zach's interference, this pursuit had become *very* personal. "I can drop you off at the hotel, if you don't want to continue."

Ruby took a deep breath. "No, I'll keep going, so

hopefully, I can protect you. You're worse than a sharp stick in the eye."

Meg shrugged. "I think the first thing we should do is put some clothes on. It's a good thing we carry an extra set, or we'd be riding into town half-naked. I'm sure we'd receive quite a welcome. Not the kind I'm looking for."

*

"You know she's going to follow us," Simon said, as they rode back the same path Meg and Ruby had traveled earlier.

"Probably," Zack acknowledged, trying to calculate how long it would take for them to get out of the ropes. He couldn't help but be worried that he had taken their clothes and left them without a weapon. What if some harm came to them because of his actions?

"Would you really leave them tied up and naked?" Simon asked. "I mean that doesn't sound like a law-abiding sheriff, if you ask me."

"No one's asking you, and no, I wouldn't have left them naked." Hell, he hadn't expected his lungs to freeze and his breath to stop when he saw Meg's breasts peaking thru the top of her chemise, his John Henry hardening at the sight of her long shapely legs. With her standing so proudly in her pantaloons and chemise, her breasts high and firm and so damn tempting, he'd wanted to forget about both Simon and Ruby. He'd wanted to take what he saw and to hell with Simon.

"You know, I think we're going to find us a nice place and bed down for a while. We'll get some rest and let her keep searching. Hopefully, she'll give up and go back to Zenith thinking we're there," Zach said.

No, he would never leave Meg naked, but it hadn't

hurt to plant that idea in her head with the hope that fear would keep her from riding after him. Still, his gut instinct told him to get prepared, she was on her way.

Simon shook his head. "I could use some shut-eye. You guys have been dragging me all over this country tonight. I haven't ridden this much since..."

Zach glanced over at him. "Since when?"

Had Simon almost slipped and told Zach something that could tell him about his way of life? His living on the fringes of the law, just one wrong step from the noose?

"Never mind," Simon said and looked away.

"In fact, let's get off the road and wait for them to pass," Zach said, pulling his horse into a groove of trees far enough off the road they were no longer visible, the brush hiding their horses.

Zach knew he would be unable to rest until he was sure Meg and Ruby passed them by. Until he knew Meg was chasing rabbits in the wrong direction, he would be hard pressed to get some shut-eye.

"You get some sleep, and I'll just crawl up a tree somewhere and wait for them to pass," he commanded, thinking of how he'd surprised Meg when he'd dropped the blanket over the top of her from the tree. Occasionally, it felt good to outsmart the other person. Occasionally, it felt devious to be the one delivering the surprise.

After helping Simon off of his horse, Zach set up his bedroll, leaving his prisoner tied up with his eyes closed. Laid out, Simon quickly began snoring. Then Zach crept off to watch for Meg and Ruby.

An elm tree grew close to the road, and Zach climbed up high enough the branches and leaves would shield him from view. About thirty minutes later, he heard horses. He watched as Meg pushed her horse, not at a full run, but a steady gallop. She passed beneath him, and he couldn't help but smile. Both girls had put on other clothes they must have had in their saddlebags.

Tension flowed like a stampede of cattle through Zach as he realized he'd been worried about leaving them on the trail in their undergarments. As they rode off, he felt an emptiness he'd never realized before. He liked sparring with Meg; he liked kissing her even more; and even though they had some unresolved issues, he was looking forward to their next encounter. Once he had Simon safely tucked away, he would pay a visit to her farm.

Then he would find Mary Lowell and hear her version of Simon's story.

Was he being led on a wild goose chase? Had Simon killed her husband?

*

Riding through the countryside, the warm spring sun beat down on Meg and Ruby as they searched for anyone who'd seen the two cowboys. Zach and Simon were missing. No one in Dyersville mentioned them, and so she'd headed north to Zenith, hoping he'd been honest and was taking Simon to jail. Yet, her gut told her he'd lied. With every mile, she sensed they were further apart, and yet she didn't turn back.

They rode as fast as they could push their horses without killing them. Exhaustion seeped from Meg's every pore, and she knew they'd have to stop and rest soon. They couldn't keep going at this pace. Yet, they rode on trying to find the elusive sheriff and his captive. Somehow, he'd given them the slip.

Meg looked back over her shoulder to where Ruby was at least four horse lengths behind her. "Can you get a move on?"

The closer they came to Zenith, the more discouragement overwhelmed Meg, leaving her tense. The closer they came to Zenith, the more Ruby slowed. The closer they came to Zenith, the more Meg knew Zach had won this time.

He may have won a skirmish, but she'd win the war.

"I've not slept in almost two days, so forgive me if I'm a little saddle sore and weary. I'm ready to call it a night, Meg."

Meg sighed. They were still a good day's ride from Zenith. Zach and Simon had to be just as tired as they were. They'd be looking for a place to hole up for the night. Meg and Ruby's horses were exhausted, they were exhausted, and the search seemed exhausted. They had to stop, rest, and regroup.

"We'll stop in the next town we come to," Meg promised to encourage Ruby, knowing she'd pushed the horses and the two of them about as far as she could safely.

An hour later, they arrived at a spot in the road that had a small rooming house, a bank, a general store, and a barbershop/bathhouse. Meg's insides cringed at the sight of the bathhouse, and yet, for a moment, she wanted to storm into the building to make sure Zach wasn't hiding in there.

"Come on, let's see if we can get a room, and get some rest," Meg suggested, throwing her leg over her horse and sliding to the ground. Her legs felt wobbly and stiff from sitting such a long time. Her buttocks ached from the hours spent in the saddle.

"Thank God. I'm so tired I've been dozing."

Ruby swung her leg over her saddle. The stirrup twisted on her foot, spinning Ruby and sending her spiraling to the ground. She landed with a loud thud beneath the horse. The tired mustang panicked and started running down the street, dragging Ruby behind.

"Oh, my God," Meg shouted. Her heart slammed into her throat, fear zipping through her bloodstream, as she watched in horror as her sister was towed down the street on her back.

Meg jumped back on her horse, spurring him after the runaway animal.

The exhausted mustang was not running at full speed, and Meg raced after the wayward horse, careful to avoid her sister's bouncing body. Leaning over she grabbed his reins and pulled the animal to a halt. She jumped off her horse and ran back to Ruby. "Are you all right?"

Her sister lay in the street, her hair and face dusty, moaning. "Meg."

"I'm here, Ruby. Are you okay?"

"My leg. It hurts."

"Can you sit?" Meg asked, staring worriedly at her sister. That had been close. Too close. All because Meg had pushed them to their limit. A careless mistake could have cost Ruby her life, and even now, she could be seriously injured.

Meg gently pulled Ruby's foot from the stirrup and helped her sister to a sitting position. She swayed in Meg's arms. Then she screamed, her face blanched of color, "Oh, my God, my back is on fire. It burns, Meg. It burns."

Meg glanced at Ruby's back and could see her dress had been ripped and shredded in several places as the horse dragged her down the street over pebbles, rocks, and a hard, dusty surface.

"You need a doctor," Meg determined.

Blood seeped from Ruby's forehead where a rock had cut her, fear reflected from her gaze, and pain left her face ashen. Meg couldn't believe this was happening. Not now, not when they were going to rest. Not when she wanted so badly to go after Simon tomorrow morning. But Ruby was seriously injured. Nothing was more important than her sister. Nothing. No bounty, no Simon, not the farm, only Ruby.

A man came running to her side. "Is she okay?"

"No, can you take those two horses to the corral for me?" Meg asked, needing the horses taken care of and fed, but knowing she'd never leave Ruby's side.

"Yes, ma'am."

What if they didn't have a sawbones? What if all they had was a healer? Right now, Meg just wanted someone to give Ruby some relief.

"Is there a doctor in this town?"

"Yes," the man responded, gazing worriedly at Ruby.

"Tell them at the corral I'll be down later to pay for their care," she told the older man, who she hoped was honest. "Thank you."

He pulled the horses down a side alley.

She had to get Ruby out of the middle of the street. There were times when she wished Annabelle was with them to help out. This was one of those times.

Meg halfway picked up Ruby. "Can you walk?"

Ruby took a step and screamed. "My ankle. I can't put any weight on my ankle."

Concern pounded like a hammer hitting an anvil in Meg's heart. If only they had stopped to rest earlier, none of this would have happened. If only she hadn't been pushing them to their limits to find Zach and Simon.

She half-carried Ruby, hobbling down the dusty street to the rooming house. When they stumbled in the door, a woman came running around the counter. "Oh, my God! What happened?"

"Her foot got caught in the stirrup, and the horse spooked. He dragged her down the street. Do you have a room?"

"I've got a room, and I'll send someone to fetch the doctor. He lives about a mile out of town. Let's get her settled into bed." The middle-aged woman wrapped her arms around Ruby, helping Meg carry her sister into the room. "Her back is going to be sore."

Her back was going to be black and blue from the looks of the scraps and burns. Even for an old tired horse, her mustang had held up well on the trip. Maybe too well.

Ruby moaned. "Hurts so bad."

The woman pulled back the quilt on the bed, and together, they tried to lay Ruby down gently without hurting her back any more than necessary.

Meg stared in shock at her sister, her face pale as she moaned in the bed. Meg had to help make Ruby more comfortable and take care of her, the best she could.

"Do you need some help with what's left of her dress?" the kind woman asked.

"I think I can get it from here. If you'd just send for the doctor, I'd be grateful," Meg responded. She took out her knife and cut the dress away from Ruby's body. It was ruined, and there was no sense in making her remove the tattered garment.

The woman watched Ruby, her face grimacing at the

sight of her wounds. "I'll send for him right now."

"Thanks," Meg said. "Oh, and could you bring me a basin of water?"

"There's one in the stand over there, but I'll bring you more water, as I think you're going to need it," she replied.

As the woman shut the door, Meg pulled the shredded garment from Ruby's body.

She moaned.

"I'm sorry, Ruby. We should have stopped earlier." Meg could only blame herself for pushing Ruby and the animals, when they were exhausted.

"Not your fault. My boot got caught. It was a silly mistake," Ruby whispered, her eyes closed. "My foot. Check my foot," she wailed. "It's swelling. I can feel it."

Meg gingerly tugged on Ruby's boot, making her scream. And when the shoe was removed, Meg could see how the ankle had swollen. Already the flesh was starting to turn dark with bruising. Meg should have watched out for Ruby better.

She walked to the basin and poured some water on a towel and came back to the bed. Gently, she wiped Ruby's face and forehead, trying to make her feel better.

"Don't leave me, Meg. Stay with me."

Meg swallowed to keep the tears from slipping down her cheeks. She had to remain strong for Ruby. This was her fault. There was no way she could go off.

"You know I'm not going to leave you. I'm going to stay right here at your side," she said, realizing how she had let her desire to catch Zach consume her and cloud her better judgment. Ruby had even tried to warn her she was becoming obsessed.

"Thank you, I was afraid you'd go after the sheriff.

Please, Meg, let it go for now," Ruby asked.

"I will, Ruby, I will," she promised, guilt gnawing at her chest for how she'd neglected to keep her sister safe. She'd pushed them past their limits. All because she'd wanted to get that bounty money.

Maybe it was time to let Zach have Simon. She'd be back pursuing him just as soon as she had Ruby settled and made certain she was okay. But for now, her sister was all that mattered.

"The doctor is on his way, and I'm going to stay right here," she said, reassuring her sister, while brushing the blonde curls away from her face. Even at eighteen, she was too young to be hunting bad men. What had they been thinking when they'd made the decision to catch criminals? They were women, not men, and this was a dangerous profession.

"Wonder if this ever happened to Papa?" Ruby asked, her eyes watering.

"Shh. Try to rest," Meg said softly, wiping Ruby's face with a damp cloth. "Is your back still stinging?"

Not since Ruby was a young girl and had torn the skin off both of her knees had Meg seen scrapes and raw places that looked so ugly. Swirls of raw skin, dust, and bruising covered her back.

Ruby gave a half-smile. "Yeah, everything hurts. There's not a place on my body that's not throbbing with pain right now."

Meg swallowed hard; she couldn't lose Ruby. She just couldn't. It was bad enough Ruby had gotten hurt, but if she were to die… What if there were internal injuries like Papa? What if she had broken something that couldn't be repaired? Meg closed her eyes and gritted her teeth. She would not cry.

A knock sounded on the door, and an older man carrying a medical bag walked in. "Hello, I'm Doc Watson. I hear you've had some trouble."

Meg stood and came around the bed. She shook his hand. "I'm Meg McKenzie, and this is my sister, Ruby."

Quickly she explained what had happened and described the external injuries she could see.

He gave her a reassuring warm smile, like everything would be all right. "Why don't you stand right over there against the wall and I'll check out our patient."

He walked over to the bed, and Ruby stared at him, her blue eyes dark with pain, her lips gray standing out against her sallow skin.

"I'm Ruby," she said hoarsely.

"I'm Doc Watson. Looks like you've had a little accident," he said. "May I sit on the bed beside you?"

"Yes." She didn't move.

"Can you tell me where you hurt?" he asked.

"All over. Everything hurts."

He smiled. "How about your head? How does it feel?"

"I have the worst headache. It's pounding, and I feel nauseous."

He leaned over and looked at her eyes. "Yes, your pupils are dilated. Probably have a concussion. Let's see what else is wrong."

A concussion? What was that?

For the next fifteen minutes, he took his elderly hands and checked out Ruby's ribs, her back, her legs, and her swollen ankle. Gently, he felt her ankle, while Ruby moaned, and Meg had to bite her lip to keep from asking him to stop. Finally, he finished.

"Young lady, you tore up that ankle pretty bad. I

don't think it's broken, but those ligaments are definitely injured. I'm going to wrap it up, but you need to stay off of it for several weeks."

Meg hung her head, thankful the bone was not broken and there didn't appear to be any internal injuries. But rest was not something Ruby did well. What would Meg do with her now? How could she continue to bounty hunt if Ruby was unable to go on? And Meg couldn't go off and leave Ruby in a boarding house. She just couldn't.

"You also have a concussion and possibly a broken rib. It's a wonder that horse didn't break your back. I'm leaving you some laudanum to help with the pain. Just take a couple of drops whenever you hurt. You're going to need bed rest for at least a week and then stay off that ankle for three more weeks. Basically, you're looking at a month of not doing too much," he said, snapping his case closed.

A month! Guilt ate at Meg's insides. She would lose her prey if she waited a month. They would lose the bounty. Yet, how could she even be considering that when Ruby lay so badly injured?

Meg had been lounging against the wall and suddenly stood taller. "We're about six hours from home. When do you think she can ride again?"

"I'd plan on staying here for at least five days, and I'd really prefer you stayed seven," he said, looking between the two girls.

Ruby groaned. "Give me some of that laudanum now. I just want to sleep."

He raised her up and gave her a few drops then laid her back down. "I'm also leaving some salve for her back. I'll come by every day and check on her just to make sure she's doing okay. Don't hesitate to send for me if she gets any worse."

Fear spiked through Meg at the memory of her father's injuries and how they'd eventually taken him from this earth. No, that couldn't happen to Ruby. It just couldn't.

"Thanks, Doc." Meg walked him to the door.

Once the doctor was gone, Ruby started to cry. "I'm sorry, Meg. I know how badly you wanted to catch Simon."

"Shh…" Meg said, sitting down beside her. "You're more important than any bounty. Just get better so we can get home to Annabelle."

*

A week later, Annabelle watched from a window as Meg and Ruby rode into the yard of the farm. She rushed out to greet them. She'd been so worried since she'd received the telegram from Meg, telling her Ruby had been injured. "Oh, my God, how are you, Ruby?"

Meg jumped down from her horse and helped to get Ruby off of hers, keeping her from putting any weight on her ankle.

"It's getting better," Ruby replied. "Won't be long until I'm back chasing bad guys."

"What happened?" Annabelle demanded, helping Ruby hobble inside the house where they sat her in the nearest chair.

Annabelle listened to Ruby explain how she'd gotten her foot tangled in the stirrup and the horse had spooked. She watched Meg move around the house, unloading their saddlebags, her face tense, her mood dark. There was more to this story than either one of them was telling.

"What about the bounty?" Annabelle asked.

"He was stolen by the sheriff," Ruby spouted off. "Ask Meg what she did to Sheriff Zach? Let her explain why we were tied up by the sheriff, not once, but twice."

"What?" Annabelle asked, glancing between her sisters.

Meg stopped putting their things away and sent Ruby a grim look. Then Meg began telling the story of how Zach had extracted his revenge for her leaving him tied up and naked in town. Her tough, older sister had hog tied the sheriff…? What was she thinking?

"You left him tied up? You saw the sheriff naked?" Annabelle asked, trying to keep the chuckle she could feel building within her from escaping.

"Yes," Meg said with a smile. "Not bad on the eyes."

Annabelle laughed out loud. Boy, would she have loved to have heard the discussion between Meg and Zach while he was tied up. But what would have caused Meg to act so impulsively? For surely she hadn't planned this scheme had she?

Annabelle shook her head. "What made you decide to leave the sheriff naked in the middle of town?" What if the sheriff had retaliated and taken Meg to jail? And why had she kept this a secret for a whole year? Had the sheriff's rejection of marrying her pained her more than she'd let on? Meg was one for keeping things close to her chest, especially if her emotions were crushed. Then she told no one of her hurt and buried her feelings deeper than a well in Montana.

"Meg, do you want to go to jail? Why didn't you tell us?"

"No, but I don't deserve to be disrespected. And I was kind of ashamed of what I'd done, so I thought it was better you didn't know."

"No, you don't deserve to be disrespected, but he's the sheriff," Annabelle said, knowing Meg felt an overwhelming sense of responsibility for her and Ruby.

"And he got his revenge by taking our bounty and tying us up." Ruby sat, shaking her head, an expression of disgust on her face. "He should at least pay us for the bounty. We caught the longrider."

"I'm going to town tomorrow to make certain he turned Simon in. I couldn't decide if he was really after Simon or just getting revenge," Meg replied quietly, removing her hat and hanging it on a hook by the door.

Annabelle had never seen Meg so obsessed. So determined to get her man. They were doing fine. They didn't need the cash, so was the sheriff the reason she was so unfaltering to catch this Simon? Or was there another reason?

"At least we kept on most of our clothes," Ruby said, propping her foot on another chair.

"What? What do you mean you kept on most of your clothes?"Annabelle stared at her sisters, shock rippling through her. "He made you remove your clothes?"

Meg shrugged. "The second time he caught us he made us strip down to our pantaloons."

"That pervert. How dare he do that to my sisters." Her chest tightened as anger bloomed throughout her. No one hurt one of the McKenzies without retribution. Annabelle was ready to storm into town and show Zach just how dangerous the three of them together could be. Meg may have left him naked, but Annabelle could think of worse things that could happen to a man. Especially if something bad had happened to one of her sisters because of his nonsense.

"He was trying to get even with me, but I think it got to him, when I removed my shirt and pants," Meg said with a laugh. "I watched his face, and he didn't have the look of a man who was certain about his actions."

Ruby winked at Annabelle. "Oh yeah, he definitely had his brown eyes trained on Meg."

"We lost him after that, and then Ruby got hurt. Tomorrow, I'm going into town. I want to see if there are any other bounties we can bring in."

"Leave it alone, Meg. You're not going out by yourself," Ruby warned.

"I agree," Annabelle responded. "One of you hurt is bad enough. I can't take care of both of you. And I can't go with you right now because one of us has to take care of Ruby. Plus, there's spring calving. You're going to have to wait," she warned her sister, but somehow she felt like Meg wasn't really listening. Determination oozed from her older sister and she seemed obstinate to finish their commitment.

"We're so close to having the bank completely paid off," Meg said quietly.

"It can wait," Annabelle demanded, staring at her older sister, her hands on her hips, her feet spread apart. Sometimes Meg forgot how dangerous this profession of capturing criminals could be. It was almost like she thrived on putting away men who'd committed a crime. Sometimes, she thought she was invincible. But they all knew that wasn't true.

It wasn't often the two younger sisters ganged up on Meg, but this time she had to see reason. They needed to sit tight and wait until Ruby healed enough so she could go hunting again.

"I'm just going to check things out. Once Ruby is

well, we'll finish what we started."

Annabelle stared at Meg. "We're not as hungry as we were. We've built up our supplies, the bank account. Leave it be, Meg."

"Let it go," Ruby said. "You're not thinking clearly."

Annabelle watched as anger, disappointment, and even determination seemed to flit across Meg's expressive face. Oh yeah, something about this latest bounty was eating at her and she'd be like a dog with a bone until this was resolved.

"Let's wait and see what tomorrow brings," Meg replied as she walked out the door to put the horses up.

Ruby shook her head and glanced at Annabelle. "She's not going to let this go. She's fixated on getting Simon because of Zach."

*

Early the next morning, Zach sat behind the sheriff's desk, closing out the monthly accounting records, making sure everything balanced before he left on the road again. The door opened, and he glanced up, his heart jumping into his throat.

Meg strolled through the door, looking like a ray of sunshine. Only, he had to remember, those rays sometimes burnt a man to a crisp.

Her auburn hair curled down her back in waves, and her emerald eyes flashed with amusement as she stared at him. Why did he always feel like she could see right through him? That she knew what he was thinking?

Why did she make him want to grab her, pull her into the nearest cell, and show her how a man in control dealt with a woman like her?

"Meg."

"Zach."

His eyes looked her over from head to toe, the memory of her standing so proudly out on the road in her chemise and pantaloons slammed into his mind, so real and vivid he could smell the spring flowers and hear the birds chirping. The sight of her standing in his office had his body tightening up in ways he'd long forgotten. "I see the journey in your pantaloons didn't seem to harm you."

She smiled at him, one of those I'm-going-to-eat-you-for-lunch grins, as she took a seat across from him and put her boot up on his desk. "How many lives do you have, cowboy? The rattlesnake didn't get you, and somehow you managed to hide yourself and Simon very well."

"Sometimes it's better to stop and rest before you travel on. That's what I did."

It had taken everything he knew to keep Meg from finding him and Simon. And even then, he'd gone for miles, glancing behind him, sure, she would discover them again.

"Looks like your beauty sleep didn't work too well," she quipped. "You're still carrying a grudge on your shoulder like a sack of potatoes."

He laughed and then checked his shoulders. "Me, carry a grudge? Yes, I am, but it's not sitting on my shoulders. It's lower."

The damn woman had left him exposed, sitting on Main Street naked. Nothing had stung so badly as when she'd ignored him when he'd said he was going to marry her. She'd paid no mind to the fact that against everyone's advice he'd planned on standing up with her and the sin-buster.

A blush stained her cheeks, and it was all he could do to keep from jumping over the desk and pulling her into his arms again. In the wee hours of the morning, he'd awakened, remembering that last kiss, dreaming of how her lips felt beneath his, wanting to experience them again.

No woman had ever gotten beneath his skin like Meg. It felt like standing on a porch while watching a Texas twister churn toward you. If you weren't careful, you'd get slammed.

"Too bad," she said, her chin rising defiantly, her eyes flashing with disdain.

He leaned back, crossed his arms over his chest, and gazed at her. God, she was a beautiful woman, and yet, she dressed and acted like a man. Was he wrong to want a soft woman who'd let him wear the pants in the family?

She glanced over at the empty jail cells. "Where's Simon?"

He'd known this question was coming, and he didn't know how to answer her. He couldn't tell her Simon had hanged, as there hadn't been a trial. He couldn't say he'd left him in another jail, as she could check and find out he was lying, and then he could lose the job he loved.

He sighed and chose the answer he was sure would cause him the most trouble, but would allow him to retain his job. "He got away."

She jumped up from her chair. "What do you mean he got away? You're a lawman. How do you lose a prisoner?"

"When he knocks you out cold and takes off, that's how," he replied, hoping she wouldn't seek Simon out. Praying she'd give the pursuit a rest.

Zach had some business to take care of first. Then he would ride out, find Mary Lowell, and hear her story. Hopefully, he'd learn the truth regarding Simon then handle the situation in the most law-abiding way.

"And you didn't go after him?" Meg asked her eyes wide and her mouth open in disbelief. She shook her head and gazed at him with a weird look on her face. "What kind of sheriff are you?"

"A damn good one," he responded as a curl of frustration tightened his fists. He'd made a promise—a vow that held him hostage.

She shook her head at him. "A damn good one for who? The criminals?"

"No," he said. "I'm going after him."

"Something's not right. You would never have let a prisoner get away and not hunt him down."

"Leave it be, Meg. I'm going after him tomorrow," Zach demanded, standing and coming around the desk. "Don't even think about going after him."

"Why?" she asked. "Why is he different than all the other prisoners I bring in? Why should I stay away from him?"

"Because he's dangerous." Zach placed his hands on her shoulders, wanting to shake some sense into her. God, she was so defiant, so reckless, so brave and stupid. She would place herself in danger just to earn this bounty.

"That's never stopped me before," she said in a daring tone.

His hands moved from her shoulders to cup her face, and he stared at her, his gaze intent on trying to see inside her soul. To see if she would listen to him and stay in town or if she planned on pursuing Simon.

He stared at her luscious lips, longing to taste her again, needing to see if there was still passion between them. Wanting so badly to kiss her. To taste her again.

To plunder some sense into her way-too-smart brain.

"You can't go after him," he whispered, unable to stop himself as his mouth came down on hers. His lips assaulted hers, pouring all his resentment of the situation into her mouth as he moved over her lips, indulging and holding her mouth captive. He kissed her with all his frustration from her ignoring his proposal. He kissed her with all the pent-up passion that had long been denied for her tempting curves and her luscious mouth.

Suddenly her hands came up between them, and she pushed away. She stepped back from him. "That's enough, Sheriff. Don't forget I'm still that same pants-wearing woman who is going after Simon. He's mine, and I won't be bringing him back to your jail, so he can conveniently escape again." She spun on her heels and walked out the door, her boots ringing against the hardwood floor.

"Damn," he said. "The chase is on again."

Chapter Four

She'd never thought of Zach Gillespie as stupid. But how could he have let a known killer escape and not hunt him? What kind of lawman let a man wanted for murder get away? If he hadn't interfered with her bringing him in, Simon would be sitting in jail, awaiting trial. She'd be five hundred dollars richer, and the bank loan would be paid off.

She kicked the sides of her horse, spurring him toward the house. Gritting her teeth, she let the frustration of their last conversation wash over her like spring's flash floods. There was still plenty of daylight, and she could be halfway to Dyersville, where she'd last seen Simon, by nightfall.

Yet, as she pulled up in front of the farmhouse and threw her leg over the saddle, her biggest battle of the day lay ahead. They had agreed never to hunt alone, but they hadn't planned on Ruby getting hurt when Annabelle was needed at home. They would just have to listen to reason or not.

She slid to the ground and marched into the house, determined that no matter what was said she would be on the road within an hour. She would be in Simon's hometown tomorrow. Maybe he wouldn't be there, but maybe he would. No matter, the hunt was on again. And this time she'd win. This time he wouldn't escape. This time he would go to jail.

When Meg walked into the house, Ruby looked up from her chair with a frown on her face. "What happened?"

Meg didn't say a word. She went into her bedroom and pulled out her war bags. She tossed in two extra pairs of clothes, grabbed her blanket roll, and carried the bags into the kitchen.

"What are you doing?" Ruby asked, her blue eyes wide with alarm. "Simon wasn't there, was he?"

Meg grabbed some leftover biscuits, put them in a tin along with some dried fruit, and shoved the meager rations in her bags. Where she was going, she wouldn't need a lot of food.

"Damn it, Meg, talk to me. You can't go after him alone. Wait a minute, and I'll get my things and go with you," Ruby said, rising from the chair.

"No," Meg told her. "You're not going with your ankle in that kind of shape. I can't be worrying about you. This job I'm doing alone."

"We made a promise we would always hunt together," Ruby said, her voice rising.

"Well, sometimes promises have to be broken," Meg yelled back. Her stomach clenched, and her limbs stiffened as determination pulsed through her blood. It wasn't like she wanted to go by herself, but she had no choice. "This time it's just me."

Annabelle chose that moment to walk into the house. "What's all the noise about? I could hear you guys clear out in the garden."

"Meg's going after Simon…alone."

"No, you're not," Annabelle said, taking a step into the living area, where the three sisters took positions like three prizefighters circling the ring. "We made a deal there would always be two of us."

"So fire me. I'm breaking the deal," Meg said, pulling on her long coat, which she knew she would need tonight. "For every day we linger, the trail gets colder."

"Meg, wait. I'll go with you. Let me just gather my things," Annabelle said.

"No. You're needed here with Ruby. It's spring calving season. I can do this without your help."

Annabelle stopped and stared at Meg, her green eyes flashing with anger. "We stick together. We're like the three musketeers. Don't do this. I won't have you go missing or learn I have to bury my sister. You can't do this without one of us by your side."

Meg took a deep breath; her heart was pounding in her chest like a runaway locomotive. She had to follow Simon. She had to finish this, so her sisters wouldn't have to ever bounty hunt again, even if that meant she'd die trying.

"I'm leaving. I'll be back, or I'll send you a telegram in a few days and let you know I'm all right," Meg said, walking toward the door. Part of her knew she was doing wrong, but she refused to stop. She had to go after him like the moon chased the setting sun, like a bull pursued a cow, like a good sheriff chased a criminal.

Or at least, like a good sheriff *should* chase a criminal.

Simon had become a token that Zach and she were fighting over, and she was determined to win this time. The bounty would be hers. Simon would go to jail. The bank loan would be paid in full, and neither Annabelle nor Ruby would ever have to ride after a bad man again.

Meg closed the door, her chest aching, her stomach rolling, knowing in her heart she was hurting her sisters, yet unable to stop herself. The bounty was hers to bring in, even if that meant leaving Ruby and Annabelle.

*

Two days later, Meg walked into the saloon where she and Ruby had first confronted Simon. She pulled her hat down low and tried to appear nonchalant and small, as she sat down at a table. Keeping her head down and her eyes lowered, she glanced around the room.

The same men were sitting at the bar. The same saloon girl strolled amongst the men, touching them, offering her pleasures. The bartender was tossing out beer and whiskey, the piano player was banging on the keyboard, and the poker players were slinging cards. It was Saturday afternoon, and Meg did her best to blend into the wall.

Her auburn hair was swept up into her hat, and her clothes were even more masculine than normal. Papa had always told them he tried to appear as if he belonged in whatever situation he found himself. Meg hardly felt as if a saloon was where she fit in best, but she'd been here before.

"Can I get you something to drink?" a young woman in a dress that had her bosom swelling over the top asked.

"Whiskey," Meg replied, lowering the tone of her voice. She kept her eyes downcast, barely looking at the men.

The swinging doors slammed against the wall, and Frank Jones, the meanest hombre this side of the Rio

Grande, stepped into the saloon followed by Simon. The two men were laughing, as they settled in at the bar to drink.

Meg took a deep breath, her lungs squeezing tighter than a corset. He was here. How did she arrest him and get him out the door? How did she get him away from Frank without taking a bullet?

Suddenly, she was filled with doubts, wishing Annabelle or Ruby was here to help her. They hunted as a team. She was only one mean-ass woman against two of the worst outlaws in the state. She could get the local sheriff, but it was doubtful he'd do anything. She was by herself, just like she'd wanted, but now she wasn't quite so certain.

Or she could simply walk out the door and wait until the timing was better. Wait until Simon came out of the bar, unaccompanied and drunk. All the bravado she'd felt back in Zenith had disappeared.

For the next hour, she watched as Simon and Frank talked over a couple of drinks. Finally, just when she was beginning to think they were going to drink until the sun set and the moon rose high in the night sky, they stood and headed for the door.

She threw her money down on the table. Once they stepped out of the saloon, she rose and followed. Quickly, she walked through the swinging doors and out onto the wooden sidewalk. She glanced around looking to see which direction they'd gone, when she heard the click of a gun.

Her heart slammed into her throat and began beating like a galloping horse. Of all the greenhorn mistakes, she'd forgotten the first rule of safety—to check the sidewalk before walking into the open.

"Why, look who's here," Simon said.

Meg whirled around and stared into the barrel of Simon's ugly six-shooter, dangling from his fingers, pointed at her midsection.

"Bounty hunter, Meg McKenzie," he said with a laugh. "Where's the good sheriff? Usually wherever you are, he's not far behind. He's been chasing your tail harder than most criminals."

Meg shrugged, fear riding her hell-bent to nowhere. "The sheriff who let you get away? I left him back at the hotel. He'll be along shortly." It was a lie, but she needed him to believe Zach would be making an appearance any moment. That he was lurking around the corner just waiting on Simon to step out.

The outlaw took her by the elbow and started leading her down the street, past the saloon. Meg knew once they left the populated area she'd be at their mercy. She dug her heels in. "Whoa, boys, I'm not going anywhere with you two."

Simon poked the gun into her ribs, while Frank removed her gun from its holster. He gave her a big ugly grin, blew her a kiss, and strolled down the street, leaving them behind.

"Where's he going?" she asked, fear spiking through her like a big gulp of whiskey.

"He'll be back," Simon reassured her. "He wants to join our party tonight."

She'd kill them both before she let them touch her.

Simon tugged on her arm, pulling her down the street. "You're not dragging me across the country again. You're not going to keep me tied up, while you and the sheriff play tag. No. This time, you're going with me, and we're leaving town now," Simon said. "Where's your horse?"

"I'm not going anywhere with you. And I don't have a horse."

"Good try! But that's your horse there. I recognize him from our last adventures together," Simon said, yanking her with his gun poking in her ribs.

There was still something about this man. A twinge that tugged at her and made her think she was missing an important detail, but she didn't know what. They stopped in front of her horse, and Simon pointed to the saddle. "Get on and don't try anything funny, or I'll shoot your horse."

She shook her head, knowing she couldn't let him see her attachment to the animal, or he was just as good as dead. "It's not my horse's fault you're an outlaw."

He smiled. "No, but it would be your fault if I were to shoot him."

"Nah, horses can be replaced. But you…your heart is black, and I'd not have a second thought about putting a bullet in you."

"That's not very ladylike," he said.

"I'm not a lady," she responded.

Simon smiled and taunted, "True, but you don't have a gun, do you?"

"Not yet," she promised.

"Shut up and get on your damn horse," he commanded, poking the gun in her ribs again.

Slowly she climbed on and considered gigging her horse and taking off, but he held her reins. She wouldn't have minded dragging his body behind her if she'd known he would lose the pistol.

Frank rode back down the street with Simon's horse. He handed the reins to Simon, and he climbed on.

Without a word, Frank turned and rode off, leaving them alone.

"Where's he going?" Meg asked, despair choking her, her pulse pounding, knowing she had to put up a brave front or she'd be lost.

"You sure are a noisy bitch. Guess you'll just have to wait and see. Let's go," he said.

Simon rode beside her as they headed out of town, her fear escalating with each passing mile. This was why her sisters hadn't wanted her to go off on her own. This was why they'd agreed to always have a second person. Now she wondered if they would indeed be burying her body or if Ruby and Annabelle would ever know what had happened to her.

And what would Simon do when they stopped? Kill her?

Meg sighed. She wouldn't give up without a fight. She had too much to live for. Too many dreams she'd yet to accomplish. A town full of people she needed to show that she truly was a woman. A woman with feelings.

They passed tall pine trees, the birds calling from the branches, and a cool breeze blew against her neck. The sun slid down the sky, and darkness would soon surround them. When they stopped, she would make some kind of move. She had no choice, but to try to escape.

"Where are we headed?" she asked.

"To a place where we can dispose of the body," Simon told her, smiling.

Her stomach tightened as revulsion rose, leaving her nauseous. He was trying to frighten her, and though she had on her brave face, her insides were quivering like she was cold.

"Why aren't you at home, married with a man of

your own, and raising a passel of kids?" Simon asked.

"Not many men want to marry a woman who dresses in pants and can outshoot and out ride them," she said, trying to make herself unattractive in his mind. "You men want the pretty, petite women who dress, look and act frail. There's not much that's fragile about me."

Simon laughed. "You remind me of my mother. She was never a delicate woman. In fact, she ruled our home with an iron fist. Still does."

"Then what happened to you? Are there other brothers and sisters?" She needed as much information about Simon as she could glean from him. For once she escaped, she would return with her sisters to cash in his six-shooter.

"I'm the baby of four," Simon said behind her.

"Is your mother still alive?" Meg asked. Fear growled like an angry serpent in her stomach at the thought of what would happen when they stopped.

"Oh, yes, she's a smart woman, except when it comes to men. And she's very protective of her children," Simon said. "Don't mess with her sons, unless you want to get hurt."

"Even the ones who are in trouble with the law?"

"You're asking a lot of questions," Simon said, his voice harsh, ignoring her statement.

She could feel the anger radiating from him. Meg tried to act like it was nothing, but somehow she thought she'd just found an issue that maybe if she could learn who the man's mother was she could exploit. "Just passing time."

They rode along in silence for a few minutes, Meg thinking of ways she could escape. She knew that if they killed her, her sisters would make sure these men hung from a noose or they would extract their own revenge. But she didn't want her sisters coming after them. She wanted to escape. Then she would pursue the longrider again. Only next time, she'd be even more cautious. Next time she wouldn't make a greenhorn mistake.

"You asked me why I hadn't married. Why haven't you found a good woman and settled down?" she asked, not really caring. "You could be eating three cooked meals a day, instead of riding from town to town."

He didn't answer her, and she knew something she'd said had affected him, but which statement? Which question was churning in his brain, triggering it to fester until he broke?

The sun beat down on her, its rays feeling more like summer than spring, causing her to sweat. She wanted to lean over her horse and ride away as fast as she could, but feared he'd shoot her. And he still had her gun. Sure, she had another one in her saddlebags, but she liked the gun he'd taken. She'd do whatever it took to get the weapon back.

A horse whinnied and stepped out in front of them from the bushes, startling Meg. A rush of warmth and pleasure flooded her body, and she smiled at the sight of Zach, sitting on his horse, his hat low over his head, his gun pointed at Simon. God, she was so happy to see him.

"Sheriff," Simon said laughing, as he pulled on his horse's reins, halting the animal. "I've been expecting you. It seems anywhere Miss McKenzie is, you're not far behind." He looked between the two of them. "Is there something you need to tell me? Maybe a wedding being planned?"

"No," Meg responded defiantly, yet still thrilled to see Zach. "I'm too much woman for him. I wear pants."

Simon sat back in his saddle like he was greeting an old friend. He seemed relaxed, almost at ease, like he wasn't afraid. Still, Zach had a gun pointed at his middle.

"Untie Meg's hands and give her back her gun," Zach demanded.

"And if I don't?"

Zach shook his head. "Don't give me an excuse. God, I'd like to shoot you right now."

A smile lifted Simon's lips. "Just asking." He reached over and tugged on the knots that had kept her hands tied to the saddle horn. In a matter of moments, she was free. She shook her wrists, letting the blood flow back down into her digits.

"Now her gun," Zach said patiently.

Simon pulled her gun out of his saddlebag and placed it in her hand. "Do you know how to use that thing?"

Anger churned inside her at the fear she'd ridden with for the last couple of hours. She clenched her fists, and when he leaned over, she threw a right punch, hitting him smack in the face.

Blood spurted from his nose. He stared at her with disbelief that she'd actually struck him. "Ow!"

She smiled. "Try me. I'd be happy to show you just how good a shot I am."

His hand flew to his face. "Damn, woman, you can throw a punch. What did I do to you?"

Quickly, she shoved the gun back in her holster. "You held me hostage. I don't do captive well."

"And how many times have I been your prisoner?" he asked.

She shrugged. "I don't have a bounty on my head."

"What now, Sheriff?" Simon asked, moving his horse away from her.

For the first time, she saw a glint of respect in his gaze. She doubted he would bother her again.

"Give me your gun. I'm taking you to jail. It's what I should have done a week ago," Zach said, reaching over his horse and pulling out Simon's weapon. "We're done playing games."

It's what I should have done a week ago? What was he saying? It almost sounded like he'd deliberately not taken Simon to jail. Maybe the prisoner hadn't escaped from Zach. Maybe Zach had never turned Simon in. But he was a lawman. Sworn to uphold the law.

Meg had never seen Zach so determined, so manly. She almost wanted to turn herself in, but that was stupid. She'd done nothing illegal.

Zach dropped down from his saddle and took Simon's hands. He began to wrap them in rope. He tied him to his saddle horn, much the same way Simon had tied Meg.

Once Zach had Simon secured, he turned to Meg.

"What in the hell are you doing out here alone?" he asked. "It's bad enough when you and Ruby are on the prowl, but alone? Do you want to die?"

"I'm earning a decent living," she said, "and this is my prisoner."

Zach and Simon both started laughing.

A sizzle of anger zipped along Meg's spine. Did they think she was funny? She'd earned more in the last year than she had the entire time she'd worked as a seamstress. More than both of her sisters had earned as a waitress and a housekeeper. They could laugh all they wanted, but they were doing much better.

"Yeah, honey, you did real well with that one. I think I just saved your butt. You were tied up," Zach said, climbing back on his horse.

She shrugged. "It was only a matter of time before I had the upper hand. I wasn't afraid."

Hell, who was she kidding? She'd been scared out of her mind, worrying what Simon planned for her. She'd known being alone would be tough, but this wasn't what she'd expected.

Laughing, Zach rode over to her side. He grabbed her reins and pulled her horse in close. "Damn it, woman. What if I hadn't followed you? What if he'd taken you to his hideout? What would you have done then?"

Okay, she'd give him a little credit, but not much. Being alone with Simon had frightened her, but she wouldn't have surrendered to that fear.

"I'm a survivor. I would have fought. I would have survived, and then I'd kick his ass for hurting me. Don't ever think I'm weak." She pulled her horse away from his and followed Simon.

*

Zach watched Meg's ass swaying on the back of the horse. She sat a saddle better than most men. She could shoot better than most men, she was smarter than many men, and yet, there was something soft and vulnerable about her that made him want to wrap his arms around her and protect her.

Even after the incident with the washtub, he wanted to safeguard her, and while he'd never concede it was his fault, it would have gone so much better if he had stood up to those men and told them she was beautiful, and he would be proud to call her his wife.

A part of him didn't want anyone to realize that Meg was a beauty because he wanted to keep her all to himself. And right now, most men in town were afraid of her. Most men in town were afraid of all the McKenzie girls, especially after Annabelle and Ruby had been fired from their jobs last year. Slowly, the news had travelled about how Annabelle had threatened to shoot Rusty, and Ruby had threatened to shoot Clay's carrot.

The stupid boy deserved her taunts, but still, that had a way of making men walk a wide path around the girls when they came to town.

With startling clarity, Zach realized Simon was spurring his horse.

"Simon, stop!" Zach yelled.

"He's getting away," Meg screamed. "Halt or I'll shoot." She pulled out her gun.

"Stop, Meg! You can't shoot him," Zach cried, knowing he could never let anyone shoot Simon. He was stupid, but he was innocent of the murder charges, and Zach had to prove he was still a good man.

"Like hell, I can't. He's wanted dead or alive."

"I'm ordering you not to shoot!" Zach yelled, spurring his horse faster. He had to stop her. He couldn't let her fire her gun.

Meg turned to glance back at Zach, shaking her head as she took off after Simon. Two ugly hombres pulled out from the side of the trail, and Simon raced toward them.

One of them pulled his gun and pointed it at Meg. Zach's blood turned colder than a dead man as he watched the criminal aim at Meg. She ducked just as he fired. She spurred her horse and pulled her own gun. She fired once and struck one of the hombres, sending him plummeting to the ground.

Damn, she was good.

Zach's horse sped past Meg just as she raised her gun

again. This time she was aiming for Simon. This time she was aiming to kill.

Zach hated Simon for his cowardliness, he hated him for how he was living his life, but still...he couldn't let her shoot him.

He spurred his horse and pulled in front of Meg, just as she fired her gun. The bullet slammed into his shoulder, knocking the breath out of him. The reins slipped from his fingers, and he felt himself falling.

The ground rushed up at him, and he crashed into the earth.

Zach watched in slow motion as Simon glanced back at him, saw him laying on the ground, and continued riding.

Darkness settled over him like a blanket, and Zach knew he was dying.

Chapter Five

Meg stared in disbelief as Zach fell off his horse, his body smashing into the ground with a wallop. Her heart slammed into her throat, and she stopped breathing. *No. No. No. Not Zach.*

Not the man she'd almost married and who still held a tiny chunk of her heart, if she were honest with herself.

And she'd shot the sheriff, the town of Zenith's law official. What kind of crime was that? She never missed her target. She'd been aiming for Simon, but the bullet had struck Zach, and now, he lay sprawled on the ground, not moving.

Simon glanced back and galloped away with the gang of outlaws, their horses kicking up the dust as they disappeared over the hill, leaving Meg and Zach behind. God, she wanted to go after them, but she couldn't leave Zach. She'd shot him! It was her fault he was hurt.

She pulled her horse to a halt beside his body. *Oh, please don't let him be dead.* She hadn't meant to injure him. She couldn't live with herself if she'd killed him.

Jumping down from her horse, she ran to his side. "Zach," she cried. "Zach, open your eyes."

He lay unconscious, his lashes dark against his pale

skin. She put her ear against his mouth. He was breathing, but barely. She placed her hand over his heart and felt its steady beat.

Her lungs seemed to expand once more as relief surged through her. She almost felt light-headed. He wasn't dead.

The wound in his shoulder was a small hole that trickled blood. The bullet had passed through his back into the muscle of his arm, where it protruded from the frayed skin it had tried to exit. That piece of lead wouldn't be hard to remove, unless he never regained consciousness.

She checked the back of his head, and he appeared okay. Maybe the fall had just knocked him out. Gripping him, she ran her hands down his firm arms and legs, checking for broken bones. Finally, she sat back and gazed at him, guilt eating at her insides like a horse chewing a carrot. He seemed intact, just unconscious, but still raw shame crushed her.

What if he never woke up? What if she'd killed him? All the pain from their breakup rose up, squeezing her chest and making her nauseous. He couldn't die. She hadn't meant to hurt him. She had to get a grip and think about her surroundings. How could she take care of him?

The sun was beginning its descent below the horizon, casting long shadows on the trail. Meg realized she needed to gather wood and build a fire before dark. She walked over to his horse, grabbed the reins, and pulled him over to her own horse, where she staked the animals. Then she gathered enough firewood to last them the night.

Over the years, she'd learned how to quickly set up camp, and soon she had a fire going and water boiling.

She undid the cinch and tugged Zach's saddle off his horse. Carrying everything over to their campsite, she went through his saddlebags to see what kind of rations he might have and if he had anything she could use to treat his wound.

She unfurled his bedroll and laid it out along with the supplies she'd found. Then she rolled his heavy body onto the bedroll, close to the fire. He moaned as she turned him over and over gently and slowly, trying to keep from doing any additional damage.

At least, he was making noises as she moved him. That was a good sign. Now she needed to remove the bullet and stitch up his wound.

When she had him next to the fire, she brought out her knife. She wiped the blade with a clean handkerchief then stuck it in the fire for several moments, sterilizing the blade.

She tugged his shirt out of his pants and unbuttoned the garment. His hard-muscled chest gleamed in the firelight. Tenderly, she pulled his arms and gently lifted his injured shoulder, removing the shirt from his body. He lay there naked from the waist up, and she couldn't help but admire his hardened muscles, his abdomen a rippling cascade of firmly toned skin.

Sitting cross-legged on the ground, she picked up Zach's head and put it in her lap. She tilted his body, so she could see the damage in the firelight.

Carefully, she wiped away the dried blood from the wound with a damp rag. Brushing his hair back from his face, she gazed at the man she'd almost married. Why did she feel more attracted to him now than she had over a year ago? Why did the thought of him dying have her chest tightening and her eyes brimming with tears?

She had to help him. She had to remove the bullet. She had to save this aggravating, tin-star wearing man.

"I'm so sorry," she said, her voice quivering almost on the verge of tears. She reminded herself to remain strong for Zach. There was no choice, but to remove the bullet.

With a deep breath, she placed the tip of her knife into the wound and began to dig the lead out of his shoulder.

Suddenly, he grabbed her arm. She glanced into his big brown eyes dilated with pain. "What the hell are you doing?"

Her heart slammed into her chest, racing like a puppy running for joy. "Zach, you're awake."

His eyelids drifted down over his eyes then back up woozily. "When someone's poking you with a knife, it's kind of hard to sleep."

"You were shot," she said, hoping his mind was clear and he remembered what had happened. "I'm digging the bullet out."

He shook his head. "No. Not you. Anyone, but you. You tried to kill me."

She stopped what she was doing. How could she explain it hadn't been intentional? "No. I didn't. And there's no one else to dig the bullet out. We're alone on the trail."

"You shot me," he said, his brown eyes flashing with painful annoyance, his voice accusatory.

She paused and bowed her head for a moment as regret washed over her. Raising her head, she stared back at him directly, unflinching. "Not on purpose. I was aiming for Simon, and then there you were in between me and the outlaw."

"You shot me," he said again, stunned like if he said it several times he could believe she'd actually hurt him.

"You rode in front of me just as I fired," she said, all her defenses riding to the forefront.

"You didn't have to pull the trigger," he responded, his eyes squinting with anger.

"You didn't have to ride in front of me," she replied, trying to remain calm, yet getting agitated. She hadn't done it on purpose. Holding the knife to the side, she didn't touch the wound, but waited for him to give her the okay.

Zach took a deep breath and sighed. "You'd argue with a dead man."

"You came pretty darn close today."

He closed his eyes and swallowed, his throat convulsing over his Adam's apple. "I guess they got away?"

What did he expect? They'd ridden off and left them over an hour ago. The sun was sliding down below the horizon. They'd be alone tonight.

"Yeah, it's just you and me and the horses. So let me finish before rigor mortis sets in."

A bewildered look crossed his face. "That's for dead people."

"Yeah, I know."

His eyes contemplated her, his brows drawing together in a frown. "You're not going to make it worse, are you?"

"Not unless you accuse me of shooting you again," she responded, guilt gnawing at her insides, like a dog with a bone. She'd been horrified when she saw the damage her bullet had done to his shoulder. Watching him fall from that saddle, knowing he'd been shot was the worst.

"Well, you did. You shot me."

"I know," she said, hating that it was true. "But you rode in front of me."

He stared at her with resignation. "Do it quick. It hurts like hell."

"I will. Now take a deep breath. This won't take long." She started digging into his flesh with the knife tip, cutting the tissue away from the bullet. Finally, after what seemed like hours, but was probably less time than it took to make coffee, the lead slipped into her hand. A trickle of blood flowed from the open hole in his shoulder.

She sighed, releasing the breath she'd been holding. That had been worse than the time Ruby had sliced her hand with the butcher knife or when Annabelle had fallen into a prickly pear cactus and Meg had had to remove all those stickers. Digging out the very bullet she'd put in his shoulder had to be right next to watching her father die. Why did this cowboy seem to cause her nothing but anguish?

"I got it. We're done. All I have to do now is stitch you up," she said with relief.

Zach moaned and gritted his teeth. "If you look in my saddlebags, there's some whiskey I've been saving. Use it to wash out the wound."

When he'd been out cold, she'd already found the fire juice. "It's right here beside me," she said, opening the bottle. She took a big swig then poured the alcohol on the wound.

"Damn woman!" he gulped a big breath of air. "You could give a man some warning before you set him on fire," he said, wincing from the pain.

Ah, she hadn't considered how the alcohol would feel in an open wound. That must burn a hundred times worse than a scrap to the knee. "Sorry, I'm not a doctor. You're doing well I didn't kill you."

"Not once, but twice," he said, his brown eyes filled with pain. "Hand me that bottle." After she passed it to him, he took a big swig of the alcohol.

"Yeah, about that. I don't know what happened. I was aiming for Simon. I never miss and then you were falling," she said, taking a clean rag and wiping his shoulder. His skin felt smooth to the touch, and she enjoyed him lying here in her lap, a little too much. Warm little butterflies were flitting through her abdomen like they were chasing each other, leaving her warm and tingly.

"Guess you're not as great a shot as you thought," he said, taking a second swig from the bottle.

She frowned. She never missed. Never. "I'm a damn good shot," she responded, wondering, could he have ridden in front of her on purpose? No, he wouldn't be so foolish. He wouldn't have acted so stupidly. Would he?

"You went through my saddlebags," he accused.

She nodded. "I know all your secrets, Zach Gillespie."

"What secrets? There was nothing in there but some clean clothes, rope, and hardtack."

"And a bottle of whiskey," she said, liking the way the alcohol made her feel warm and cozy and safe and secure. Like everything was going to be fine.

"Doesn't every man carry a bottle of whiskey?" he asked, looking up at her as she finished holding the clean cloth to the wound to stop the blood flow. The bleeding was minimal, but she still wanted to stitch him up to keep the dirt out.

She hated hurting him yet again, but she had to take care of him, since it was her bullet that had laid him low.

"I guess Papa did. He never told me." She gazed down into Zach's earthy brown eyes, and a warmth she hadn't expected filled her. He had beautiful eyes with lashes that were long and brows that arched with expression. Why was she still attracted to him after what they'd been through? "You better take another sip of that whiskey. I'm about to start sewing you up."

"I don't think I want you sewing on me."

She glared at him. "Fine. Then ignore my comment about the whiskey."

"You'll probably stitch your initials in my shoulder. You worked for Ho Chinn until he fired you. Was it because of bad stitching?"

The urge to jam her needle into his flesh was overwhelming, but she knew that wouldn't be nice, and he'd already suffered a lot at her hands today.

"Why in the world would I put my initials in your shoulder?" Like she wanted some woman to come bringing him home to her? She had no use for this cowboy. She'd done her good deed, and now it was time for him to stand on his own.

He took another swig of the whiskey. "Because you'd leave your mark on me?"

She laughed. "I don't lay claim to you. I don't want someone to bring your dead body back to me."

He grabbed her hand, halting the needle. "You almost did."

The way he said those three little words brought back memories of the night they'd kissed in the moonlight. The hope she'd had after he left that evening that maybe, just maybe, she'd found a man who would help her and grow to love her. But that was a silly dream, which had burst in the bathhouse like a cloud in a thunderstorm.

"But I learned the truth about how you really felt about me, so you're still free as a bird. I'm surprised some dress-wearing woman hasn't claimed you yet."

There were other single women in town who would have hitched their wagon to the sheriff. In the past year, why hadn't some stupid, proper woman calf-roped him?

"Hasn't been one I'm interested in. I'm beginning to think I prefer my women wearing trousers," he said, his eyes staring warmly into hers.

Her heart slammed up into her throat, sending a shower of butterflies through her midsection. "You need to be careful what you say. I'm about to stick a needle in your skin, and you really want me to be gentle," she said, her voice low. Why was he flirting with her so outrageously? And why did his voice send warmth cascading through her like a hot summer night?

He smiled. "That's my Meg, running from her feelings."

What was he talking about? She didn't run from anything. This past year she'd faced enough bad men to make her rethink about ever marrying. "Your head is in my lap. I'm not going anywhere. And I'm not your Meg."

"You could be."

"Leave it be, cowboy."

He closed his eyes for a moment then took another sip of the whiskey. "So tell me why did Ho Chinn fire you?"

Meg remembered the weeks she'd slaved over all the mending Ho Chinn had let accumulate. She'd worked twelve hours a day, stitching up rips and sewing on buttons until her fingers were bloody. "I was fired because he wouldn't give me a paycheck, so I took the cash that he owed me from the register."

Zach squinched his eyes shut when she poked him with the needle. Quickly and efficiently, she zipped it through his flesh, closing the wound. In just a matter of moments, she was finished.

He opened his eyes and glanced up from her lap. "Are you done?"

"All finished with the front. Let me take a look at your back to see if we need to stitch up the entry wound."

He rolled over, moaning as he moved, placing his face right between her legs, the top of his head inches from her crotch. Warmth spiraled through her, putting a little catch in her breath.

"Don't be getting any ideas there, cowboy," she warned, her voice sounding breathy. His head being so close to her womanly parts was creating all kinds of tingly feelings.

He sighed. "I'm wounded. I'm hurting. I feel like someone took a two by four to me. You have nothing to be worried about. Although I must say, this is a very interesting position. One any other time, I would enjoy."

She looked at his back. It was smooth and hard, and her hands itched to run her fingertips down his muscles, but she resisted. "Take another swig of whiskey then hand me the bottle."

He rose up, took a gulp, passed her the bottle, then settled back down between her legs.

"Don't get too comfortable down there," she warned.

He chuckled. "If we were naked, this could be fun."

"But we're not," she said, the image sending shivers

spiraling down her spine to right between her legs, awakening desires she'd never felt before.

She took a swig, letting the warmth of the alcohol flow down her throat, and then she poured a little on the wound on his back. He flinched as the alcohol trickled over his skin. That should keep his mind in the right place, until she could move him.

"I'm not certain I want you drinking while you're sewing on me."

"Too bad." She put the needle in his flesh. The urge to finish stitching him up and get his face out of her crotch urgent.

"Ow, woman. You just like to surprise a man, don't you?" His voice sounded muffled and vibrated between her legs.

Oh yeah, he had to get out of there. "It's the best way to get your attention." She made two quick stitches and tied up the open hole. She poured more of the alcohol over the wound.

"Damn, remind me to never let you doctor on me again," he said, the alcohol taking his breath away.

She smiled. She never wanted to have to remove a bullet from anyone. Never again did she want the responsibility of that person's life in her hands.

"You're all done," she said. "Unless it gets infected, I think you're going to live."

Thank goodness it hadn't been more serious because she didn't know how she would have reacted. Leaving Zach wounded on the trail had not been an option.

He rolled over, leaving his head in her lap and gazed up at her. His eyes, along with the whiskey, blazed a hot trail straight to her womanly parts, starting a wildfire.

"Thank you," he said. "You could have gone after

Simon, but you stopped to help me."

"You're welcome." Her words came out almost in a whisper, the very idea of leaving him behind unthinkable. "I wouldn't have ridden off and left a wounded man. Not even for a good bounty," she said, staring down at him. He was still in her lap, but at least his face wasn't planted between her legs. "How's the shoulder feel?"

"Feels like I've been shot."

"Drink more whiskey. It's going to hurt tonight."

He took another swig from the bottle and handed it back to her.

The fire crackled, and a piece of wood popped, sending sparkles flying into the night sky, reminding her of fireworks. She took a long sip. "You've never been shot before?"

"Not until today," he said, his brown eyes meeting her gaze.

"I still don't understand what happened," she said. The feel of him laying in her lap was warm and welcoming. Yet his head was positioned very close to her crotch and every time those warm dark eyes lit on her, he seemed to start a bonfire between her legs.

"Maybe you should move," she said, picking up his head and resting it back down on the ground.

Having him in her lap was just a little closer than she was comfortable with. She needed to put some distance between them. He could be going after the same bounty money, even though he was the sheriff.

"Ow," he said. "I was enjoying where I was at. I'm wounded. Help a man find a little comfort."

"Well, now, there's the problem. You shouldn't be experiencing any enjoyment right now due to your injuries."

Oh, no. She should put the fire between her and Zach. It was bad enough they were out here alone. But he was injured, and she'd had no choice but to stay the night on the trail, just the two of them.

He shook his head at her and smiled. "I kind of thought it was the least you could do after you shot me."

"Doesn't pay for you to think, does it?" she said, her voice rough. She had to get a rein on the emotions Zach seemed to create in her. An urgent need to touch him, to feel his lips on hers, to seek that next step between a man and a woman, engulfed her like a raging river roaring through her. That unknown step that would make her a woman.

"I guess not."

With a sigh, she released all the pent-up craving that had consumed her when his head had been in her lap. Once she had her emotions under control, she could concentrate on her goal. Simon.

"You need to rest, so I can take you into town tomorrow," she said, thinking she could drop him off then continue her search. They needed to part ways and the sooner, the better. She was grateful to Zach for getting her away from Simon and Frank Jones, but she had to go it alone.

"Why are you so determined to catch Simon?" he asked, completely out of the blue.

For a moment, the question surprised her. "Simple. The money is enough that it will finish paying off the bank note, and then the farm will belong to my sisters and me. We won't ever have to bounty hunt again, unless we want to."

She'd never told him about the bank note. That had

been her secret she would have revealed once he'd agreed to marry her, but now there was no need.

He nodded in understanding. "Is that why you wanted me to marry you? The bank note?"

Meg felt ashamed for a moment. She hadn't wanted to marry him just because of his money, but she hadn't pursued him because she cared for him either. In today's world, what choice did a woman have, but to snag a man? "I needed help with the mortgage and the farm. I couldn't do it all."

"Yet, you have," he said softly, taking a swig from the whiskey bottle, his dark brown eyes studying her, searching, and leaving her breathless.

"Yes, with the help of my sisters, we've managed to keep the farm. But I don't want to be a bounty hunter all my life. I have my own dreams," she said, wondering why she was telling him this.

He offered her the bottle, and while she knew the whiskey was warming her and loosening her tongue, she didn't feel the urge to stop. The liquor soothed her and allowed her to dream of things she wanted.

"Tell me what kind of dreams a girl like you has, Meg. I'd like to know," he said, leaning back against his saddle, staring at her.

She reached out and put another log on the fire. The hoot of an owl sounded lonesome in the darkness. The image of her store came to mind. The place where she had ready-made dresses for ladies to purchase and dress patterns she'd designed. She wanted a place where women could sit and chat about the latest fashions then go back to their families excited by the time they'd spent at Meg's Creations.

But first, she had to make sure her sisters were well

taken care of, the farm was in good hands, and then she could accomplish her dreams. Her desires.

"I want to own a dress shop," she said, staring at the fire.

Zach had just taken a swig of whiskey. The liquor spewed from his mouth, and he began to cough.

Her spine stiffened, disappointment hardened her stomach, and she jerked around to stare at him. "You have a problem with that?"

She should never have told him. Like all men, except for her father, no one understood her enjoyment of taking a piece of cloth and transforming it into the design she'd drawn on paper. No one understood the pleasure she received from touching satiny fabric and altering it into a beautiful gown.

He shook his head as he coughed and tried to clear his throat. He took another swig of the whiskey. "Not at all. It just wasn't what I expected. I thought a woman like you would want to raise cattle or horses or continue bounty hunting or even want to start a family. I'm kind of shocked." He glanced over her attire. "You're just not the type of woman who you usually see owning a dress shop."

Bristles rose on the back of her neck and all the pent-up rage she'd held onto for the last year exploded from her. "You're just like everyone else in town. You think I wear pants because that's what I want. Has it ever occurred to you that maybe we didn't have the money to purchase the material for me to make a new dress?"

Zach shook his head. "But you know how to sew."

"Yes, and all the new material went to Annabelle and Ruby, so they wouldn't have to wear Papa's hand-me-downs." Tears pricked the back of her lids, but she refused to cry. She'd not wanted her sisters to do without, and she'd sacrificed her own clothing for them. Was it fair? Probably not, but she loved Annabelle and Ruby.

She rose from the blanket. "I need to check on the horses and make sure everything is secure for the night."

She walked into the darkness and stared up at the night sky, her hands shaking, her chest aching with the need for someone to understand. Someone to realize she had dreams; she had desires. She longed to dress like a woman and knew eventually her time would come. All she had to do was wait. Then the naysayers could choke on the vile things they'd said about her.

Zach was no different from any other man she'd ever known. They all believed she wanted to wear pants and look like a man. But this life had been handed to her, and she'd had no choice but to accept what she'd been dealt, for now. But soon, very soon, she would change her life and turn into the woman she'd always dreamed of becoming. Once she caught Simon, there would be enough money to pay off the loan, and then she could begin her life.

*

Zach watched Meg storm off into the night. He took another swig of the whiskey and let the alcohol course through his blood and soothe the ache in his shoulder. Warmth flooded through his body, releasing the tension, except when he looked at Meg.

God, he was such a fool. She'd told him more than once how she didn't like wearing pants, but he'd thought she was just saying what she thought he wanted to hear. He'd believed like all the other men in town that she really wanted to wear men's clothing.

He was a fool. A damn fool.

He'd never realized just how desperate their situation was, even after he'd had dinner with the three girls and been served a stolen ham. Meg had sacrificed and let her sisters have the newer clothes, while she wore her father's clothing. She wore pants, so her sisters could dress like women, and Zach had laughed with all the other men in town at her clothing.

They'd ridiculed her for something she'd had no choice about. They'd ridiculed her for her self-sacrifice. The realization left him feeling queasy. Not exactly his best effort.

She walked back into the camp area she'd set up carrying her bedroll. She started to unroll it on the other side of the fire. He was impressed with everything she'd done while he'd been unconscious.

"It's kind of hard to pass the bottle to you when you're way over there," he said.

No wonder she'd tied him up and left him naked in town. He'd deserved that and more. Yet, Meg was a rounder. She was spirited and prettier than any woman he'd ever met. He feared seeing her in a dress would have every man in town chasing her skirts. And that wouldn't do at all. He kind of wanted to be the one to chase her. He kind of wanted to catch her as well.

"I've had all the whiskey I'm drinking tonight," she said, not looking at him.

Zach grinned as she stomped to the other side of the fire. He watched as she spread out her blankets and settled her saddle on the edge to lean against. "I think you need to take a look at my wound. It feels funny, like it might be swelling," he said, knowing it was a lie, but hoping she'd come check.

She frowned at him. Slowly, she unfurled her long, lean legs from sitting and strode to his side of the campfire. She bent over to look at his shoulder, and he pulled her down onto his lap with his good arm.

"What are you doing?" she cried. "I can't look at your shoulder like this."

"I lied," he said. "I wanted you here."

She stared at him, her green eyes widening, questioning. "Why?"

He took a deep breath, not knowing what to say, not wanting to apologize, yet feeling he'd done her wrong. "I didn't mean to make fun of your dreams. Everyone has to have a goal, an aspiration, and it's a lucky person whose desires are fulfilled. I hope you get your dress shop someday." He reached out and brushed her hair with his fingertips.

"Is that the whiskey talking or the man who made fun of me?"

"No, it's Zach, the man who didn't understand," he replied. She felt so right in his arms, her little derriere snug in his lap, his good arm wrapped around her. Her lips were mere inches from his. He watched as her tongue licked her bottom lip, and he wanted to groan.

Of all the times for his body to be banged up and bruised with a bullet wound in the shoulder, he couldn't do a damn thing that he wanted to do. But yet that sassy mouth of hers was begging for his attention. That sassy mouth of hers needed to be kissed. And by God, he could still kiss.

He lowered his lips to hers, his mouth greedily consuming what he'd dreamed of possessing again. His lips devoured hers, his tongue teasing and tasting the edge of her mouth. This woman was sweet temptation wearing a cowboy hat and a six-shooter. Yet beneath the tough cowgirl exterior beat the heart and soul of a woman. A woman he wanted to peel the layers off of, charm his way past her armor, and find the vulnerable lover he believed she'd hidden. Beneath all that spunky, stubborn, strong-willed persona beat the heart of a loving woman.

He wanted to find that creamy center and see if he could melt her heart.

His mouth moved over hers, sucking her lip inside, wanting…needing more from her. With his good hand, he pulled her closer, angling his mouth, his tongue sweeping the inside of her lips. She tasted of whiskey and desire, a thrilling combination any man without a bullet hole in his shoulder would have taken advantage of.

Suddenly, she pulled her mouth away from his, her breathing harsh, her eyes wide. "What are you doing, Sheriff?"

He pulled back, his shoulder aching in a rhythm that matched the throbbing between his legs. "Kissing you."

She smiled, and his heart warmed clear down to his toes and back. He loved it when she smiled at him; it got his ticker pounding every time. Not to mention that it seemed she was over being angry at him.

"You kiss pretty nice," she said softly.

He glanced up at her and frowned. "That's not something a man likes to hear. You never want your kisses referred to as nice. You want to hear stupendous, earth shattering. Maybe we should try again," he said, his lips closing in to kiss her again.

She put her hand between them. "I think it's time we called it a night. You're going to feel like someone's beat you up tomorrow."

He already felt that way, but he liked holding her in his lap, and he loved the feel of her mouth beneath his. He wasn't ready for the night to end. He wanted more. "Just tell me one thing, Meg, and then we can go to sleep."

"What, cowboy?"

"Was I the first man to kiss you?"

Chapter Six

Meg stared into the fire, her heart in her throat, her eyes burning from the smoke. She knew the wetness in her eyes was not from the campfire. She stood from Zach's lap, walked over to her blankets, and sat. She needed to put as much distance between the two of them as possible. She had to keep her focus on Simon and that bounty. Not kissing a good-looking cowboy. The alcohol and Zach had opened a vein of feelings she'd been unable to control.

Her stomach clenched and rose up in her throat. His question only made her think of how much she'd missed out on while she'd raised her younger sisters. How she'd put her own life aside until her sisters were settled. How unfair the situation seemed.

"Let me think about this. I've been taking care of my sisters and the farm since I was twelve years old. When do you think there would have been time for boys and primping and courting? So, yes, Zach, you're the only man who has ever kissed me," she admitted in the darkness.

Why did it feel like she was admitting to being a homely, ugly creature that no man had ever wanted?

Why did it feel like she wasn't worthy because no man came calling? And why, given her situation, did she feel like this was a fair representation of her beauty? Even her sister Ruby had been kissed by more than one young man.

Zach smiled. "You know a man likes being a woman's first. I feel honored."

"You don't think I'm too homely to kiss?" she asked. There had been no one to ever tell her she was pretty. No mother to reassure her, not even her father to let her know she was someone a man would want.

Zach's eyes widened, and his mouth dropped open. "God, woman, do you need those new fangled spectacles to help your eyesight? Homely is not a word that comes close to describing you. Even wearing pants, you're the prettiest woman this side of Fort Worth. I'm not sure I want to see you in a dress because I don't want to have to fight the local cowboys off."

Meg knew he was just saying this to make her feel pretty. She didn't believe him. Besides, Papa had warned the girls about listening to a man who enticed them with pretty words. He'd told his daughters to watch a man's actions. Actions revealed a man's nature.

Zach stared at her in amazement. "You really have no idea of how pretty you are, do you?"

She shrugged. "I've not had much time to spend on primping and dressing up. Between the farm and taking care of my sisters, my childhood pretty much ended when my mother died."

One moment she'd been playing dolls and the next she was handling real dolls, feeding, clothing, and caring for her sisters. While she loved them with all her heart, she longed to have had a normal childhood. Whatever that entailed.

He nodded. "My dad died when I was young. My mom remarried, and my stepfather was not the man my father was. It wasn't long until I started anticipating the day I could leave."

Even Zach had experienced death at such a young age. But the caregiver, his mother, was there. He wasn't responsible for his younger siblings. He wasn't the one they'd depended on.

"Didn't you say you had brothers?"

"Yeah, three of them."

"Do you ever see them?"

"Every couple of months," he said. "They're all grown now and out on their own."

Meg stared at him like she was seeing him for the first time. "I never realized just how little I know about you. We were going to marry, and I've never even met your family."

She wondered if he felt about his brothers the way she did about her sisters. What his relationship was like with his brothers? Were they close?

He smiled. "I really did intend to ask you to marry me that night."

Like the spin of a windmill, her mind returned to that night when she'd been waiting to find out his answer. Her hopes and dreams had all been pinned on that evening, and then she'd overheard the men ridiculing her in the bathhouse. Zach had always said he was going to ask her. Even as she made the tub ready to drag down Main Street, he'd said over and again he was going to ask her to marry him.

"I would have said yes," she replied, gazing at him intently.

"What if I asked you today?" he said staring, his brown eyes focused on her, a slight smile on his lips, though she knew he was serious.

Her heart pounded in her chest. Was Zach the man she wanted? She considered his question and how it could change her life. Then she smiled. "I'm no longer desperate. Now I'm holding out for the real thing. I want a man who will honor and protect me and who loves me. I want someone I can grow old with. You had your chance."

Zach grinned. "I didn't realize how easy I had it before. Now I'll have to work for your heart and your hand."

Was he serious? Somehow she didn't think she was what he wanted. He wanted a prim and proper woman, and even if she wore a dress, Meg had an air about her that she doubted any man would ever change. And she would never change for any man.

"Oh, I think that's the whiskey talking," she said. "You don't want a pants-wearing, bounty-hunting woman who'll hen peck and tell you what to do."

"God, I could eat those words right now, but they'd probably give me heartburn," he said. He picked up the bottle and took another swig.

A moth dove into the fire and made a sizzling noise. Occasionally, she could hear something rustling in the bushes and wondered what animal was foraging for food.

"I think they would be tough words to chew," she said, wrapping her arms around her knees, hugging them in close to her while she stared at Zach's nice firm chest. She loved watching the flicker of the flames from the fire glinting off the hard planes of his abdomen.

He shivered.

"Are you cold?" she asked.

"Yeah, a little," he said.

"Here I'll let you have my blanket." She handed him the cover from her bedroll.

"No, I'm not taking the only blanket away from a woman."

She resisted the urge to roll her eyes, knowing he probably couldn't see her in the darkness. Why was the man resisting? It was a damn blanket, nothing more. He was injured, without a shirt, and the whole argument seemed senseless. His manhood was not any weaker because she was wanted him to be warm tonight.

"Really, I'll be fine. You're the one without a shirt." Though, covering up that chest and abdomen would be a darn shame. She'd enjoyed gazing at him without his shirt on—the ripples across his abdomen, the tapering of his waist, the hint of something more just below the waistline of his pants.

"No. I'll share the blanket, but I'm not taking it from you."

She stared at him and shook her head. "Zach Gillespie, you are one stubborn mule-headed man."

"That I am. And you, Meg McKenzie, are a spirited, opinionated, beautiful woman. Now bring your blanket and your sweet little self and come sit by me," he said, motioning her with his good hand.

His earthy brown eyes darkened with desire and a need she didn't recognize. Part of her warned, *don't go over there*. The other part, her more reckless, adventurous side felt drawn to him and had parts of her body dancing to a music she'd never heard before, leaving her breasts fuller, her breathing quicker, and her mouth aching to search out his once more.

He was hurt because of her. He was injured, and she needed to keep him warm at all costs, regardless of the fact that she had this urge, this need consuming her. Sitting next to him could have dangerous consequences. Slowly, she rose and pulled her bedding closer to his. She sank down on the ground beside him on his good side and threw the blanket around both of their shoulders.

"See, I don't bite."

"Not yet," she replied, her voice sounding husky.

He laughed. "That does feel better. Here," he handed her the bottle. "Have another drink."

"I shouldn't." She took a big swig to boost her courage. She was sitting next to Zach, sharing a blanket with him, her hip close to his, her shoulder touching his, and yet it felt right. She handed the bottle back to him.

"One of us has to stay sober," she said. "I'm not injured. You are."

He shrugged and took another sip. "Oh, so you can wear pants like a man, but can't drink like a man."

She snatched the bottle from his hand and took a big swig. "I can do anything a man can do and probably better."

"If you can drink like a man, let's play a drinking man's game," he said. "Are you on?" He watched as she considered his taunt, hoping she would agree.

"What's the game?"

"Every time I take a drink I ask you a question, and you have to confess the truth. Every time you take a swig, I have to answer your question and confess the truth. The last man-woman standing wins."

She smiled. "How will you know I'm being honest?"

"I won't, but you're a sincere person, so I'm going to take your word," he said. But did she play fair?

Somehow Zach thought the woman played to win.

"What about yourself? Are you an honest person?"

There was so much he wasn't telling her—one tiny little detail that would send her scooting back across to the other side of the fire, madder than a rabid skunk in springtime. He raised his arms then halted when fire spread through his sore shoulder. "I'm the sheriff. Of course, I'm honest."

She rolled her eyes. "Even the law can be corrupt."

He shook his head. "Are we playing?"

"What's the prize?" she asked.

"Dinner tomorrow night in town. Whoever wins pays for dinner."

"How will we know when the game is over?"

"Whoever passes out first or whoever cries uncle." He knew he was weak. The alcohol would affect him much faster than it would a normal person. But Meg was not a big drinker, and hopefully, she wouldn't last long.

She grabbed the bottle from his hand and took a swig. "You first. Tell me why you're trying to take my bounty from me."

Zach smiled at Meg and knew he had to keep her off the subject of Simon. He didn't want to out and out lie to her. He just couldn't tell her the whole truth.

With a deep breath, he played into her assumptions. "Even a sheriff has needs that his pay doesn't cover."

"I knew it. You're trying to earn that five hundred dollar bounty. Why did you let him get away?"

"He knocked me out cold and disappeared. I had to get back to the jail." He hated lying to her, but had no choice.

She handed the bottle to him, obviously satisfied with his story.

He took a swig of the liquor and let it burn down his throat, leaving him warm. "You don't dress like a woman. How do you know you can make dresses that other women will want to wear?"

She smiled, and his heart seemed to melt into one big puddle. When her lips parted and the smile reached all the way to her emerald eyes, he wanted to grab her and make her his. Put a ring on her finger, make passionate love to her, and build them a home.

How could a woman's smile create so much havoc within him?

"That's easy. Papa caught me drawing a dress and knew I had a good eye for design. He would bring me catalogues whenever he came home, and I would pour over them looking at the latest fashions. Now, whenever we stop in town, I go into the local dressmakers shop and look at her dress designs. I have a collection of ideas, several designs already drawn. If I don't succeed, then it won't be because I didn't try."

While she'd been talking, her eyes had a dreamy expression of determination, and he suddenly realized how much she wanted this. This was no spur of the moment consideration; she'd been thinking of this for years. Her whole body had perked up, and he'd seen a side of Meg he'd never realized existed. She was a soft woman hidden beneath a tough exterior.

"Have you ever sewn a dress before?" he asked, wondering if she really had the talent.

She smiled. "All of my sister's clothes."

"You know you should design a dress that women could wear while riding a horse. Some kind of split skirt."

She gawked at him for a moment. "That's not a bad

idea. I wish I had my pencil and paper. I'd sketch that out right now."

He set the bottle down in front of her. She took a deep breath then took a swig of the alcohol. "When did you decide to become a sheriff?"

His shoulder pounded. He had to be careful how much he told her. Even the tiniest detail could be used against him.

"I left home when I turned eighteen. Traveled around a bit, doing odd jobs and a little ranching. Quickly, I learned I never wanted to go on another cattle drive again. Then an opening came up as a deputy in San Antonio, and when I received the position, I was thrilled. Now I'm the sheriff of Zenith."

"Are you far from your family?" she asked.

"No, they're a two-day ride away," he said. So far, he hadn't had to lie to her and that felt good. He wanted to tell her the truth, but kept hoping he wouldn't have to. "My stepfather passed away a couple of years ago, but my mother refuses to sell the small ranch she owns. I check on her often and try to help her when I can."

She handed the bottle to him. "That stuff is really starting to work. I don't think I can feel my legs anymore."

He laughed and leaned against her, rubbing his good shoulder with hers. "We've still got half a bottle to go." He took a big swig and shivered. "What's made you such a capable, determined, stubborn woman?"

Sometimes there were things that happened in a person's life that made them a strong person, and he wondered about Meg. Sure, she'd had to be responsible very young, but what else had toughened her?

She looked at him like he was crazy. "You don't

think taking care of two young girls before you're old enough to breed and have the responsibility of the farm would make you into a stubborn woman? Have you ever dealt with Mr. Green down at the mercantile? That man would just as soon gyp you as give you what you ordered. I learned at a very young age to watch very carefully as he would short me every time. There were no adults around, and I had no one to depend on. I had to learn."

He smiled and handed the bottle back to her. "Ready to cry uncle?"

She took a swig of the alcohol. "Not on your life. Tell me what you were thinking that day I walked into your office and asked you to marry me?"

He threw his head back and laughed. He'd never forget that day as long as he lived. When this beautiful young woman had waltzed into his office and asked him to marry her, his heart had almost frozen to a halt. That was probably the biggest shock he'd ever received as sheriff.

"You about gave me heart failure. I'd never had any woman propose to me, especially after we'd only spoken a few times. Yet, I was intrigued. Why in the hell was a good looking woman asking this dog-eared cowboy to marry her?" Today, he wouldn't even hesitate. He'd ask where and when.

She handed the bottle back to him. He took a swig of the drink. "If I had a do over, I would take you by the hand and walk straight out the door to the sin-buster."

"You lost your chance, cowboy," she said, leaning against him to stare up at him, their faces so close together.

"Don't count me out," he whispered, knowing he had

no idea where they were headed, but it was somewhere together. "Okay, it's your turn to answer. Why didn't you sell the farm and just move to town and get a job, instead of bounty hunting?"

Meg shook her head. "That's easy. We tried menial jobs, and we all three got fired. Annabelle wouldn't accept the owner patting her on the ass. Ruby was almost raped by that stupid Mullens kid, and Ho Chin fired me because I took my wages out of the cash drawer. He wasn't going to pay me. I had no choice but to take what he owed me."

A fierce, protective anger flowed like a river through Zach's chest. He hated Ho Chinn and now he understood why. The man always seemed to be trying to get something for free.

"Why didn't you come to me and ask for my help?" How many other women in town had suffered from these three men? When he got back to Zenith, he'd be paying them each a visit to talk about how they could be arrested.

"For what? I think men have been taking advantage of women who don't have a man for centuries. Those three men are no different from most. You can't arrest every single one of them. We stood up for ourselves, and that resulted in our getting fired. I wouldn't have it any other way," she said with a slur. "Now the bank is almost completely paid off, and we have food on the table. We're no longer starving."

He admired her spunk, her perseverance, and how she had taken her sisters from losing the farm to having the loan almost completely paid off without the help of anyone.

"I think we're going to run out of whiskey before

someone wins," Zach said, his head feeling groggy. The pain in his shoulder had dulled to a small ache, instead of throbbing with his every heartbeat.

She grabbed the bottle from him and took a swig. "There's still enough for two more rounds. Or are you ready to cry uncle?"

"No, ask away. I'll answer your questions."

"How many girls have you kissed? Made love to?"

The question sent a tremor charging down his spine. He wasn't a saint, but he wasn't a complete sinner either. Yeah, he'd kissed a lot of pretty girls when he was growing up, but not since he'd stopped running with his brothers. They were a wild bunch who'd enjoyed a good calico cat occasionally. Zach no longer played with fire for fear he'd get burned.

He shook his head. "Nope. That's two questions. You only get one."

"Then answer my first one, but you better not guzzle the rest of the whiskey to keep from answering the second," she said, her voice low and commanding.

Well, he certainly wasn't going to answer her second question. A man didn't tell a lady how many lovers he'd had. Maybe the direction of the game needed to change and quick. "I wouldn't do that. That wouldn't be fair, though, it's tempting," he said with a chuckle.

Meg swayed toward him, the whiskey clearly affecting her. "Yeah, well, who said life was fair? I think you would drink it all just to keep from answering my question."

"I can't remember how many women I've kissed. You have to understand I was raised with three brothers and well…there was a time when we were all kind of rough and randy. So I've kissed a fair number of gals."

"Damn. Am I the only woman who has only kissed one man? Even Ruby has kissed more men than me."

He reached over and drunkenly caressed her cheek. "I find that very charming. I'd like to be the man who showed you just how much fun kissing can be. But I don't think that's going to happen tonight," he said with a slur, his eyes heavy and his head feeling like it weighed twenty pounds. It didn't want to stay straight. The alcohol was beginning to affect his vision, and his mind was having a hard time focusing.

He took the bottle from her. "As for your other question, a gentleman never tells." With a laugh, he held the bottle to his lips.

"Maybe a lady never tells as well."

If only he didn't have a shoulder wound, they would be doing more than just talking. But then again, they wouldn't be out here on the trail alone if he hadn't gotten hurt. But still, the desire to prove to her that he knew she was a virgin was so tempting.

"Oh, honey, I know you're a virgin. If you haven't been kissed, you have never experienced being with a man."

She pulled back from him. "How do you know I'm not lying?"

He glanced over the top of the bottle. "If that's not a challenging statement, I've never heard one. If I didn't have this injured shoulder or had drunk almost this entire bottle of whiskey, we'd be finding out whether or not you've been with a man."

"Not unless I agreed," she said.

He leaned in close to her, his mouth mere inches from hers. Licking his lips, he stared at her full lips, her tiny mouth, and so wanted to taste her. He wanted to start at her cheek and work his way south, lingering in the juncture between her thighs, where his head had been resting earlier. Oh, there was so much of her he wanted to explore.

"By the time I got through kissing and touching and whispering how much I want you, I think you'd be mine," he said, his voice low and ragged.

"You're awfully sure of yourself," she murmured against his lips.

"A weak man doesn't get what he wants." And Lord knew he wanted her, even in his inebriated state.

"Ask me a question," she said.

He leaned back and gazed at her intently. "What do you want for a wedding present?"

She stared at him, her green eyes widening in surprise. "What did you just say?" She grabbed the bottle from his hand and finished it off.

"I said what do you want for a wedding present?"

"Are you talking specifically you or just anyone?"

"Well, hell, I'm not trying to find out for some sage hen in town. I want to know what you want from me as a wedding present," he said, not really even sure why he was asking, but knowing he was going to pursue her. He'd already made his mind up, and it didn't matter if she said no, he would hunt her down until she said yes.

She stared at him and shook her head. "Damn you, Zach. When I wanted you to marry me, you didn't defend me. When I don't want you to marry me, you start trying to court me. Why in the world would I want to marry an ornery cowboy like yourself?"

He pulled her into his arms, his face inches from hers. "Because I'm regretting my actions that night. I think having you as my wife would be a challenge I would love waking up to every day."

He covered her mouth with his and tried to focus on how he wanted to take her. How he wanted to explore her body and taste his way from her mouth all the way to her toes. How he wanted to bring the passion he sensed just beneath the surface out into the open. He wanted to feel her surrender beneath him and hear her call out his name in excitement.

He wanted Meg like no other woman he'd ever met, and yet, his shoulder rendered his arm useless, and the liquor was making him feel lethargic and drowsy. Suddenly, he felt his eyes closing and his body giving way to the numbness of the alcohol. And then he slumped against Meg.

The last thing he heard was "You picked one hell of a time to pass out, cowboy."

*

Meg awoke to birds chirping. It sounded like they were in her room at home. She wondered how they'd come into the house. She shifted on her side, and it was then she felt the large arm thrown across her middle, warmth spread across her back, and something hot and hard against her backside.

A nice delicious sense of heat skittered down her spine, landing in the region of her stomach then sliding even lower.

She opened her eyes and sat up. When she did, the world spun a crazy tilt and the memory from the night before came rushing back. Her head pounded like an army paraded through it, and her mouth was cottony with the nasty taste of alcohol.

She moaned and grabbed the side of her head. Why had she drunk so much? The memory of their drinking game came rushing back, and nausea overwhelmed her.

Zach lay on his good side, facing her, his eyes closed, his mouth hanging open as he gently snored.

Of all the insults, he'd passed clean out last night while he'd been kissing her. Right in the middle of a lip-lock, she'd realized he was no longer moving. He was no longer kissing. His eyes were closed.

And darn it, she'd been enjoying his kisses. She'd enjoyed his company and the twinkle in his eye when he'd asked her who she'd kissed. And then he'd passed out, and she'd won the game.

Slowly, she rose from the bedroll on the hard ground. She stood, and the world seemed to whirl around her. She felt dizzy and nauseous, and somehow she had to get coffee boiling.

Hurriedly, she went into the bushes and did her business then came back out and dug through her supplies. She poured water from the canteen into the pot, put it on to boil, then went to check on the horses.

With each step, her head pounded and her stomach roiled, leaving her wishing she'd never met Zach Gillespie, never consumed a bottle of whiskey, or even heard of Simon Trudeau. She hated being sick, and this was self-induced.

The horses were still staked out, and she moved them to a new area, where they could eat more grass. Suddenly, her stomach rebelled at the amount of alcohol she'd consumed, and she bent over in the grass and threw up.

Her stomach was queasy with nausea, and she felt like the devil himself was dancing in her head. When she managed to get back to the bedroll, Zach was gone. She had no idea where he'd crawled off to, but she didn't have the strength or the energy to look for him.

She laid down, thinking maybe he was behind a bush somewhere. Soon, he stumbled back to the blanket and sank down.

An awkward silence filled the air. For a moment, neither one of them said anything as everything they'd said to one another last night hung in the air like an invisible wall between them.

Finally, Zach said, "Remind me to never drink a whole bottle of whiskey again."

"I may kill you myself for tempting me to play such a silly game," she responded.

"Hell, you won."

"All I won was a headache, a stomachache, and dinner with a cowboy." Not to mention the fact he'd passed out in the middle of a kiss. Were her kisses so boring men just closed their eyes and began to snore?

Dang it, she was not happy this morning. With all the talk of kissing and weddings and gifts and then for him to start snoring.

He grimaced. "At least, your arm isn't throbbing."

"No, just my head. I should get out my frying pan and make sure your head is pounding as badly as mine."

"Believe me, it is," he said.

"How's your arm this morning?" she asked, realizing in her own misery she'd forgotten about shooting him yesterday.

"It's sore. So sore I don't know if I could control my horse. How would you feel if we just laid low today and rested?" he asked.

That would mean Simon would have a further jump on her. It would take her longer to find him. But lying here, resting with Zach, sounded like a great idea. How

Deadly

long had it been since she'd taken a day to recover? And this morning's hangover was the sickest she'd been in years. And just maybe she'd get the chance to tell him his kissing wasn't good. It was damn boring.

"I like that idea," she whispered, not wanting any noise louder than her voice right now. "As long as it involves no more alcohol."

"We're completely out," he promised. "I'll even get the coffee cups if you'll pour. I can't lift anything with my right arm."

He stood and went around to the horse and pulled out the cups. He took some hardtack out of his saddlebags and put it in a pan to heat over the fire.

"Do you remember what we talked about last night?" Zach asked.

Meg closed her eyes. He was trying to get out of asking her what she wanted for a wedding present. In the morning light, he'd decided she wasn't the woman for him, and he was looking for a way out.

"No," she whispered. "Nothing, except drinking and drinking and drinking. And then your snoring. Right in the middle of kissing me."

Zach held the coffee cups in his hands and stared at her, his eyes widened. "No, I didn't."

"You most certainly did, cowboy. Your lips were on mine, and then you went slack and started to snore," she said, pouring the coffee into their cups. "I know I've never kissed a man before, but I didn't think my kisses would put you to sleep." The nerve of the man to fall asleep while she was kissing him. If they'd been married a hundred years, maybe, but even then he'd be doing time in the chicken shack.

"No, honey, it wasn't you. It was me. The alcohol

and the loss of blood. I passed out cold. I don't even remember what we were talking about. The last I remember, you were telling me how you were fired by Ho Chin," he said. "It wasn't your kissing. It was me."

She stared at him. He didn't remember asking her what kind of wedding gift she wanted? Well, good. "You took bigger sips than me," she admitted.

"Your hangover still seems worse."

"That's because it's my first and hopefully my last." She laid back down on her bedroll and watched him heat up their hardtack. She didn't even know if she'd be able to keep the biscuit down. Her stomach was in an all-out rebellion at the moment at what she'd consumed last night.

He took the hardtack out of the fire and handed her the biscuit. "Breakfast is served."

She sat up, and her world spun again. Closing her eyes, she brought the coffee up to her lips then slowly opened them. "Do you have any idea where Simon went?"

He shrugged his shoulders. "There's a place I know of, and he might go there."

"Then we should leave now and go after him."

"And do what?" His look was filled with disdain. "Are you going to go racing after him? I don't think so. Neither one of us feels like chasing him."

"No, but it has to be done." Sometime today, she had to get up on her horse and ride after Simon. Soon, just as soon as her head could manage to stand up straight and her stomach wasn't bucking like a wild horse.

"It can wait a couple of days. I think we should rest and get my arm checked out by a doctor. Then we'll be refreshed and ready to take him on once again."

"We? Who says we're going to do this together?" she said. Did he think they were going to stick together? Oh, no. He sure as hell wasn't getting this bounty. It was hers and hers alone.

"I did," he replied.

"You'll steal the bounty for yourself, just like you did last time," she responded. She could feel her stomach muscles tightening at the idea of losing the bounty again. No, Zach couldn't win this time.

"No, I won't," he promised. "Once we prove his guilt, then the bounty will be yours. If we prove he's not guilty…it won't matter. We'll work together."

"You know he's guilty."

"No, I don't. But I intend to find out, just like I do with all my clients," Zach said.

Meg raised her brows and stared at the handsome sheriff. Did he believe Simon was above suspicion? She wanted to laugh, but knew instinctively he wouldn't think it was funny.

"The boy is about as innocent as the hurdy-gurdy gals down at the bar. But you keep on thinking that, and soon I'll have him tied up and turned in, and I'll be walking away with the bounty."

Chapter Seven

The next day they rode into Dyersville. Tension radiated from Meg like the heat of a potbelly stove. Zach sensed that if he weren't careful, she'd be riding off without him the moment she could sneak away. Still, he had no choice but to leave her, while he did some business in town. Some business Meg didn't need to know about.

"Let's get a room here tonight, and then in the morning, I'll take you to where Simon may be hiding," Zach said, thinking it wasn't a complete lie, but not really believing Simon was still there. After being shot, he'd watched Simon ride off with Frank.

Somehow he feared the man had not listened to his advice and was now long gone and that made Zach question Simon's claims of innocence. They needed to locate Mrs. Lowell. Zach wanted to hear her side of Simon's tale and learn from her how the situation had played out.

"As long as we get two rooms," Meg replied, sliding down from her horse.

"Of course," Zach said. "Is it okay if I help you get your things into the room?"

She stared at him. "Nope. I can manage on my own. I know how I like things done."

"Remind me to never let you drink alcohol again."

"Remind me to never let you kiss me again, since you'll fall asleep."

"That was only one time," he said, frustration spiraling like a tornado through his mid-section, tightening his stomach into a knot. Of all the times for him to pass out. "And I'd been drinking with you."

"Sad when a woman can out drink a man."

The woman knew just how to put a burr under a man's saddle and stick him on a regular basis. "I'd been shot. I lost blood. I could have died."

"That's what happens when you ride in front of a bullet."

Shaking his head, he took a deep breath and decided to keep his mouth shut. It would be less painful.

She raised her brows, her eyes flashing that impatient, irritated message only Meg could effectively convey. She'd already slid her saddle off and was standing there, waiting for him. "Get a move on, cowboy, or be left behind."

Hurriedly, he untied the cinch and pulled the saddle off his horse. "Remind me again, why I want to keep you along?"

"Because I'm such good company," she retorted, walking ahead of him, her pants swaying with the swing of her hips as she entered the hotel.

It took about ten minutes to check in. Their rooms were across the hall from one another, close enough he could keep his eye on her. Yet they were separated, and after the last two nights on the trail, it would feel good to get cleaned up and sleep in a bed again. It would be good to put some distance between him and Meg just for a little while.

They walked up the stairs and down the hall to their respective rooms. He glanced at her as she put her key in the lock and turned the knob. She opened the door and set her saddle inside. Then she turned to shut the door, and their eyes met across the hall.

"Why don't you rest and get cleaned up, and then we'll go to dinner at seven," he said, not really wanting her to leave his sight, but knowing he had things to do.

Her eyes appraised him like a schoolmarm grading her students' exams. "Am I dirty?"

He shook his head. Since he'd fallen asleep while kissing her, she'd not given him any slack. She'd been touchy and irritable. He'd hoped it was because of a hangover, but maybe not. "No, I love my women to have that dusty glow about them with a smudge of mud on their pants and smelling of campfire smoke."

"Sarcasm doesn't become you, cowboy." A faint smile turned up her lips, and then she flashed him a haughty glance. "Plus, you look a little weather worn yourself."

"That's why I plan on taking a bath."

"Ohhhh... You're going to the bathhouse?"

He smiled and shook his head at her. "Yes, I am. Do you want to go? Though, I'm not certain the sheriff in this town would be as forgiving, if I'm found naked in the middle of Main Street."

"It's a tempting thought," she said with a smile. "But you'll be on the lookout for it next time. I think that trick's retired."

"Good, I can enjoy my bath in peace. But first, I'm going to take our horses to the livery stable, find a local doctor, and have him check out my arm. When I get back, we'll go eat some dinner. Is that okay?"

There were other places he needed to visit, but she didn't need to know that. Still, he didn't want her leaving without him again. She needed to wait in her room.

She raised her brows. "When did you start having to ask my permission?"

He frowned. Damn, every step of the way, she was going to make his life a living hell. "I don't, but I lost the bet, and I'm buying you dinner. You'll be waiting here for me when I return?" he asked, needing something that would keep her from riding off without him.

"Worried I'm not going to be here when you get back?" she countered.

How could he deny that was exactly what concerned him? "Yes."

She smiled. "I'll be here tonight. You promised me you'd take me to where Simon could be hiding out tomorrow. I'm giving you that much time."

"Tomorrow," he promised, knowing Simon was probably long gone from the place he would take her, but still he needed to check.

"Okay. See you later," she said with a shrug and shut her door.

As soon as Zach had piled his saddle and saddlebags in the room, he left. It didn't take him long to drop the horses off, and then he headed to the doctor.

The old sawbones examined his shoulder and gave him some salve to put on the wound. The doc told him Meg had done an outstanding job, and he should heal in about three to four weeks. The shoulder had turned black and blue. Even now, Zach could see some tinges of green where the bruising was starting to fade, but not quick enough to suit him. The shoulder was sore and often ached with a dull throb, but he would live.

The doctor wanted him to take it easy for several weeks, but Zach knew that wouldn't happen, not with him trying to prove Simon's innocence and keep Meg from catching the outlaw.

Last, he went to the sheriff. The two men had once been good friends, but now, when Zach walked in the door, he could see the suspicion in the lawman's eyes. He didn't deserve that scrutiny, but yet, he couldn't blame the man.

"Zach, how are you?"

"Healing from a bullet wound. Got it chasing after Simon," he replied, the memory of lying on that ground as Simon rode away still painful.

"Sorry to hear that."

"Can you tell me if he's been seen in this area lately?" The town wasn't far from where he hoped Simon was hiding. And Lord knew, Simon wasn't smart enough to stay out of town and hidden from the law.

"Why should I tell you anything, Zach? I'm not sure which side of the law you're on," the sheriff said.

Ouch. That hurt. But the sheriff wouldn't be a good lawman if he weren't cautious.

"I'm on the side of justice, but before I can hang him, I need to be certain he's guilty. I want to find Simon, bring him to the authorities if need be, but first I want to talk to the widow Lowell. I want to hear from her lips that Simon killed her husband. Can you tell me where to find her?"

Zach would do whatever he needed to do to keep the promise he'd made. Once he finished his investigation, he would either prove Simon's guilt or his innocence.

Once he fulfilled his commitment, then he would feel free to either release the criminal or hang him.

"She took her kids and moved off the farm and back to Cryer Creek, where she's from. Be careful when you talk to her, she's grieving her husband something terrible, and those boys of hers are not happy someone shot their father."

Zach couldn't blame them. He'd be furious if someone had shot his father. His own father had died plowing the field one afternoon. "No matter what, I want to learn the truth, and then I'll do whatever the law says."

The sheriff nodded. "Glad to hear that. Last time Frank was seen around here was two days ago. But he left town the moment I spotted him."

"Thanks. I'll keep looking for him. If I learn anything about the shooting, I'll let you know."

"Zach, I spoke to the woman. She identified Simon. It was him."

Still, Zach had to hear the words from her lips, and then he wanted to confront Simon and hear his reaction. Simon blamed Frank, and the woman blamed Simon. Somehow, he had to learn the truth.

"I have to keep a promise and investigate, Sheriff. I can't accept his fate until I know for certain."

"Understand."

"See you round," Zach said and walked out of the sheriff's office.

This was not good. Simon had made some wrong choices in life, had never been on the right side of the law, but he'd never murdered anyone in cold blood. He'd never shot anyone; he'd never even hurt someone physically. But if he'd killed that farmer, then he would swing from the end of a rope. Still Zach had to speak to the dead man's wife.

He hurried down the sidewalk, his next stop Sarah's Fabric Shop. When they'd ridden into town, the idea had slapped him upside the head as they'd passed the local dress shop. Why didn't he buy Meg a dress? Something she could wear to dinner tonight. As he neared the building, he glanced in the window and saw Meg talking to a woman.

Shock rippled through his mid-section like the tat-a-tat-tat-tat of gunshot. Surprised, he watched her through the glass as the woman showed her different designs. They looked at the dresses displayed in the windows then moved over to the rack.

Peeking like a stalker, he watched as Meg touched the dresses, her fingertips caressing the material the way a man wanted a woman to touch him. She would pick a dress off the rack and hold it up against her, tilt her head to the side and smile. It was like watching her in her own fairy tale. Her face was soft, her green eyes twinkled, and a smile graced her lips. She laughed, the sound rippling along his spine causing his breath to cease.

The dress, a green silken material, made her emerald eyes shine, and her red hair turned even more auburn. The garment seemed made for her, and even he could see the longing on her face.

Her expression was close to rapture, and suddenly he understood that owning her own shop would make her very happy. She handed the dress back to the woman, thanked her, and started for the door.

Zach stepped around the corner of the building, so she wouldn't see him. He watched as she strolled toward the hotel, her head high, her buttocks twitching with every step, leaving him aching to touch them.

He'd been on his way to buy her a dress, and now she'd just made his selection even easier. Whatever doubts he'd held disappeared. Somehow he felt like he owed her this gift. She deserved to be treated like a woman, and he was just the man to make her feel special tonight.

When he walked in the door, he glanced around at the bolts of fabric, the dresses displayed, hats and shoes, and everything a woman desired.

"May I help you?" the young woman asked.

"Yes, I need the dress that young woman was holding up sent over to Spencer's hotel. It's for her," he said, smiling and feeling out of place like a stud horse at a tea party. Yet, certain of his purchase.

"It's beautiful. I'm sure she'll love it."

"Can you have the dress and all the undergarments sent to the Spencer hotel to room 201 to Meg McKenzie," he asked.

"I'll take it over personally," she told Zach, smiling as she quickly wrote up his ticket.

Zach stared at the dress as warmth filled him at the idea of seeing Meg in the flowing green emerald material that matched her eyes, her red hair streaming down her back. The woman had earned a dress after everything she'd been through, and while he'd never understood before, now he realized that deep inside Meg wanted to be just like any other woman. She wanted to be feminine and pretty and be treated like a lady.

Life had given her a man's world with a man's responsibilities, and she'd handled them well. But secretly she longed to be a woman.

"Thank you, ma'am," he said and walked out the door.

Next stop was the bathhouse, so he could get cleaned up in time to take Meg to dinner. He couldn't wait to see her in that dress, and he couldn't wait to spend time just the two of them alone.

*

Meg heard the knock on the door of her hotel room and thought if that was Zach ready to go to dinner, he could just wait. She'd ordered a bath, but they'd said it would be at least twenty minutes. Maybe it was early. She intended to spend some time soaking in that tub. It wasn't often she was able to relax and pamper herself, and today she'd planned on doing just that.

They knocked again, and she hurried across the small room. "Hang on. I'm coming."

She threw open the door and gazed with surprise at the woman from the dress shop. "Yes?"

The woman smiled at her and swept into the room without being invited. "Your gentleman friend purchased the dress and asked me to deliver it to you."

"Gentleman friend?" Meg stared at her in surprise. "Zach?"

"He didn't give me his name, but he was a very nice looking cowboy," she said as she laid the box on the bed and then motioned for Meg to open it.

Meg walked over to the bed, her heart racing inside her chest. She knew instinctively what lay inside that fancy box. Though she knew she should tell the woman to take the dress back, when she lifted the lid, she gasped. That beautiful green satiny cotton dress lay wrapped in tissue.

"Oh, my God," she cried, knowing she didn't want to be beholden to Zach, but she just couldn't refuse this dress. She'd loved this creation in the shop. It was the one she'd promised herself that someday she would sew a replica. It was the one her heart had fancied until she'd had to either walk out of the shop or purchase the dress.

"Oh," was all Meg could say as she pulled it from the box. "It's so beautiful."

"And you'll look lovely, dear," the woman said. "He also included new undergarments."

Meg looked inside, and her brows rose. "He didn't pick them out, did he?"

The woman laughed. "Oh no, he asked me to choose the necessary garments. "

Meg stared in wonder at the dress, her heart slamming up into her throat as tears pricked her eyes. She'd never owned anything so beautiful. She'd never experienced a dress so stunning. For all his faults, Zach Gillespie could be a generous man. A man she could fall in love with if she wasn't careful.

"Well, I better be going, but I wanted to bring it over to you personally, since I knew you'd been looking at this dress before he arrived."

"When did he get there?" Meg asked, wondering how he knew.

"Right after you left," she replied. "You couldn't have been gone for more than a couple of minutes before he walked in."

For a moment, she wondered if he'd followed her, but knew that couldn't be true because he would have seen her visiting the sheriff, to learn all she could about Simon.

Though, the sheriff hadn't been forthcoming with information. He had, in fact, seemed reluctant to speak to her. She'd left the hotel not long after Zach and gone to the telegraph office to send her sisters a wire to let them know she was okay. Then she'd paid a visit to the sheriff and finally the dress shop. Any time she had the opportunity, she visited the local women's shop, gathering ideas, looking at what was available and filling her head with plans.

After that she'd returned back here to the hotel, where she'd laid down for a little nap and then a bath.

"Well, I better get back to the shop. I knew you'd be thrilled he'd purchased the dress for you. I just had to see your expression."

"Thanks," Meg said and walked the woman to the door. She hated owing Zach. She hated she didn't trust him about Simon, but she loved this dress, and frankly, it was the exact thing her wounded pride needed right now.

Suddenly she couldn't wait to go to dinner with him tonight. The thought of wearing this beautiful gown was more than she could fathom. For the first time in a very long time, Meg felt a rush of excitement. Tonight, she wanted to look gorgeous. Tonight, she wanted to act like a young woman who wasn't a bounty hunter, but a normal woman being courted.

*

Zach stood in front of Meg's door, nervous as a preacher at a gunfight. He tugged on his bolo tie one more time to make certain it was straight. He hoped the dress fit her and she was happy he'd sent her the garment. Meg was different from most of the women he'd encountered in his life, and sometimes the things he thought would make her happy sent her temper to the moon and back.

They'd never had a chance to court or spend time getting to know each other. Tonight, he wanted this time for them, to show her there was this growing thing between them he wanted to pursue.

He licked his lips then knocked on the door. It flew open, and there she stood. His breath left his body in a mighty swish; his groin tightened as this vision in green stood before him. For a moment, he couldn't breathe.

Her auburn hair hung loosely down her back, with soft curls around her face. And that dress clung to her curves even more than the pants, to which he'd grown accustomed to. But this dress showcased her neckline, leaving him aching to place his lips along her chest. The material plunged to reveal the curves of her breasts at the fitted bodice then swelled at her hips. And the color…that dark green matched her eyes and made them shine like emeralds in the night sky.

She reached over and touched her finger to his chin, closing his open mouth. "Cowboy, you're going to catch flies if you leave your mouth open."

"Meg," he gasped. "I knew the dress would look great on you, but I don't think I can take you out of the room wearing something that makes you so pretty."

The woman bounty hunter had morphed into a lady— a proper lady he would be honored to have grace his arm tonight.

She laughed and twirled for him. "It's gorgeous, Zach. Thank you, but why?"

He shrugged. "I thought it was time someone did something nice for you, Meg. You take care of your sisters, and well, I wanted to do something special just for you."

Meg reached out and grabbed his hands. "Thank you from the bottom of my heart. This dress is so pretty. I was going to decline it, and then when I took it out of the box, well…I just couldn't. I had to have the dress."

His heart swelled with pride as she thanked him again. No other woman had ever made him feel so special, so loving, so right. This small gift had made her day and left him ready to protect her until he took his last breath. "I'm glad. You deserve it," he said. "Are you ready to go to dinner?"

"Yes, I'm starving. It seems like forever since we've had something decent to eat."

"What? You didn't enjoy my hardtack biscuits?"

She took his arm and pulled the door shut behind her. "Let's just say they'll do in a pinch. A desperate pinch."

They walked down the stairs and out onto the street. He frowned at every man who looked in her direction and sent them a glare that would have sent most men running.

"Where are we going?" she asked, oblivious to the attention she was receiving from the too young and too stupid males on the street. She was hanging on his arm, and they were gazing at her like she was hot apple pie for the taking. That slice of pie could get you killed.

"Zach," she said loudly, trying to garner his attention.

"Yes?" he replied, coming back from staring at the young bucks. Maybe buying her a dress wasn't such a smart move; for suddenly, she was a hot commodity in this small town where women were scarce.

"Where are you? I asked you a question."

"I'm sorry. We're going to the restaurant right down the block there. See it?" he asked and telegraphed yet another "touch her, and you'll die" look to some young fool.

"Yes," she said, squeezing his arm tightly. "Smile, it's supposed to be fun tonight."

"I'm sorry. It's just I'm not accustomed to men

ogling you." What could he say? He'd silently warned those young bucks they were courting death.

"They're looking at my pretty dress, not at me."

"I don't think men give a damn about a dress. It's what the dress is covering that has their interest."

She turned and looked at him, her face blushing. It was the first time he'd ever seen her cheeks redden, except in anger.

"Why, Meg, you're blushing."

"Oh, stop it, I am not."

"Well, it certainly looks like you are."

"It's just my lipstick."

"We're here," he said, steering her toward the door. He opened the portal, and they stepped inside the restaurant. The smell of roast beef and potatoes smacked them in the nose, and he felt his stomach growl.

After they had been seated and their order placed, they stared at one another. For the first time, silence came between them, and then she smiled that bewitching way that always sent tremors from his groin to his heart.

"What did the doctor say about your shoulder?" she asked.

"He told me the next time some woman shoots me I should make sure she goes to jail," he said, teasing.

"What about the next time some cowboy gets in front of my gun? Did he tell you what I was supposed to do then?"

"We didn't talk about that." And he wouldn't. No one needed to know he'd ridden in front of her gun to stop her from shooting Simon. No matter what, he didn't want the man dead.

"Shame. He probably would have told you it's not safe to ride in front of a *bullet*," she replied.

He smiled. If only she knew the truth, she'd be madder than a room full of hornets.

"So what did he say?"

"He said whoever took out the bullet did a fine job, and I should rest for the next two to three weeks. Like there's a chance of that happening."

"I'm glad my stitching met with the doctor's approval, unlike the man who questioned my technique that night."

He shrugged. "Just wanted to make sure you knew what you were doing."

"I'm quite capable with a needle," she taunted, her green eyes challenging him.

God, he wanted to scoop her up from her chair and carry her back to their hotel and do unspeakable things to that smart mouth of hers. Things that would have her begging him to take her.

They stared at each other across the table. He had a hard time taking his eyes off of her. There was such a change from the bounty hunter Meg to the ladylike Meg. He liked both personas, but ladylike Meg could have her pick of any man. Would she still want him?

Nick Hargrove, the owner of the stables, stopped at their table. "Zach, good to see you."

"Hi Nick, how are you?" He wanted the man to disappear. He didn't want him to ruin tonight, and he didn't like the way he was eyeing Meg. It wouldn't take much for Zach's temper to flare, especially if Nick started talking out of both sides of his mouth.

Nick ignored Zach and turned to Meg. "I haven't met your lady friend. My name is Nick Hargrove. I own the local stable."

"Oh, our horses are there right now. Meg McKenzie,"

Meg said, shaking his hand.

Zach could feel his lips tighten. Nick had his eyes on Meg. He'd better not say anything that would screw this up for Zach. He watched the man's eyes linger on her, and he wanted to jump up and smack him.

"Thanks for the business." Nick turned to Zach. "How's your mother doing? I'm sure she's upset—"

Zach quickly interrupted him. "Mom's great. I hope to get by to see her in the next few days. How about your mom? How's she doing?" he asked, trying to change the direction of the conversation.

The waitress delivered their dinner, and Zach had never been more glad to see food interrupt a conversation.

"Well, I'll let you folks eat. Good night," Nick said and walked away.

"Your mother lives close by?" Meg asked.

"She lives about a half day's ride from here," he replied, wishing Nick had kept that bit of information to himself. Somehow, he needed to them to talk about anything other than his family. "I know your mom passed away when you were young. Do you have a tintype of her?"

"Nothing. Except my memories and I cherish those," she said, taking a bite of her food. "What about your mom? Tell me about her. You told me she ruled your house with an iron fist."

He shrugged, not wanting to talk about his only parent or the past. "When you have four rambunctious boys, you have no choice but to make certain they know who's in charge."

"I wanted brothers," she said.

"I wanted sisters," he replied. "And every time

mother had a boy. But my brothers are important to me." Zach feared being this near to his mother. He didn't want to run into her. It was bad enough the owner of the stable had stopped by and acted like he knew Zach. Meg was no fool.

"Were your parents happy before your mother died?" he asked.

"Very. Of course, Papa was gone a lot, and it was just the three of us and mother. When he came home, my mother would be so excited to see him. There would be laughter, and we would have such a great time until he left again," she said with a sigh. "Papa was only gone for about four months a year. When spring came, he always came home and worked the farm. When money got tight again, he'd go hunting."

The waitress came by and refilled their water glasses. Zach had barely touched his dinner; instead of concentrating on the food, he'd focused on Meg. He reached across the table, unable to stop himself, and touched her hand. The feel of her soft skin sent tremors straight to his groin. She raised her eyes to his, questioning as he rubbed the back of her hand.

"You're not eating," she remarked.

"I'm full." How could he tell her the hunger he felt had nothing to with food and everything to do with her? He knew she was off limits, even if she was just across the hall.

She pushed her plate back and stared at him. "Last year, when we were talking about marriage, I never even considered your family. At the time, there was so much on my mind with Papa's death and the bank mortgage. I just never thought about how we would be joining our families."

He shrugged. "I knew your family. Everyone in town knows the McKenzies."

They weren't known in a bad way, but rather considered to be eccentric—their father for his strong bounty hunting skills, their mother for her fierce independent nature up until the day she'd died. Each one of the girls had some small piece of gossip tied to them. Something that would make you sit back and reconsider them.

"Yeah, well, sometimes we're well known for reasons that are not so good."

"The Gillespie boys could get into trouble as well." He continued to rub his fingers across the back of her hand, and all he could think about was how much he'd like to slowly peel the layers of clothing from Meg. One by one, he'd like to unwrap her new garments from her and explore her womanly body from head to toe.

She looked at him, her green eyes darkening, and he knew she could feel the tension building between them. "Let's order dessert."

Zach signaled the waitress over, and Meg ordered apple pie. When the waitress set it down before her, he watched her break off a piece with her fork and place the sweet fruit in her mouth. She closed her eyes, her tongue trailing across her lips for crumbs, and for a moment, he thought he would carry her out of that restaurant and back down the street to their hotel. He could imagine carrying her up the stairs and into his room, where he would throw her down on the bed and rip the clothing from her body.

He closed his eyes, took a deep breath, and released it slowly, trying to bring the rush of pleasure under control. This night couldn't last much longer without him exploding.

"Zach," she said, her voice a delicate whisper that seemed to caress his skin.

He opened his eyes, and she held her fork to his mouth. Like a bird, his mouth gaped, and she slid the fork between his lips, giving him a bite of the hot apple pie. "That's delicious."

"Really tasty. Am I am boring you?" she asked. "Are you about to fall asleep on me again?"

God, if only this woman knew what she did to him. She'd realize he was struggling to keep from acting like a savage and carrying her away. "Never, Meg. Never. Let's just say watching you eat that dessert is getting to me."

Her brow furrowed like she didn't understand. He smiled and leaned across the table. "I love the way you relish your pie, and I can only think of how much I'd enjoy you."

Her emerald eyes widened then darkened with the realization of what he meant. She picked up her fork and placed it between her lips and savored the pie once again, licking her lips.

Zach groaned. "Meg, you're pushing me."

She smiled. "Am I? I've never pushed a man before. Is this how it's done?"

She'd never had the opportunity to flirt and thank God! She was a dangerous woman when she dressed like a woman and tried out her feminine wiles on him.

Zach motioned to the waitress. "Check, please."

Meg leaned across the table, her breasts pushing against her dress. "What are we going to do now?"

Oh, that was a question he'd love to answer his way. "I'm going to take you back to the hotel, kiss you senseless, and then lock you in your room." There was so much more he'd like to do, but he would be wise to take a step back and let the embers she'd ignited cool. For once she learned the truth, she'd be madder than momma bear in springtime.

"Are you certain you can stay awake?" she teased.

Even the thought of sleep was something he knew would be elusive. "Oh, honey, sleep is going to be very difficult tonight. I'd say damn near impossible."

She smiled. "If I decide to let you kiss me, I'll keep that in mind."

The waitress brought the check, and Zach quickly paid her. Oh, she would be kissing Zach if he had anything to say. He planned on showing this woman the power of his lips.

He stood and offered Meg his hand. She took it and gazed at him that way that had his heart doing a wicked dance. A mischievous smile graced her face like she knew exactly what she was doing.

"I think you need to go back to wearing pants. You're a lot safer than when you wear a dress."

Meg cocked her head at him, her emerald eyes giving him an uncertain look. "How is that?"

"You're not a seductive wench who flirts with me over dinner and then teases me when she eats dessert." Entwining her hand through his arm, he strolled with her out of the restaurant.

"You poor man. You've been mistreated all evening. How should I make this up to you?"

Zach could think of a half dozen ways, and they all started and ended in the bedroom. But the chances were pretty good Meg was a virgin. "You can kiss me."

She reached over and gave him a peck on the cheek

as they walked down the sidewalk. His cheek burned where her lips had touched. Heat spiraled through him, and he pulled her tight against his body. "That wasn't exactly the kind of kiss I wanted."

"Oh, I'm sorry," she teased and brought the back of his hand up to her lips. She kissed him and let her tongue trail across his skin, sending shivers racing down his spine. God, he was going to grab her and carry her to his room if she didn't stop teasing him.

They entered the hotel, and he tried to appear normal, though his pants were tight against his erection, and he was certain his face was flushed with excitement from Meg's kiss. "You know you're playing with fire," he said. "I'm going to get my kiss."

They took the stairs slowly, as she lifted the front of her skirt to reveal her boots beneath her dress. She turned those velvet green eyes on him, and he thought he would be scorched from the heat reflected in her gaze.

"Better know how to put out a fire," she said softly.

"Oh, honey, I can quench a flame," he promised.

She smiled as they walked down the hall. He noticed a note hanging on his door and grabbed it, stuffing it in his pocket. He wasn't interested in reading any notes right now. Not with Meg's hand on his arm. She turned toward her door and pulled a key out of her reticule. With a twist, she unlocked the door and twisted the knob.

Glancing back over her shoulder at him, she smiled. "Good night, Zach."

He grabbed her arm, pulled her toward him until she slammed against his chest. "Not so fast. I think you owe me this."

He covered her mouth with his, his tongue sliding between her lips, his arms wrapping around her pulling her close. This woman had made him crazy during dinner tonight. He'd wanted to swipe the table clear of dishes and lay her down, push her skirts to her waist, and have his way with her right there in the restaurant. The thought had crossed his mind more than once.

He pushed her against the doorframe, pressing his body into hers, letting her feel his erection that was filling his head full of images of the two of them—her body gleaming in the moonlight, him pumping into her over and over again until they were both sated.

A moan escaped her lips, and he reached up, holding her face between his hands, angling her mouth for a deeper kiss. Then he slid his hands down her face, her neck, her shoulders until he reached her breasts. He could take her right here in the hall. He wanted her that badly.

She pushed him back, her green eyes wild, her auburn hair mussed from his kisses, and her breathing harsh and labored.

"Damn you, cowboy. I don't know what you've done to me," she whispered. Then she pulled him into her room and shut the door. "But you're going to make it right."

Chapter Eight

Zach was the luckiest son of a bitch this side of the Red River. He couldn't believe Meg had pulled him into her room and shut the door, her mouth still on his, her hands running down his chest. He twisted her around and slammed her against the door, his mouth consuming hers like a man starved, though he'd just had dinner. He took her hands in his and raised them over the top of her head, pinning her to the door, while his mouth plundered her full and inviting lips.

He leaned into her body, pressing against her, needing to feel her breasts against his chest, the touch of her body against his. She seemed to fit in the hollows of his body's embrace like this was where she belonged, and he marveled at the way they melded together. He left her mouth and nibbled his way down past her ears to her neck.

"God, you smell so good," he said, taking a deep breath of her, his cock hardening as he continued his way down to the swells of her breast.

All night long he'd stared at her chest, wanting, needing to touch her breasts, kiss his way over that white strip of flesh that had billowed above the fabric of her dress. He longed to bury his face in her cleavage and tried to remind himself to slow down. Take deep breaths.

He dropped her wrists, wrapping her face in his hands, and brought her mouth to his again. He pushed his tongue past her lips and caressed her mouth like he was dying of thirst, and she was his fountain of water. Her sweet lips tasted of pleasure, and he sampled her mouth, sweeping his tongue across her full lips.

She pushed him away, her breathing harsh, her eyes wide with wonder. She walked over to the desk in the corner and lit the lantern. When she returned, she twirled around, giving him her back. "Help me out of this dress, cowboy."

He pulled her to him, kissing the back of her neck, nipping her gently with his teeth. "Are you sure?"

"Stop dawdling and help me out of this," she whispered, her voice husky with need.

She didn't have to tell him twice. He was undoing the buttons like a man seeking gold. When he finished, his hands reached inside and slowly pushed the dress down. She stepped out of the garment then lovingly placed it on a chair. She turned to face him, and he thought he was going to die of need right there in the middle of the room. His heart raced like a stallion chasing a filly at the sight of her in the new undergarments he'd purchased today.

"Meg," he drawled, needing her more with each passing minute, his manhood swelling tight against his pants, his blood pulsing and centering between his legs.

She was gorgeous, and it was all he could do to keep from ripping her chemise and pantaloons from her body.

Her breasts swelled above her chemise, and he reached for her, needing to feel her in his arms, but she stepped back. With a slowness he found maddening, she pulled the chemise over her head. God, she was more beautiful than he'd dreamed. She was stunning, and he started pulling his shirt out of his pants. He opened the buttons, his eyes never leaving hers as she shimmied out of her pantaloons.

Then she stood before him naked, and he thought he'd died and gone to heaven. Only being inside her could be any better than this.

"Hurry up, cowboy. You're falling behind."

He moved faster, shucking his boots, unbuckling his belt, and unbuttoning his pants. He reached his long johns and suddenly felt shy. Then he remembered she'd already seen him without his clothes, and he pulled his long johns down.

They were both naked. For a moment, they stared at one another.

"Oh, cowboy," she said, her voice a husky growl.

Then they were moving toward each other. Their arms outstretched. They came together, flesh against flesh, and Zach only knew he needed her like the earth needed rain. His mouth claimed hers, as he led her to the bed. They landed arms and legs tangled together on the soft quilt.

She laughed. "Now you can slow down. We've got all night."

"Easy for you to say," he whispered, the feel of her naked skin causing his blood to pulse with need.

He moved his palm down her body, caressing her silken skin until he found her breasts. The feel of her soft skin, her nipples tightening beneath his touch, was almost too much to bear. He'd wanted her for what seemed like forever. He'd dreamed of her just like this, lying in his bed, his hands and mouth teasing her body until she cried out his name.

But that had been a dream, and this was reality. A reality he couldn't believe.

A low, throaty growl escaped him as he caressed the hardened pebble of her nipple. She was soft as satin for sale in a shop window, as he trailed his hand over her breasts.

He put his mouth to her breasts, savoring their sweet taste. She gasped and arched her back toward him. Her hands grabbed his hair and held his mouth to her hardened kernel.

Meg was a strong woman who wasn't afraid of danger and knew how to take care of her family. She was the type of woman a man would feel proud to call his woman and one he knew would always have his back. She was the type of woman who would care for their children. She'd make a great wife, yet there were secrets between them that could tear them apart.

He pushed the thoughts aside, promising tomorrow he would tell her, just give him tonight.

He skimmed his hand down her body, past her ribs, past her belly button, down her smooth stomach, to the wispy curls covering her womanly folds. She moaned a deep, throaty purr beneath his touch as he slid his fingers into her moist center.

She grasped his naked back, running her fingers across his shoulders, down his muscles, her fingers leaving hot trails of desire branding him with her touch. She tossed her head from side to side, her auburn hair splaying across the pillows as she called his name.

"Zach," she moaned as she cried out his name, sending desire rippling through him.

While he'd lost his virginity many years ago, he

wanted her to always remember the first time they were together as memorable.

"Kiss me, Zach," she cried, her mouth searching for his again.

He moved his lips over hers, wanting to consume her. God, he loved it when she called out his name, like he was the only person she needed and wanted. Like he was the one person in this world she could depend on. He wanted to give her everything. He wanted to fulfill all her wishes and have those emerald eyes gaze at him like he was a man she believed in.

He placed her hand on his cock, and she wrapped her fingers around him, but he felt her touch all the way to his heart. He slid her hand up and down his shaft, and it felt as if the world moved. He knew he wouldn't last long. He couldn't hold off forever. The feel of her fingertips gliding up and down him was rushing him to the edge, pushing him ever closer.

"Zach, please," she cried, not understanding what she needed.

"Honey," he said and moved over her, spreading her legs apart with his knees. If this was her first time, he wanted to make this as painless as possible, but right now, he was throbbing with such urgency he didn't know if he could hold off much longer.

He pushed into her and felt the resistance. He slowly thrust, stretching her, and she cried out just as he felt her maidenhead give way. And then he was inside her, surrounded by the feel of Meg. For a moment, he let her catch her breath and grow accustomed to the feel of him deep within her body. She was so tight, and he loved the way she moaned as he slowly began to move with her.

She opened her eyes, her pupils full and dilated in the

light of the lantern. She stared at him, her gaze holding him hostage, her body tormenting his, with Meg filling his empty soul. He'd never expected this evening to go like this, with the two of them spending the night in the throes of passion. He'd never thought she would invite him into her bed. But she had and right now, he felt like he would die from the sweetness he was experiencing in Meg's arms.

She gripped his shaft with her inner muscles, and he thought he was going to lose it right then. Sweet, sweet friction stroked him, surrounded him, their hips moving in rhythm with fierceness, an intensity, which surprised him. He plunged deeper into her, and with every driving movement, she matched him.

Burning resonant pleasure encompassed him with each long stroke and swirled him closer to the edge. She met every pounding thrust of him, gripping his erection, consuming him with a wildness that drove him to the edge.

Passion filled him until he thought he would burst from the feelings Meg evoked in him. The sensations were so stirring and felt so right; he was shocked at their joining. He'd never experienced these types of emotions before. They startled and overwhelmed him.

He reached for her head and brought her mouth to his, devouring her with a hungry kiss that consumed him, holding her lips firmly against his. She shuddered, pulling away from him.

"Oh God," she cried, her body racked with tremors.

As he felt her orgasm rock through him, he relinquished the tightly controlled rein he'd been holding onto as he shuddered his release deep within her.

"Meg," he cried as the pleasure he'd felt in her arms

imprinted onto his soul. He'd never experienced anything like this before. He'd never felt so whole, so complete, and so loved in all of his years. Yet, there were secrets between them that could tear them apart.

In the glow of the lantern, they lay together, their breathing harsh, their naked skin warm against one another's. Meg didn't say anything, and he rolled them over onto their sides and pulled her up against him, not wanting her far from him.

What had just happened to him? Never before had sex been so gratifying, so emotional it left him stunned. What had Meg done to him to make him think of more than just one night together?

He kissed the back of her neck, his lips touching her heated skin. "Thank you," he said.

"For what?" she asked, perplexed.

"For letting me be your first," he replied, his voice husky. He'd never been someone's first. He'd never had a woman trust him with her virginity.

"It was pretty darn special," she said quietly and yawned.

The air cooled their bodies, and he felt her shudder. He pulled the covers up over them, not ready to leave her side. Wanting to see to her comfort.

"Are you staying?" she asked.

"I'm not going anywhere," he replied and pulled her tightly in his arms. "Give me a little time, and we're going to do this again."

"For a man, you're not too bad," she said sleepily.

He laughed and rubbed his mouth against her ear. "Oh, honey, you have no idea. This was our first time. The next time it'll be even better."

All he needed was a few minutes, and he'd be ready

to go again. Just a few minutes to enjoy the feel of her sweet womanly body snuggled against his. He'd never dreamed it could be this good between them.

She yawned. "I can hardly wait. Just let me rest for a moment or two, and I'll be good."

He leaned in and kissed her shoulder, his lips leaving a wet trail all the way to her ear.

She shivered. "Cowboy, if you don't stop, I'm going to make you regret that."

Her words challenged him and made him move his lips down her shoulder as far as he could reach. He wanted to flip her over on her back and kiss her luscious breasts. "How? Nothing can make me regret kissing you."

She laughed. "I'm going to reach down and yank on your tallywhacker."

"Yank away, honey. Yank away," he said, his voice gruff, his member already starting to swell again. God, this woman, could stir him like no other.

In the morning, he would tell her everything. They would have an honest discussion that would hopefully not destroy what they'd created tonight. He sighed and wished he'd told her sooner, before she'd branded herself all over his heart.

*

Meg awoke in the hours just before dawn. They'd made love several more times, and each time had been better than the first. And the first had been pretty darn good. She knew this was how babies were made, but she hoped and prayed they hadn't created a child. She wasn't ready for a little one. She wasn't even certain of her relationship with Zach. All she knew was they'd had so much fun yesterday afternoon and then again last night.

There was something about him she craved. She couldn't seem to get enough of this lawman.

Zach was a special man. They had a good time together. He made her laugh. She liked his spirit, and she loved the way he looked at her like she was the only woman who existed and there was no one else for him. Yet, there were still unresolved issues between them. Issues she needed answers to. Like Simon. What was Zach's connection to Simon?

She slipped from the bed, needing to find the slop jar and clean up a bit before she woke Zach and sent him back to his room to dress.

Last night had been the best night of her life. She loved the way he'd made her feel, the touch of his skin against hers, the way his smile seemed to trigger the rapid beat of her heart. It would be so easy to allow herself to give her love to Zach, yet her gut was warning her something wasn't right. And one of the first things Meg had learned when she started bounty hunting was always to listen to those gut instincts. They could keep you alive.

As she took a sponge bath, she couldn't help but think about Simon. They were going after him today. Hopefully, they'd find him. Soon, he would be in their custody, and then this life would be behind her. She would be free of the note from the bank and able to open her own dress shop.

Then she could think of Zach, and they could talk about where they would go from here. Would they have a relationship or just a simple roll in a hotel bed? But first, before anything could be decided, she needed to find Simon.

She glanced at the dress Zach had bought for her and

smiled. The silkiness of the material against her skin had made her feel like she was the richest woman in Dyersville. The way Zach had escorted her through town had made her feel like a lady, like a woman with a man. Her man.

Part of her longed to put that dress back on and be like any other woman in town, but she knew now was not the time. Hurriedly, she pulled on her bounty hunting clothes. She loathed putting on the man's pants and shirt. Someday soon, she would burn every single stitch of men's clothes she owned. Soon, she would develop into the woman she dreamed of becoming.

A smile graced her lips when she saw his pants lying in the floor where he'd kicked them off last night. He was as bad as her sisters, leaving his clothes tossed about. She reached down and picked them up.

A piece of paper floated to the floor. She knelt, her fingers snatching it from the ground and went to stuff it back into his pants, when she remembered the note left on his door.

She glanced at the paper, and her heart shattered as if a dozen bullet holes filled her fragile organ. The words sent a ripple effect over her that spun around crazy in her head as she realized the impact.

That son-of-a-bitch!

Immediately, she went to her saddlebags and found what she needed. She pulled out the lengths and walked over to the bed.

Zach lay curled on his side, his hand outstretched. Quickly and efficiently, she spun the roll of rope out. First, she wrapped the rope around his outstretched wrist, and then she tied the cord around the post of the iron bed. Then she worked on his second hand. She was tying his ankle down when he awoke.

He tugged at his arm. "Hey, what are you doing? Meg?"

"You know, cowboy, last night was pretty darn special. So special I was entertaining fancy ideas of marriage and kids and the two of us and all the things girls dream about. Things a woman like me has no business coveting."

"What happened?" he said, rapidly blinking the sleep from his dazed eyes.

"Your note," she said, grabbing his leg and spinning the rope around and tying it to the bedpost. Now he was laid out on the bed, trussed up, his tallywhacker standing at full attention.

Meg felt the tears spring to life behind her eyes, ripping her heart to shreds. He'd used her. He'd taken advantage of her, and now she knew the truth. But she refused to cry.

"I didn't read the damn note. What did it say?" he asked.

She yanked it out of her pocket. "It says, 'Zach, Frank and your brother Simon were last seen leaving Dyersville on the road to your Momma's late this afternoon.'"

Zach groaned and shook his head. "Let me explain. I was going to tell you this morning."

"What's to explain, cowboy? Simon is your brother. Blood's thicker than water, and you would never have let me catch him. You've kept his identity secret, hoping I would lead you to him."

How could there ever be anything between them if she turned in his brother? How could he forgive her? Yet, how could she let this bounty go and risk everything she'd worked so hard for in the last year? The bank note would not be resolved; her dress shop would be in jeopardy; and her sisters…they would have to continue being bounty hunters.

She had to get Simon. She had no choice.

"That's not true. I made a promise to my mother that I would make certain he's guilty before I turn him in. That's why I wanted to find Mrs. Lowell. I just need to keep my promise to my mother. If he's guilty, you'll get the bounty."

"No, Zach. I don't believe you." She shoved her hat on her head.

"What are you doing?"

"I'm going after Simon. I have to find him before you do."

Last night had been something she'd never dreamed of experiencing. Last night he'd made her into a woman. And now this morning, she was back to square one. Back to needing to catch this bounty, to catch the most wanted criminal. His brother.

"Damn it, Meg. Don't leave me tied up like this for the maid to find. Let me go with you, and we'll find him together. The bounty is yours if he's guilty."

She shook her head, not believing a word of what he said.

"Thanks, cowboy, but I'm not taking any chances. Hang out here while I go find your brother," she said. "In fact, on second thought, I better stuff that ornery mouth of yours. It can be rather noisy." She walked over, shoved the tail of his long johns in his mouth, picked up her saddle, and walked out the door, shutting it firmly behind her.

"Mrrrrrr," he screamed through the cloth.

Meg leaned against the wood, her heart shattered like a glass window. He'd lied. He'd never told her the truth. How could he turn in his own brother? No wonder Simon had escaped once. And now she would be the one to bring him to justice. Zach would never forgive her for handing over his brother.

The maid walked down the hall and glanced at her. "Is everything all right?"

She shook her head. "He's not feeling well. He's pretty sick with an upset stomach and diarrhea. I wouldn't recommend going in there for a while."

The maid's eyes grew wide. "I'm so sorry. Does he need a doctor?"

"No. It's best if we just leave him alone for a while. Let the worst of this pass."

Sharp shooting pains gripped her middle at the thought of what she'd done to Zach, especially after the best night of her life. How could he ever forgive her a second time?

"I'll tell the other girls not to disturb him," the maid advised.

"Thank you, that's so sweet of you," Meg said. She picked up her saddle and walked down the hall. There was a hole the size of Texas in her heart. Once again, she'd gone off and left Zach tied up and naked because for the second time, he'd disappointed her.

Only this time she'd left him after having the best night of sex a girl could ever dream about...even a virgin. She'd never imagined how she'd feel after spending the night in his arms. She'd never imagined the pain of leaving him once again.

How could Simon Trudeau be his brother? She wiped a tear away and went to find her horse. Zach's mother lived somewhere close by, and Meg knew just the person who could tell her where.

Chapter Nine

Meg held her head up high and walked through the small town. Her heart was bleeding from the pain of Zach's betrayal, and tears threatened to fall from behind the carefully constructed dam that barricaded her emotions.

He hadn't really lied, but he'd failed to tell her that Simon, the man she was hunting, was his brother.

Last night had been beautiful, more than she'd ever dreamed possible, but this morning the sun had risen to shine a light on his deceit. How had he kept this a secret for so long? Why hadn't she realized the reasons for Zach's elusive behavior regarding Simon?

She'd been so stupid not to think Simon could be one of his brothers. She hated feeling dim-witted. She hated being misled. And now Zach's deception felt like he'd gutted her and left her on the side of the road to die.

Walking into the barn, carrying her saddle, she noticed his horse alongside her mare. Damn, even their horses had bonded. Well, maybe that was a good thing.

"Can I help you?" Nick Hargrove said, gazing at her with interest. "Say, aren't you the woman Zach was with last night?"

"Yes, I'm Meg McKenzie. We met at the diner."

"Sorry, I didn't recognize you this morning."

She wanted to roll her eyes, but refrained. No, she wasn't dressed in her finery, but she was still the same woman. She still had the same auburn hair and the same green eyes. How difficult could it be to recognize her? "Not a problem. I'm a little overdressed today."

He grinned. "How can I help you?"

"I need to pick up my and Zach's horses. I'm taking his horse to his mother's, while he stays here for a couple of days." She leaned in and whispered conspiratorially, "He had too much to drink last night and forgot to tell me where his mother lives. Can you give me that information? I know she lives close by."

If the man were as smitten as she hoped, he wouldn't question why Zach had forgotten to give her the necessary information. She tried to blink her eyes at him the way she'd seen Ruby smile and bat her eyes at men in the past. It just felt awkward and silly.

The man smiled at her. "Let me get those horses for you." He disappeared into the corral and returned with her horse and Zach's. "I'll give you directions. She's a nice woman and doesn't deserve the heartache her son, Simon, has given her."

Laughter bubbled up in her chest. Not only had her flirting worked, but Meg suddenly understood Zach's nervousness from the night before when Nick had stopped by their table. He'd been worried when Nick motioned his mother that Nick was going to say something about Simon. Another realization of how Zach had deceived her.

Fire burned her stomach like she'd eaten way too many hot peppers. Zach had played her for a fool. She wouldn't forget how he'd sweet-talked and made her feel like a lady, for her only to learn he'd forgotten one very important piece of information.

"Do you plan on being out there long or are you coming back to town?" Nick asked.

"Depends," she said. "It could be a quick visit or it could take a while."

If Simon were there, she'd be back in town later this evening. But if he were gone, she'd be on the hunt once again.

"If you come back into town, maybe we could have dinner. That is if there's nothing between you and Zach."

Meg smiled. Whatever had been between her and Zach had sizzled out like fire in the rain. Once again, she was a woman alone. Six months ago she would have been delighted to have dinner with this nice young man, but now, her heart was shattered, and she didn't want anything to do with the male gender. Even the idea made her insides cringe with revulsion.

There was a soreness between her legs that reminded her of the treachery of dealing with the male species. She wanted nothing to do with this man or any other one.

"Thanks, but I don't know when I'll be back this direction," she said, thinking even if she came back, she'd never be interested.

No matter what, Zach had left an impression on her heart and then he'd broken it.

Nick grinned at her like he was the best thing this side of the Rio Grande. "Well, if you come back through, look me up."

"Thanks, I've gotta go. I'd like to be there before nightfall."

"Oh, it will only take you about two hours."

"Thanks, that's good to know," she said, picking up her saddle.

When she stepped outside, she quickly saddled her horse then attached the reins from Zach's horse to her saddle horn.

Zach wasn't going anywhere until he found himself another ride. A twinge of regret filled her conscience, but he'd deliberately withheld information about Simon. There had been numerous times he could have told her about his brother, and he'd chosen to keep Simon's identity a secret.

Play with fire and eventually you're going to get burned. She'd just burned Zach. He would be hoofing it for a while.

This way she would have a head start on capturing his brother.

*

Meg stared at the two-story rambling home where Zach had grown up. The place looked homey and inviting, with wide porches where a family could gather in the evenings. It appeared spacious and roomy compared to her small farm. The house had a coat of white paint with a rose bush blooming in front and several rocking chairs gracing the porch.

For the last hour, she'd stared at the house, waiting to see if anyone moved about the place, but so far no one had come through the door. No sign of Simon or Frank, and she wondered if anyone was at home. Finally, she gave up and rode into the courtyard area.

She looped the reins around the hitching post in front of the house and tied Zach's horse, knowing she would leave it behind for him to find. Climbing the stairs, trepidation galloped through her bloodstream like a racehorse as she knocked on the door. Could Simon be here?

The door opened. A small woman wearing a prairie dress, her gray hair pulled into a bun, greeted her. "Yes?"

"I'm looking for Mrs. Gillepsie. Is she home?"

"I'm Patricia Gillespie Trudeau," the woman said, frowning at her. "That's my son Zach's horse. What's happened to him?"

Now it was starting to come together. Zach's mother had remarried.

"Zach's fine. I expect him to catch up to me any time now."

"What did you do to him?" she asked.

Oh, his mother really didn't want to know Meg had left him butt naked and tied to the bed in a hotel room. This whole day had been one exercise after another in frustration. "Nothing. You should be asking what he's done to me."

The woman frowned. "Zach's a good son. I don't have to worry about him. Why do you have his horse?"

"I'm leaving it here for him. I'd like to talk to you about your son Simon."

The woman sighed, her look no longer friendly at all. "Who are you?"

Meg thought for a second about lying to her, but then decided no, she wanted no part of deceit. "I'm a bounty hunter looking for Simon."

"He's not here. Why should I help you?"

"Why should I leave Zach's horse?"

"Because you don't want to be a horse thief."

"And you don't want your son Zach, a lawman, to have to turn in his own brother."

The older woman frowned, her eyes narrowing in

suspicion. "Why did you take Zach's horse?"

Meg crossed her arms and gazed at the older woman. She looked a lot like Zach. She had the same earthy brown eyes, the same smile, and tough chin. Meg determined she was going to be honest with her, even if it got her nowhere. "We were riding together, me and Zach, chasing Simon, but I didn't know our criminal was Zach's brother. This morning I learned the truth, and I left Zach tied up in bed. When I got to the corral, I took off with his horse."

The woman stared at her, her mouth hanging open in disbelief. Then a smile curled her lips, and she started to laugh. "I think you need to come in, sit down, and tell me this story from the beginning. You're telling me a lot this old mind doesn't comprehend. I mean, no one has ever gotten the best of Zach Gillespie. What's your name, girl?"

"Meg McKenzie."

The woman smiled and opened the door to the house wider to let Meg come through the portal. "You're that girl Zach was going to ask to marry."

Meg stepped through the door, removed her hat, and shook out her hair.

So it'd been true, he really had planned on asking her to marry him the night she'd tied him up and left him in town. He'd been serious.

"I'm sure you're wondering how I knew, but he came to visit me and told me all about you." She glanced at her clothes. "He said you liked to wear men's clothes."

"I hate wearing men's clothes, but it's all I have," she said and remembered the beautiful dress Zach had bought for her. God, how she wished she hadn't left the dress behind. She'd loved it. But she couldn't take the dress and hate him at the same time. Though, she loathed going off and leaving that gown.

Patricia patted her on the arm. "Have a seat, Meg. I want to hear this story about you and my son. Then, if I think it's right, I'll tell you everything I know about Simon."

An hour later, they were still talking, and Meg felt like she'd found someone who reminded her of her own strong-willed mother. She liked Zach's mother and thought that if she had married Zach, they would have gotten along. But there was no chance of that ever happening. Now that she'd learned of Zach's deceit, how could she ever trust him again? Though, somehow last night, he'd loved her body and soul enough to own a chunk of her heart. But without trust there was nothing. And there was no point in dreaming fanciful dreams of a man who she couldn't have faith in.

"Tell me about Simon?" Meg asked. They'd talked about Zach and Meg the entire time with Meg telling her everything, except the fact they'd slept together. That little piece of information Patricia didn't need to know.

The older woman shook her head and let out a deep sigh. "My sons mean the world to me. I love them all, but he's been the most difficult one to raise. My biggest regret is marrying Simon's father. Mr. Gillespie had been dead and gone for four years when I met John Trudeau. He was a fast-talking French man who swept me off my feet and had such great visions. We were married soon after we met, and then the real horror began."

She paused for a moment and gazed around the room as if searching for her husband. "I got pregnant with Simon, and John began to visit the saloons. For years, I put up with him coming home smelling of whiskey and other women. Then one day when Simon was about fourteen, his father didn't come home. We went into town to look for him, and he was standing in the middle of the street embroiled in a gunfight. While we watched, he was shot and killed. I don't think the boy ever recovered from seeing his father shot dead."

Meg felt a little compassion. The memory of her own father's death washed over her like it was yesterday and not a year ago. The sight of his body lying helpless in the bed wrenched her stomach, and she realized how much her own life had changed because of his death. "That had to be hard. How about your other kids? How did they take it?"

Zach's mother laughed, a hard sound coming from her tiny body. "My other sons were old enough that they knew this was a blessing because John would never be coming home drunk again. I think my second marriage is the reason Zach's a sheriff. I think he wanted to make certain no other family had to put up with a sorry drunk."

"He's told me he loves his job," Meg said, knowing Zach enjoyed being the town's sheriff.

"And he's good at it," Patricia said, gazing at Meg.

"Yes," Meg admitted, though she could still outshoot him.

"His brothers are important to him. He's the oldest and he looked out for each of them when they were growing up. He loves them. Even Simon."

The image of Ruby and Annabelle came to mind, and Meg thought about how much she loved her sisters. Obviously, Zach loved felt the same toward his brothers. Only her sisters had never committed a crime.

"Yes, but he told me he'd take Simon in if he found out his brother had killed that man."

"He told me the same thing," Patricia said, staring off into the distance. "I love all of my sons, even Simon. And if he killed someone, it will break my heart, but I know Zach will have to do his job. He will turn him in. But I asked him to investigate and find out the truth. Simon said he didn't kill that man. That Frank killed him. I don't know, but before I watch my son hang, I have to learn the truth."

Meg felt her anger toward Zach simmer down. How could she stay mad at a man who was doing something so his mother could live with the consequences of his actions? How could she be angry with him when he was only a dutiful son to a loving mother?

She could be mad because he didn't trust her enough to tell her. All he had to do was tell her that Simon was his brother and he was going to find out the truth before Simon hanged. A simple conversation. A simple acknowledgement that there was a connection between him and Simon.

But oh no, he'd kept his secret for as long as possible, would still be hiding his brother if she hadn't learned the truth from his silly note.

"Do you know where Simon is?"

Patricia shook her head. "I don't. He was here for a while, but I've not seen him in over a week. Zach told him to stay here and lay low until we learned the truth, but he's gone and that makes me doubt his innocence."

Meg didn't know if Simon was innocent or guilty, and frankly, she didn't care. There was a bounty on his head. It was up to a jury to determine his guilt or innocence. She wasn't the executioner. She was just the deliverer.

"Let me fix you another cup of tea," Patricia said,

getting up.

Meg glanced at the clock. It was getting late in the afternoon. Zach would be arriving soon, and she wanted to leave before he showed up. She had no idea where she was going, but she hadn't spoken to the widow Lowell. If she were the only witness, it would be imperative nothing happened to her. She could be in danger. If Simon had shot her husband, he might want to see her dead as well.

"Thanks, but I should be going. It'll be dark soon, and I'd like to get on down the road a ways and set up camp.

The woman stared at her. "Do you enjoy catching criminals?"

Pausing to consider her question, Meg thought about it for a moment and then slowly shook her head. "Not really, but it beats being a saloon girl, and it pays better than being a seamstress. And I'm in charge of myself."

Bounty hunting was a tough, dangerous job. She'd be glad to hang up her spurs and guns forever. But right now, it was the best paying job where she was in control, not working for a man who refused to pay, a restaurant owner who thought he deserved free desserts from his waitresses, or a spoiled college boy who didn't understand the word no. Soon, this would all be behind her and her sisters, and they could live like normal folks.

The woman smiled. "That's why I'm a rancher. I have control over my destiny. Sounds like you're a self-sufficient woman, as well. Don't ever let a man take that away from you."

"I'm doing my best," Meg said as she rose from her chair in the small kitchen and pushed it under the table. "It was great to meet you, Mrs. Trudeau. I'm sorry I'm going to be the one who turns your son in."

"What will you do with the money?" Zach's mother asked.

"It'll pay off the note on my family farm. Then my sisters will have a place and won't have to be bounty hunters any longer."

She nodded. "What will you do, Meg?"

The image of that green dress came to mind, and her heart clinched in sorrow. There would be other dresses like that one in her future. She would make certain of it. "I'm going to open up a dress shop."

The woman's eyes widened in disbelief.

"I'm good with a needle, and I love to create dresses. It's just that there's never been the money for me to own a dress of my own." Meg hated admitting she had no money for a dress. And when she got home this time, the first thing she would do was buy herself a fancy new dress and let the people of Zenith see she could be a lady.

Patricia nodded, her large eyes shining with understanding. "I hope you don't find Simon, but I do hope you get your dress shop. And if you see Zach again, tell him I said he should have married you."

"Thanks," Meg said, knowing with certainty it would have been a mistake. "We weren't ready."

"What about now?"

"Ha, now it's impossible. He's tied up in a hotel room, hating me right about now, and well, I'm not real happy with him either."

The elderly woman smiled, her facial expression tearing at Meg's heart. It reminded her of Zach so much she could feel tears welling up and she pushed the hurt down.

"Zach is like his father. Stubborn to a fault. He needs

a strong woman who can challenge him and put him in his place. He's a good man, but he'd walk all over a woman who doesn't have a backbone. You have a backbone."

Meg almost thought the woman was going to tell her to marry her son. And while part of Meg's heart was interested, the other part was reminding her they had no trust between the two of them. What else was Zach keeping from her? What else had he lied about?

"Thanks for the cup of tea. When Zach shows up, tell him I've gone after Simon."

*

Zach had had enough of Meg's games. If that woman ever came near him with a rope again, he'd use her own rope to hang her. Twice now she'd tied him up and left, and he'd had all he was willing to take from her.

The final straw was taking his horse and leaving him with this old nag he'd had to rent from the livery stable. And Nick had enjoyed sticking him with the slowest horse just this side of six feet under.

Zach had pushed the old nag until he feared she was going to drop dead right here in the middle of the road and leave him walking. Finally, the old homestead came into view, and when he saw Meg walking down the steps, he kicked the side of the old gray mare.

Meg looked up and saw him riding toward her. She rested her hand on her gun, and he knew he was still in a lot of trouble.

He pulled to a stop in front of her, leaned over his horse, and shouted, "I should arrest you for stealing my horse."

She gave him that cold stare that sent a chill straight to his heart. "Just try. There's your horse." She pointed to the courtyard. "I'm just aching for a chance to knock some sense into that empty brain of yours."

Ice cold fury seethed within him like a snowstorm in July. "Empty brain? I'm not the one who has a thing about ropes. I'm beginning to wonder if you secretly want some man to tie you up."

"You've already done it to me twice."

He smiled, remembering the satisfaction in tying up Meg and her sister. Yet, he hadn't enjoyed leaving them that last time on the road in their pantaloons.

"And you've done it to me three times. Leaving me tied to the bed for the maid to find. That was downright humiliating."

Her green eyes flashed with amusement, which only made him madder. She thought his humiliation was funny?

"Well, it's better than shooting you, which is what I really wanted to do," she replied, walking down the last two steps.

"You've done that too. Don't forget."

She halted in mid stride, her eyes widened and her breath came out in a whoosh. "Oh, my God! You let me believe I'd accidentally shot you when you rode in front of me to keep me from shooting your brother. You're dumber than a tortoise in the desert."

He frowned, knowing she'd now fully realized he'd placed his own life in jeopardy to save his brother. Yeah, maybe it had been a dumb move, but it was the kind of thing a man did when he loved his brother. And even with all his faults, he still loved Simon. "You weren't supposed to shoot."

She threw up her arms, her face contorted in rage. "If I'd known he was your brother, I wouldn't have. But somewhere along the trail, you forgot to mention you were kin," she said with a sarcastic tone to her voice.

They stared at one another, each one breathing hard. Finally, Zach couldn't stop the words from flowing from his mouth. He knew they were bad, yet he could no more stop them than the creek from rising during a flash flood. "You're hunting the man. What was I suppose to say? Don't hurt my brother? Yes, he's a known criminal, but there's a chance he's innocent. I'm trying to save him. You want me, the lawman, to ask for special favors for my brother?" The very idea had his guts turning inside out. He was a respectable man of the law, and he did not take advantage of his position. His conscience cringed.

"Yes, was that so hard to say? Would it have made a difference? I can't say, but at least, you would have trusted me enough to tell me the truth. At least then, we could be working on building trust between us and not destroying our friendship."

"I don't ask for special favors for anyone!" he fairly shouted at her.

She laughed, which sent anger rippling through him because he knew the irony of the words he'd just said.

"Oh, yes, you do, cowboy. Don't lie to yourself. You want people to ignore the fact that your brother could be guilty while you try to prove his innocence. But what if he's guilty?"

Zach hated her at that moment because her words were true. And as much as he didn't want to accept them, they made him feel dishonorable. And he'd always prided himself on being honorable. "Yes, I'm trying to protect him until I know he's guilty. Once I'm convinced he's done wrong, then I will turn him in. I've said that all along."

"Not to me you haven't. Because I didn't know he was your brother."

Silence filled the dusty courtyard. She untied the reins to her horse and climbed up into the saddle. With ease, she backed the horse and turned him toward Zach.

"I'm going after Simon," she said. "Don't even think about stopping me. Don't follow me. Don't come near me," she said emphatically, her voice trembling with anger. "We're done."

"I'm going to find him first," he said. "And we're not done." He didn't know what he wanted, but he wasn't through with Meg. He wanted to explore this thing between them. He wasn't ready to profess undying love, and she'd probably shoot him if he did, but he wasn't ready for this to end either.

"By the time you rid yourself of that nag, I'll be down the road, and you'll have no idea where I'm going."

"I'll find you, Meg. I will hunt you down, and wherever you're at, I know Simon won't be far away. You can't hide from me."

She spurred her horse and rode down the lane, leaving him behind. She raised her arm in the air with a clenched fist to let him know how she felt regarding his words.

God, the woman was infuriating. She probably thought she'd won this little skirmish, but he'd win the war. He'd find her.

Chapter Ten

Meg spurred her horse down the lane away from the house. She didn't know where she was going, but she thought her first clue would be wherever the widow Lowell resided. If she was the only witness, could Simon possibly be thinking of doing away with her? No one to say that the farmer hadn't drawn first. No one to prove Simon's guilt.

Except that would mean Simon was definitely guilty, and even as angry as she was at Zach at this moment, the thought of his brother hanging, wrenched her heart and filled her with sadness. Mrs. Trudeau didn't need the heartache of knowing her youngest son would hang. That he had killed someone.

If Simon was nowhere near the widow, then maybe he was innocent. Seemed way too simple, yet it also made sense.

For the next hour, Meg pushed her horse, hoping to stay far ahead of Zach, needing distance from the deceitful man. After talking to his mother, she understood his reasons, but why couldn't he have been honest with her? Why hadn't he told her Simon was his brother?

Would it have made a difference? Maybe, but probably not. Still, she deserved to know. If it had been one of her sisters who'd committed a crime, she would have explained to Zach that nothing came between blood. Nothing. And while she hoped her sisters would never do such a horrible thing, even so she would do everything to protect them. She'd been caring for them since they were kids, and it was hard to even think about letting them go now.

In so many ways, she was more their mother than their sister. She could understand Zach's feeling of protectiveness toward his brother, but without trust, they had no chance as a couple.

And he was a lawman. He was risking everything to fulfill his promise to his mother. What would this do to him as a person if he had to turn his brother into the law? Would he throw his ethics to the wind and let his brother go free? Either one was a terrible choice. One that Meg would not want to make.

As the afternoon sun waned, she glanced behind and saw Zach had indeed caught up to her. He was probably half a mile back. She ignored him, hoping she could reach the town before nightfall. Knowing that was probably impossible.

She rode until the sun sat just above the horizon. Shadows like whispers of darkness filled the trail. With little sleep the night before, her body craved rest. She had no choice, but to stop and make camp for the night. Hopefully, Zach would keep his distance. They were not sharing a camp, a bedroll, a whiskey bottle—nothing.

She had just gotten her fire started when he pulled into her camp.

"Mind if I join you?"

"Yes, I do. Keep your distance."

They weren't sharing a camp tonight. He would do his best to sweet talk his way back into her life and into her pants, but she refused to accept him yet again.

"Can't we at least talk?"

"Cowboy, you should have talked weeks ago. That was the time to talk."

"You're just not going to give up, are you?"

She stared at him and shook her head. Like a stampede of cattle, she could feel the anger building at his attitude. "I slept with you, believing there was a chance of something between us. You, on the other hand, were too busy keeping secrets."

"Damn it, Meg, you don't understand."

"What's there to understand? You're honest with the people you care about. You respect them and tell them the truth, even if it's ugly. Even if they don't want to hear the bad news."

"I was going to admit to you this morning Simon was my brother. I was going to be honest with you then."

Meg shook her head, wondering how long before he caught on to the fact he'd waited too long. Was this a man trait? Or was it just Zach?

"Why are you always just a little too slow, cowboy? Too slow to ask me to marry you and now to tell me Simon is your brother. Our relationship would be so different if you'd been honest and forthright with me both times."

Zach strode away, but he didn't walk far. Maybe ten feet, where he began to set up his own camp.

He hadn't responded to her last comment, and in fact, he almost seemed to want to run away. Could it be that when he began to see her point of view, he tucked his tail and ran? This big strong cowboy maybe had a problem admitting he was wrong?

She watched him gather his firewood, and soon he had a bigger fire going than hers. He disappeared into the woods, and later, she heard a gunshot. When he walked back into camp, he was carrying a skinned rabbit.

As he roasted the rabbit on a spit over his fire, the smell made her mouth water, and her stomach let out a healthy growl. Any meat would taste better than the hardtack sticking to the roof of her mouth.

He took his dinner off the fire and held it up for her to see. "There's more than enough for both of us. Come join me and you can have some."

"I don't eat with deceivers."

He shook his head. "Suit yourself. But it's really good."

The smell was driving her crazy. Her stomach growled again, and she wanted to run over there and grab a piece, but she refused. She wouldn't let him tempt his way back into her heart. She just couldn't.

Zach sauntered over, his swagger matching his ego, as he brought her a piece of the rabbit. "Here. Swallow this with some of that pride."

Argh, she wanted to hit him. She wanted to slap him for being so nice and thoughtful, and oh, she wanted that piece of rabbit so bad. Her mouth was watering at the sight of that grilled piece of meat. But he was right, her pride remembered the anguish of reading that note this morning, and her throat closed up tighter than a virgin in a whorehouse.

"No, thank you. I'm not hungry." Her stomach growled once more, illuminating her lie.

He smiled at her and took a bite. "Okay, suit yourself,

but this tasty little guy is a lot better than a rock hard biscuit.

She ignored his comment and watched as he took another bite. Then his face changed. His eyes drew together, as he frowned. "Meg, don't move." His voice was serious, calm and deep.

"Go away, and leave me alone. You can't tell me what to do."

A moment ago, he'd stomped out of her camp, unable to face her when the talk became too serious, but now he was back offering her food and trying to tell her what to do. The man was more than a nuisance.

"I'm serious. There's a rattlesnake about a foot behind you."

She shook her head at him. "We've already played that game. You're just trying to get even with me for pulling a snake trick on you. I'm smart enough not to fall for your lies."

Suddenly, he dropped the rabbit, whipping out his six-shooter and firing at a spot behind her, causing her heart to leap in her chest. She jumped almost clean out of her skin.

"Damn it, cowboy, that's enough. Get your tail out of my camp before I pull out my gun and shoot you. There's no snake behind me. Pretending to shoot the varmint is not going to convince me it's real. Get out of my camp, now!"

He walked behind her and reached down. When she turned around, she saw the three-foot rattler hanging limply in his hand. Her heart leaped into her throat, her blood racing faster than a fox chasing a squirrel.

"Now there's some good eating," he said with a triumphant, manly smile. "Now I'll get out of your camp and leave you be."

Meg began to shake, nausea gripping her insides like bats on a cave wall. She jumped up and gazed around her camp. Where there was one snake, there could be two.

"Stop," she said weakly to Zach. She walked to the edge of the clearing, leaned over and wretched. Shivers overtook her as she realized if Zach hadn't come over to her camp to bring her some rabbit, that snake would have bitten her. There was no telling how long it had been lying there. One wrong move and it would have struck, probably killing her.

"Meg, it's dead. This one wasn't even in your blankets," he said with a smile.

"I hate snakes."

He stood there, holding that damn rattler, looking like a man who'd just won a fight with the devil. She wanted to hate him. She wanted to kiss him. She wanted him to wrap his arms around her until she felt safe again. And she had no idea when that might be.

All thoughts of arguing over who was right or wrong suddenly seemed insignificant. Nothing mattered, except the fact he'd probably just saved her life.

"Yeah, me too. Nasty critters. Mean as the devil."

"But where there's one…"

"Oh, there's probably another one somewhere." He stared at her. "The safest thing you could do is move to sit around my fire. It's bigger and hotter and safer."

She stared at him for a moment, and the thought of that snake's partner or family or just another rattlesnake being close by was enough for her to swallow her pride and take him up on his offer. With conditions.

"All right, but you sleep on your side of the fire, and I sleep on my side. No sharing blankets or bedrolls. Your clothes stay on at all times."

He smiled. "You're not going to make this easy, are you?"

"Make what easy? We're sharing a fire and that's all. There will be no reconciliation. It's over." She was saying the words her head was telling her to say, but her heart was still pounding loudly in her chest and glancing over at that snake had her wanting to be as close as possible to Zach.

She kicked some dirt over her fire, dousing the coals, then picked up her blankets and saddle while Zach carried the snake and pulled her horse over to his camp.

Maybe she was silly for letting a snake send her back to Zach, but it was only for one night. And tomorrow, she'd ride alone.

*

Zach's eyes had almost popped clean out of his head at the sight of that rattler lying there all coiled up, its head down, its beady eyes gleaming in the firelight. The poisonous serpent had watched Zach up until the moment he'd fired his gun.

Why it hadn't rattled was beyond Zach, but the fear that had flashed through him like a springtime flood was enough to have aged him right out of his youth and into middle age. Meg had been sitting on her blanket less than a foot away from the snake. Close enough it would have gotten her in one single strike. Close enough it could have killed her so very easy.

For a moment, Zach's heart had leaped in his throat as terror sped through his veins like a runaway horse. Meg injured or hurt left him with the strangest empty feeling.

The idea of her not being in his life confused him,

left him wondering what being with this woman had done to him. He watched her settling in across the fire and enough warmth filled him his dick hardened and his thoughts churned. He wanted her back in his bedroll. He wanted her close, so he could protect and love her. He needed her like warm sunshine and rain.

Why was he always slow to react with Meg? Did she have reason to be angry with him or had he just been doing what he had to do? Yes, he should have told her Simon was his brother, but there had just never seemed like the right time, and he'd kept hoping she'd give up on pursuing the man.

But no, Meg was as stubborn as they came, and like a dog digging for a bone, knowing sooner or later he'd recover what he'd lost, she was determined to find Simon.

He skinned the snake then put the meat on a spit and laid it across the flames to cook.

Meg sat on her blanket across from him, her hat pulled low, her arms wrapped around her knees. "Your mother is really nice."

"Thanks," he said, thinking how weird it was that Meg had met his mother.

"I feel bad for her that I'm going to catch Simon."

Zach shrugged. "I may catch him before you."

She looked up and gazed at him. "Are you going to turn him in this time?"

That was a question Zach had struggled with every day. His head was telling him he had to turn his brother in, but his heart kept repeating *this is your brother*.

"I know you find it hard to believe, but I only let him stay at my mother's while I tried to learn the truth."

Meg shrugged and gazed into the fire. "Funny thing,

cowboy, I'd have a real hard time turning one of my siblings in, too. If you'd been honest with me, things would have been different."

"How? You'd still be mad." How could he admit to her he'd been wrong? He should have told her from the beginning Simon was his brother, but he'd hoped it would never come to this. He'd believed he would discover his brother was innocent, and they would laugh about how Zach had almost had to turn Simon in. Maybe even go to the saloon and drink a draught once it was all over.

Meg smiled. "I still would have gone after Simon because that's what I do. You should have told me he was your brother when you tied me and Ruby up and left us in that alley."

He shook his head. "Maybe so, but when you're the sheriff, it's hard to say it's your brother who's got a bounty on his head. When you put on the badge, you never think about choosing between your profession and your family." He lowered his head and stared into the fire. "I may have to help end his life. How do you think that makes me feel? No matter what he's done, he's still my brother."

Meg sighed and hugged her legs tighter. Zach wanted to go over to that side of the fire and wrap his arms around her, but somehow knew he better stay on his side of the fire or send her running back to her camp. He didn't want her away from him. He actually wanted her closer than across the fire.

"I feel sorry for you and your mother, but my job is to take him in, and that's what I'll be doing," Meg said, her voice somehow soft. "It's not just the fact that you didn't tell me about Simon it's the whole principal of the thing. I thought we had something, but how can we if you can't be honest and forthright with me? How can I follow you if you're not truthful with me from the beginning?"

Zach shook his head. "I was going to tell you this morning."

"Oh, that would have made the morning pleasant. The sex was great, and oh, by the way, Simon is my brother."

His insides clenched and sizzled like water hitting hot coals of anger. How could he blame her for being so upset with him? He'd done this not once, but twice now to her. She was right, but his damn pride refused to tell her the truth. "That's why I didn't tell you the night before."

"Don't you think it would have been better if you'd told me before we had sex?"

Zach frowned, shook his head, and stared off at the sky. "I messed up, Meg. Nothing about this has been easy."

"Don't do it again," she said before she laid down, rolled over, and gave him her back.

"Does that mean we're going to have a relationship?" he asked, feeling somewhat hopeful that maybe she was getting over his lie. "Does this mean we have a future?"

She didn't roll over. "No, it means if you want to live, don't lie to me again."

God, the woman could hold a grudge better than any woman he knew. But maybe she was right. He should have told her weeks ago that Simon was his brother, but he feared the knowledge would change how she felt about him. He feared he would appear less a man and a bad sheriff.

Her voice called out from the other side of the fire. "Just so you understand. This changes nothing. I'm still going after him."

Zach sighed. "I didn't expect anything less."

*

The next morning they rode into the town of Vera Cruz, with Meg in the lead and Zach following behind her. He'd not slept well last night, his mind going over and over again the way Meg had made him feel about lying to her.

He didn't want to withhold information from her, but at the time it'd seemed the right thing to do. Now, he knew it was the worst thing he could have done, and it had ruined his attempts to win Meg's heart. And he *wanted* to win Meg's heart. In the last few days, it had become the most important thing on this journey. Watch over Meg, keep her safe, and find Simon.

They pulled up in front of a small house. Meg threw her leg over her saddle and slid to the ground. She tied her horse to the hitching post. Without glancing back at him, she walked to the door and knocked.

After tying his horse next to hers, Zach hurried to catch up.

He curled his hands into fists. What they were about to learn would lead him to a decision regarding his brother. Part of him feared what he would soon hear, and the other part of him felt confident Simon would be cleared.

A middle aged woman in a long skirt covered by an apron answered the door.

"Is Mrs. Lowell living here?" Meg asked.

She frowned at the two of them, gazing at Zach's tin star pinned on his chest. "Who are you?"

"I'm Meg McKenzie, and this is the Sheriff Zach Gillespie."

She opened the door wider and motioned them in. "Come on in. I'm Mrs. Lowell. Have a seat."

They walked in to the rudimentary two-room cabin. A stove graced one corner of the front room, and the back room was a bedroom.

"We're hunting Simon Trudeau for the murder of your husband," Meg said. "I'd like to ask you some questions about what happened that day."

"He's been in town, you know," she said, her voice trembling. "My kid saw him."

Zach saw the fear in the woman's gray eyes, and he wanted to reassure her that Simon would never harm her, but he couldn't. He wasn't as certain as he once was about his brother's innocence.

Mrs. Lowell hung her head and sighed. "My kids are now working to try to support us since my husband's gone. We're reduced to living in this shack, instead of our homestead, and I've not left the house for fear he'll see me and realize where we live."

"Do you think he would come after you?" Meg asked.

"I don't know. I mean it's my word against his. If I weren't talking anymore, it could just be swept under the rug, and everyone's life would go on. My husband is still six feet under, but that man would still have a life."

Zach swallowed the tight lump that had formed in his throat. He couldn't ask any questions, as he felt strangled with the fear that had grabbed him. He loved Simon, and if he'd killed this woman's husband, Zach would be forced to turn him in.

"So tell me what happened that day," Meg said.

The woman took a deep breath, glanced over at Zach then began her tale.

*

Annabelle and Ruby rode into Dyersville determined to locate their sister. Fear spurred Annabelle on. She'd left the care of the farm with her cousin, Caroline, with the promise as soon as Annabelle located her eldest sibling and talked some sense into her, she'd be home. The talking sense part might be a tad bit ambitious, but she had to know Meg was all right. She'd never been this long on a hunt without checking in.

Dust drifted up from the hooves of their horses, coating her boots. The town was like any other sleepy western town with the essential businesses people needed to survive, and some that people thought they had to have to live.

"Where do you think she would have gone?" Annabelle asked as they rode side-by-side through the town.

"The sheriff, the saloon, and maybe the livery stable. You take the sheriff. I know a girl who works the saloon. I'll speak to her, and then we can meet back up."

"Let me help you off your horse. We need to spend the night here to let you rest. I don't want you reinjuring that ankle."

"It's fine. You worry too much."

"And you don't worry enough."Annabelle helped Ruby slide from her horse, her sprained ankle still swollen and tender. "Can you make it into the saloon?"

"I'm fine. You go talk to the sheriff."

As Ruby hobbled into the saloon, Annabelle watched long enough to make certain she made it into the rowdy establishment, knowing with certainty she could hold her own. If not, then Annabelle would soon be along to give Ruby any support she might need.

Thirty minutes later, they both arrived in front of the livery stable at the same time.

"Any luck?" Annabelle asked.

"Yes, Meg was in the saloon two days ago. But they haven't seen her since. How about you?"

"Nothing. That lawman's lips were sewed tighter than a corset. I'm hoping we can learn something here."

The two women walked into the livery stable. Annabelle watched a good-looking tall man approach them. "Nick Hargrove, how can I help you ladies?"

Her stomach clenched. The man was as phony as fool's gold. Ever since she'd worked at Rusty's café, she could spot a lady's man from a mile away. She should probably thank Rusty's wife for giving her the opportunity to learn what kind of men to avoid.

"Have you seen a red-headed woman wearing men's clothing in the last few days?" Annabelle asked.

"Why?"

"She's our sister, Meg McKenzie, and we're trying to track her down," Ruby said, staring at the man, her blue eyes zeroing in on him like he was a target.

Annabelle was proud of the way Ruby had become a strong woman in the last year. Being a bounty hunter, she'd quickly learned how to hold her own and didn't think twice about hauling some criminal in to the law. This wiseass would do well not to make her mad.

"She was in here day before yesterday. She took Zach Gillespie's horse and was headed to his mother's ranch, last I heard. Zach was pretty angry at her for leaving him without a horse."

"Where does his mother live?" Annabelle asked,

doubting Meg was still there, but hoping she'd know where Meg had headed. "We've got to find her."

The man gave her directions. "You can track his horse prints because the right front leg only has five nails in that shoe. The other three have eight. Damn horse has a weird hoof."

"Thanks, that's good information. We'll pay Mrs. Gillespie a visit."

"Oh, it's not Mrs. Gillespie. It's Mrs. Trudeau."

"What?" Ruby frowned at the man and shook her head. "Zach's name is Gillespie."

"Yeah, she remarried after Mr. Gillespie died."

Ruby flipped her blonde hair back off her shoulder. "Dear God, then Simon Trudeau is Zach's brother."

"Yes, ma'am," the man said, leaning against the barn door and staring at Ruby like she was steak and he was starving. "You girls passing through or will you be coming back?"

Suddenly, Ruby seemed to take notice of the way he was observing her, and her hand shifted closer to her gun. She stepped back away from the open door. "We're just passing through. Come on, Annabelle. We've got to warn, Meg."

Chapter Eleven

"**Y**ou okay, cowboy?" Meg asked gently, her heart aching at the sight of his drawn face, his eyes a torturous brown as they rode away from the cottage.

Zach had barely said five words to the woman. Before they'd left, he'd expressed his condolences for the death of her husband, but he'd never admitted Simon was his brother or whether or not he'd been convinced Simon had killed the man.

"Yes," he said, his voice gruff. "I really believed he was innocent."

Meg turned her horse toward town, her body swaying in the saddle. "I don't know what I would do if one of my sisters had killed someone. Ruby said she almost shot that Mullins boy when he tried to rape her. I was tempted to kill him myself." She glanced over at Zach. "You know this means we have to bring him in."

"Yeah, I know."

Sadness filled Meg's soul like an overflowing well, her heart breaking at the sight of Zach slumped in the saddle, clearly upset about what the Lowell widow had told them.

"What if she's wrongly accusing him? What if she

just wants to get him in trouble?" Zach asked, his voice filled with desperation.

"Do you believe she's lying?"

He sighed, the sound loud in the lengthening Texas shadows. Their horses plodded along the road, kicking up dust as they rode into town. "No, I think she's telling the truth. I just don't want to believe it."

Meg nodded. She understood, and for once, Zach had her complete sympathy. Mrs. Lowell had been his last chance to clear his brother's name. And now he was faced with the situation he'd dreaded. Now he would have to turn his younger brother over to the authorities, where he'd face trial and possibly hang. But he'd also have to tell his mother, whose heart would be broken that her youngest son had murdered a man and would pay for his crimes.

"Sometimes a man has to face the fact he's been wrong. You've helped me see that in the last few days. First, with the realization how much you really want to be treated like a woman, which then helped me realize how badly I've treated you. And now Simon. I feel like I've not been thinking very clearly with either one of you."

Meg turned in her saddle and stared at him. His brown earthy eyes were dark, and she wanted to wrap her arms around him and comfort him. "That, cowboy, is quite a confession."

"Well, it's true."

"So what are you going to do about it?"

He pulled his horse close to hers and yanked up on her reins, stopping her. "I'm going to work hard not to be stupid when it comes to you. I don't have any other dark hidden secrets. Just a longing to be with you." He reached over, his hand coming behind her head as he brought her mouth to his. He kissed her like a man who'd lost everything and needed to be reassured that he was still alive. He kissed her like a man whose well was empty, drained of all feelings. He kissed her like a man who longed for only her.

She pulled back when their horses snickered and did a side-step. Her hand reached out to caress his face. "It's getting late. Let's find a hotel and bunk in for the night."

She knew exactly what she was telling him. He needed her tonight, and she could no more deny him than the sun could keep from rising in the morning. Maybe she desired him as much as he needed her.

*

Darkness cloaked the small Texas town as Meg and Zach walked up the stairs, their boots making a hollow noise. Zach turned the key, flinging open the door to the room they'd rented for the night. Maybe she was crazy for agreeing to share a room with him, but the news of Simon's guilt had been like a poison spreading through his body. She'd seen the way his expression had closed off, his eyes vacant and distant, his shoulders sagging and his speech becoming one-syllable answers. It was like Zach had disappeared into the cavern of his mind.

Yet, how would she have felt if the accusations were against one of her sisters? How would she have reacted to the knowledge that Annabelle or Ruby had killed an innocent man in cold blood? How would she feel if she were the person who would have to turn her sister over to hang?

She couldn't do it. She could never deliberately harm her sisters. Sometimes she'd like to, but there was no way she could take them to the law, knowing they would hang for their crimes and be out of her life forever.

They closed the door behind them, and she glanced at the big bed in the middle of the room. She turned her gaze to Zach's large brown eyes. She let her saddlebags drop to the floor, her eyes never leaving his, her heart beating inside her chest like a drummer in a military band.

Hot sultry silence filled the room. The kind of tension and heat that crackled the atmosphere before a summertime thunderstorm. And then he moved swiftly and deliberately toward her. His hands gripped her face, cradling her head like she was the most cherished person in the world as his mouth descended to hers. And, oh God, how she wanted this kiss. Needed him like she was a flower and he was the rain.

His lips moved over hers, making her body seemed to bust out singing the "Hallelujah Chorus". A tingle of desire shot straight from her lips to her groin. He pulled her tight against his body, letting her feel the solidness of his chest, the rock hardness of his manhood snug against her belly. She opened her mouth, seeking his tongue, needing him, wanting to comfort this big strong man who tantalized her, made her crazy with anger, and left her laughing with pleasure. Only Zach had the power to make her feel so many different emotions all at the same time.

Only Zach…those words flitted across her mind like the aftermath of a bad storm, when you realized you had survived and the blessed rain had cleansed the earth. Could she be falling in love with this man? Absolutely not! They irritated one another; they made each other madder than a bear in springtime. Yet, she couldn't keep her hands off him.

His hands slid down her face, her throat, lingering on her breasts as he gripped both of them. Their lips came apart, and she slowly opened her eyes.

He was gazing at her. "God, I need you so much tonight."

She reached up and touched the side of his face, her fingertips feeling the bristles of his beard, the smoothness of his lips. He could make her so angry, yet this afternoon, she'd felt like her insides were being cannibalized at the devastating realization that Simon was guilty.

And Zach would suffer because of his crimes.

"What are you waiting for?" she whispered, the words escaping, acknowledging the desire that consumed her.

Zach walked her to the bed. He pulled the shirt from her pants and undid the buttons. He pushed the garment from her shoulders, his lips connecting with the side of her throat, trailing down her chest to the tops of her breasts. Lifting the bottom of her chemise, he pulled the garment over her head, leaving her breasts exposed to his gaze.

"Oh God, Meg. You're so beautiful." His words were like raindrops of desire filling her well with much-needed assurance that he wanted her.

Meg arched her back as he lifted her breasts to his mouth. His tongue laved her nipple, sending tingles racing through her. She grasped the back of his head, holding his mouth in place. A moan escaped her lips as he nipped her nipple with his teeth, sending sparks cascading through her.

She'd never known such arousal was possible until Zach. She'd never known it was possible for a man to need a woman and for her to ache with passion and pleasure.

He reached for her pants and quickly unbuttoned them. He kissed his way down her stomach as he slowly pushed her pants down. Kneeling on the floor, his mouth lingered above her womanly center, sending a spiraling cascade of desire straight between her legs.

She gasped for air, wondering what he would do next as his breath moved her auburn curls. With a gentle push from him, she fell onto the bed. He moved between her legs, spreading her open like a flower. Her heart felt as if it would burst out of her chest as he lowered his mouth to her center. The first touch of his tongue on her most intimate womanly parts had her shooting up off the bed onto her elbows. "Zach, what are you doing?"

"Lay back. Let me love you," he commanded.

She lowered herself back to the bed, and he bent over her, placing his mouth on her center. Between her legs, a firestorm began to build, like a wildfire out of control. Reverently, his tongue licked her moist folds. Her hands gripped the bedspread, while he caressed her. Just when she didn't think she could stand another second of his mouth upon her, his teeth nipped her, sending her bucking against his mouth as desire spiraled within her.

"Oh, God," she cried as her hands found the top of his head. She no longer wanted him to stop, and she wasn't certain she would ever let him come up. Pressure began to rise in her, and her breathing increased until she thought she would explode from the pleasure.

"What are you doing to me?" she gasped, her hands running through his hair, holding onto him to keep herself tied to the earth.

He didn't respond but inserted two fingers into her as

his tongue lapped at her center.

The pressure reached a peak she could no longer control. With a cry, she felt herself tumbling over the edge of a precipice, falling. His gentle hands grasped her as her body shook from the pleasure that had overtaken her. Like a river crashing over the falls, she tumbled headlong with exhilaration. She completely lost control in Zach's hands.

The man had wrung her out and laid her low. As her heart rate slowly returned to normal, she felt her heart swell with emotion.

She released his head and he rose from the bed. With tantalizing slowness, he unbuttoned his shirt while he stared at her. She lay completely naked, spread eagle on the bed, her breasts rising and falling as she recovered from the passion they'd just created.

His eyes were dark with some hidden emotion that touched her soul and left her wanting more. She needed him in her arms. She wanted him. Now.

Desire filled her body and left her with an ache. An ache for this man.

She had no previous experiences to compare what they'd just done, but now she wanted Zach inside her.

He sat on the bed beside her and began to pull off his boots. She ran her fingertips along his naked back. Her fingers gliding over the stitches he still bore from the shooting. His shoulder was now a mass of green and purple and yellow as it healed.

"Does it hurt?"

"No," he whispered. "Your touch is healing me."

She sat up and leaned against his back, kissing his shoulders.

"Woman, stop. Or we're going to be finished before

we even get started." He stood and stepped away from the bed while he shucked his pants. Soon he was striding toward her, his manhood hard and rigid and sticking straight out in front of him.

And she lay back, eagerly anticipating him.

As he crawled up on the bed, she reached out and touched his face, bringing his mouth down to hers. Eagerly, his lips sought hers, and she tasted herself on his mouth. While her hand caressed his cock, gripping and rubbing the flesh up and down, his legs spread hers wide. His fingertips wrapped around her hand, and he helped her guide his penis to her opening.

Then he was stretching her wide, sliding between her folds, as he entered her body.

A sigh escaped her as she felt him within her, and a completeness filled her. She glanced up into his brown eyes and felt him push deep within her. With each thrust, she felt like he was imprinting his name on her heart. With each thrust, she sank deeper and deeper into his gaze. With each thrust, she felt her defenses melting away and her heart opening up like a flower to receive him.

"Zach," she moaned. "Please…"

"What, Meg?" he asked, his breathing heavy.

She didn't answer him, not really understanding what she needed, but knowing they were rushing toward that avalanche of feelings once again. Wanting him there with her as they reached the summit and plunged over the edge.

As he made her his once again, she could feel her boundaries slipping away. She'd never been in love before, but with a sureness she found disturbing, she suddenly wanted to give all of herself to him. To follow him across the prairie and back and let him be the man who fathered her children. The man she grew old with. The man she gave her heart and love to every day.

With each thrust, she found herself holding back tears. Zach was the one who made her heart sing with joy. Zach was the one she sought when she walked in a door. Zach was the man she loved with all her heart.

Tension and power and love filled her to near overflowing as her breathing sounded more and more harsh as she reached her peak. She felt Zach rise up and thrust into her deeply.

"Oh, God," he cried as he came, his body shuddering with release.

He plunged into her one final time as she cried out in ecstasy. Her own release roared through her body, sending shudders rippling through her. She clasped him to her, holding him as tight as she could, wanting to somehow absorb him into her soul, where she would hold him tightly and cherish these moments together.

They lay there, their bodies clasped securely as if the world could not interfere. For several minutes, they held each other as their breathing returned to normal and their heartbeats slowed. But Meg would never be the same. This joining had changed her, fulfilled her in ways she'd never considered. She knew that after tonight, no matter what the future held, she would be forever changed.

Zach rolled her to the side, pulling her up tight against him. She listened to the beating of his heart next to hers. What happened next?

"Meg," he said softly into her ear.

"Zach, hold me," she cried as a lone tear rolled down her cheek. She loved Zach Gillespie, and that was a dangerous predicament.

"Always," he said gruffly in her ear as he pulled the sheets up over them.

*

Zach lay beside Meg, his heart heavy, his soul burdened, his body satisfied. God, this woman had not only made him forget the awful mess he was dealing with, she'd made him feel like a man who was capable of taking care of her, of protecting her, of being there beside her each day. She'd loved him like no matter what happened tomorrow, tonight he was all that was important.

His chest felt tight with fear for what the morrow would bring, yet Meg had comforted him and left him more satisfied than a man had the right to feel. She was everything a man could want in a woman, and he'd once stupidly doubted she was woman enough for him. All his doubts had just been dynamited into the atmosphere. If anyone here were weak, it was him.

"You okay?" she asked, her voice soft and breathless.

How could he answer that question? His heart was in his throat, filled with satisfaction, emotional attachment, and something that could easily turn into love for this woman. He was also bereft at the knowledge of his brother. The little boy he'd helped take care of, the man he'd loved, had killed a stranger and now would pay the consequences of his actions.

Had Simon not thought about how his crime would affect his family? His mother? His brother the lawman? Or how it would end his life. For those five seconds of pulling the trigger and a demented feeling of satisfaction, he had destroyed his family.

A lump filled Zach's throat. He swallowed, trying to wash away the pain that held a tight grip on him.

"I'm good," he said, knowing he lied. A sigh escaped from his tightly closed throat. "God, Meg, being with you is the best damn thing that has ever happened to me on the worst day of my life. I'm so torn up inside, yet here you are, soothing me better than any doctor could ever help. I just wish things were different."

Zach knew the morning would not be good, but Meg had made him feel like she would always be there. That she would wrap her arms around him and soothe away the day's hurts. God, he was nine ways a fool to not have married her that same day she'd asked.

She took his arm and wrapped it around her middle section, snuggling up solidly against his chest. "Tell me some good things about Simon. Tell me about the happy times."

Memories of Simon as a little boy flooded his mind, filling his throat with tears. How could Zach turn him into the law? How could he let his brother hang?

His chest ached from the tightness that held it hostage. "At first, me and my brothers hated that little brat baby who took our mother away from us. My youngest brother was four when Simon was born. I was eight years older and out comes another squallin' baby. We went back to playing outside once we learned we had another brother."

"So when did you start to like Simon?" she asked softly, her big green eyes staring up at him like emeralds shining in the darkness. That piercing gaze seemed to touch his soul like a warm gentle caress.

"The first time I remember protecting him was when he fell into the river while we were all out fishing. Mother had told us we were not to go near that river, but like typical kids, we disobeyed. He slipped into that raging water, his little head bobbing up and down like a cork on a fishing line. I had to go in after him." He sighed the sound heavy in the room as he remembered the way terror had filled him as he'd jumped into the churning whitewater of the river.

"I didn't think I'd ever find him. My brother Matt threw me a rope, and once I found Simon, he pulled both of us to shore. Scared me senseless. When mother found out, it was the worst whipping I've ever received, not to mention all the chores she gave me to teach me responsibility." He'd never forget the memory of his mother's face, going all white and then red with fury, or the way she'd swung the paddle, making it damn near impossible to sit down for a couple of days.

"Then there was the time he didn't want to go to school, so he trapped a skunk and put it in the schoolhouse. I thought his time to meet his maker had surely come after my mother took the switch to his hide. One thing I can say about my mother, she never spared the rod. She may have broken the rod on our backside, but it was never spared."

"What did the school do?" Meg asked, snuggling against him.

Zach laughed as all the memories of Simon's childhood flooded him with emotions that left him happy, yet sad. "We went to the local church for the next week, while they aired the building out. Simon spent his free time scrubbing the smell out of the schoolhouse."

Again, his mother the strong disciplinary force in their home had dealt out punishment. But though all four boys were raised the same, Simon had ignored his upbringing and chosen a life of crime.

Meg giggled, her fingertips trailed down his arm, her

touch soothing, yet his heart still ached with the memories of his brother.

"Simon was always a boisterous child, getting into trouble at a young age. It was almost like he had no fear. One time when he was about ten, he decided he wanted to go into town. So he walked the ten miles without Mother knowing where he went. When she found him two days later, I thought she would kill him. She'd been so worried."

Pain wrenched through Zach, and he hugged Meg closer, needing the feel of her sweet womanly body to comfort him. What would he do? He loved his job as Sheriff, but a lawman turned in a criminal, not helped him escape. But this was his brother. This was the brother he loved.

"When he was fifteen, he came down with pneumonia. We almost lost him again, and my mother was up with him around the clock, putting poultices on his chest. It was then that I realized I loved all my brothers and didn't want to lose any of them. They mean the world to me, and if Simon died, there would be a hole left in our family."

God, he didn't want Simon to die. He didn't want to watch his mother's face as her youngest son hanged. He couldn't do it. He couldn't hurt his mother anymore. She'd suffered the loss of an infant, the loss of two husbands, and now the loss of a second child. What more was she supposed to endure?

"When did Simon's father pass away?"

Zach thought back to that awful day when his brother had gone into town to find his father. It had changed the brother he loved forever from a good kid to a cold man. He'd never been the same. "He was fourteen when he watched a man shoot his father."

Zach had loved his own father immensely and couldn't imagine seeing him gunned down in the street over a card game. James Simon Trudeau had been accused of cheating, and Zach knew for a fact the man was known for how he could work the cards. Only this time, the cards had gotten him killed.

"If he knew how it felt to watch someone you love die from a gunshot wound, why would he be the one who killed that farmer? Why would he inflict that pain on someone else?"

Zach thought about this for a moment. Maybe Meg was right. Why would Simon kill another human being? Maybe this was all just a big misunderstanding. Maybe he'd wake up in the morning and this would all have been a nightmare. "I don't know, unless he was trying to get even. Unless he wanted those kids to feel the way he'd felt as a young man. But that seems so cold. And my brother has never been a cold-blooded killer."

Meg grabbed his hand and brought it to her lips, giving him a kiss. "Are you going to be able to turn your brother in? Can you take him to the sheriff?"

The idea was gut wrenching and left Zach in a cold sweat. He loved being in law enforcement. He loved being a small town sheriff, and he thought he was a good one. But the idea of turning in his brother, letting a circuit judge decide Simon's fate and carry out a hanging, left Zach terrified. Watching Simon be put behind bars... He didn't know if he could do it.

"I don't know. I keep going back and forth. The irrational part of me wants to let him loose to head for Mexico. But I'd lose my job as sheriff. I'd be giving up the job that brings me joy, and God knows what I'd become then. But he's my brother. My youngest brother and my mother doesn't deserve the heartache and the pain. She asked me to help him. Not to take him to his hanging. So what am I to do?" His insides felt like someone had torn him asunder.

"But as a lawman, you have to think about his victim's family. Did they deserve to lose their loved one? They've gone through all the emotions you're experiencing and more."

She was right. Five minutes of violence would forever scar two families.

"I would be so angry if someone had shot and killed one of my loved ones. I'm sure they feel the same. You do what your heart and your head say. You make the decision you can live with the rest of your life."

It was simple, heartfelt advice, but which one did he choose to give up? His integrity or his brother?

"But what is that, Meg? What is it?"

*

Early the next morning, Meg came wide awake at the sound of someone pounding on the door.

"Open up, Zach!"

Oh no! Oh, dear God, no! She recognized that voice and pulled the sheet up over her head just as the door crashed open.

Zach sat straight up in bed and reached for his six-shooter.

Good golly, the grapevine telegraph, she was in so much trouble.

"What the hell?" Zach scrambled up in bed. "What are you doing crashing in here without waiting for me to answer the door?"

The sound of boots rushing into their room had Meg

shaking with nerves.

"Where's Meg? What have you done with our sister?" Annabelle asked.

Meg felt herself shrink even further down in the bed. The bed shifted, and she realized Zach was sitting on the side with the sheet wrapped around him. If he pulled on that sheet any harder, she would be exposed.

"Uh, she's not here," Zach lied. "Last I saw her, she was riding out of town."

There was silence for a moment and then Annabelle asked, "Where was she headed?"

Zach shrugged. "She didn't tell me. She's still searching for Simon."

There was silence then the sound of boots walking across the floor. "If you're lying, I'll come back and find you and your whore. I'll send you both to hell if something has happened to Meg."

"There's no whore in my bed," Zach defended her.

Oh, this could not be good.

"Any woman lying in bed with you, Zach Gillespie, has got to be a harlot. You turned down courting our sister, so obviously your taste runs toward loose women."

That seemed like such a long time ago, but Annabelle's memory was longer and older than dirt for such a young woman. She could remember what happened ten years ago like it was yesterday. And she hadn't forgotten how Zach had treated Meg.

"What then…?" Annabelle asked.

"If she's left town, then whose clothes are these? That looks like Meg's pants and that's definitely Meg's hat laying there," Ruby said, walking over to the floor where Meg had dropped her clothes.

The sound of a gun cocking had Meg's nerves skittering like fireflies down her spine.

"You've got five seconds to tell me where my sister is before I start plugging your naked ass full of holes," Ruby said.

Oh, horse hockey, how was she going to stay hidden under the blankets with them threatening to shoot Zach? Shooting him a second time would not be good, and Annabelle was just mad enough at men and their treacherous ways she wouldn't think twice about plugging Zach. And Ruby would shoot anything that moved.

But oh, my God, were they going to be mad.

"Your time is running out, Sheriff. Where's Meg?"

Meg let the sheet slowly slide down her neck as she rose up on her elbows. "I'm right here."

She watched as her sisters' eyes widened and their mouths fell open. "Close your fly traps and step out into the hall while Zach and I get dressed."

Annabelle shook her head and pointed her gun at Zach. Slowly, she pulled back the hammer. Now both girls' pistols were trained on Zach. "If our Papa were here, he'd be hauling your sorry ass off to the sin buster. There would be a wedding before noon. What have you got to say for yourself, Sheriff? You ready to marry our sister?"

Chapter Twelve

"That's enough, Annabelle. No one is getting married today," Meg said, hopping out of bed and dragging the sheet with her.

Of all the lousy timing, this had to be the day her strong-willed sisters showed up and discovered her in bed with Zach—the morning Meg had planned to ask Zach his intentions regarding Simon. If Zach were going to turn Simon in, she'd help him capture the criminal. But if Zach meant to let Simon go free, she wanted no part of the brothers.

She would not participate in hiding a known felon, even if he were the brother of the man she loved.

Zach quickly grabbed the quilt and wrapped it around his waist, covering his privates.

Ruby picked up Zach's pants, shirt, and boots. "I think you better get out of here while we have a little chat with our sister." She shoved the clothes in his arm, along with his gun belt. "You might want to give us some time before you come back."

Zach turned and stared, his brown eyes searching Meg's. "I'll meet you at the café."

"Yes," she said, her heart ripping in two at the sight

of him leaving with things in such an uproar. She didn't want him to go. They needed to talk, to decide what their next step would be before they went any further. She had to know his plans for Simon. She needed to know their plans for them.

He nodded, picked up his hat, and shoved it on top of his head as he backed out of the room, his arms full. His earthy brown eyes gazed at her like he longed to say something. "Ladies."

As soon as the door closed, both sisters started talking at once.

"What the hell are you doing? Are you crazy?" Annabelle said, whirling around to face Meg, her reddish blonde hair swinging onto her back.

Yes, Meg was crazy in love with Zach, and while part of her believed it was a good thing, another part was frightened. She loved Zach, the lawman, the man who played by the rules and stood for honor. Not the man who would help his brother escape from the consequences of his actions. What about justice for the dead man? What about his family? Which one would Zach choose?

"You warned me away from kissing boys and here you are in bed with the sheriff? Have you lost your mind?" Ruby spouted at her.

Maybe Meg had lost her mind out here in the wilderness, following Simon from town to town. But most definitely, she'd lost her heart. Somewhere along the trail, she'd fallen in love with Zach, and that scared her worse than a Texas rattler. Even worse than the wrath of her sisters.

"You don't have to be the sacrificial lamb any longer. We don't need you to marry Zach," Annabelle said.

Meg wasn't the sacrificial lamb. In fact, she hoped to start her own life very soon. She wanted out of the bounty hunting business. She wanted to be a dressmaker. She wanted to own her own shop. This life on the road chasing bad guys was tough, and she'd had enough.

Ruby tossed her blonde curls behind her head. "Marry? Meg, we're so close to paying off the loan, and then we can all do what we want. You can continue bounty hunting or work the farm, but you don't have to get married."

Meg knew she didn't have to get married, but secretly, she longed for Zach to ask her again. This time she wanted him to do it the old-fashioned way, with him down on one knee. She wasn't marrying any man who had a gun stuck to his head forcing him to marry her. That wasn't happening.

"Papa would have made him marry you, if he'd caught you in bed," Annabelle said, loud enough the people in the next room could hear her.

"No one is forcing me to marry anyone," she said quietly in response to her sister. "No one."

"Meg, you could be pregnant," Annabelle said. "That baby would need a father."

"Shut up, Annabelle. I'm not pregnant. I'm not."

"You don't know that for certain," Annabelle whispered.

The very thought sent Meg's heart racing through her chest like a cattle herd stampeding the plains. She couldn't be pregnant. Now was not the time in her life for a baby, especially one out of wedlock, since there was no guarantee Zach intended for them to marry.

"You told me a girl should never lose her virtue," Ruby said, throwing her clothes at her.

Maybe virtue wasn't as worthy an ideal as she'd once believed. Being with a man who filled her heart with love seemed way more important than being a virginal miss.

"We've been looking everywhere for you, scared out of our minds, and you've been holed up here fornicating with Zach," Annabelle said in a disgusted tone.

"Not hardly," Meg said, shaking her head at the absurdity of Annabelle's assumptions. "We didn't check in until late yesterday evening. So no, my time has not been spent fornicating in hotel rooms."

"With Simon's brother," Ruby declared. "The sheriff is Simon's brother."

Somewhere along the trail, her very savvy sisters had learned the truth regarding Simon's family and his connection to Zach.

"You know Zach is Simon's brother?" Meg said while her sisters continued to talk all over each other.

"Yeah, we were coming to tell you," Annabelle replied. "But it looks like you already know. Is that why you haven't caught Simon yet? Normally, you'd have had your man and been home by now. We've been worried sick something happened to you. Then that gossipy stable owner, Nick, told us Simon was Zach's brother, and we doubled our efforts to find you. We were scared for your safety."

Meg's heart warmed as she realized she would have done the same if she had been the one left behind. "Simon got away and we haven't found him since," Meg said, slipping on her pantaloons and pulling her chemise over her head. She dropped the sheet and pulled on her pants and shirt.

Both sisters stopped and stared at her. Finally, Annabelle said, "What's going on Meg? It's not like you to lie with a man."

Meg hung her head for a moment as defenseless feelings swept through her, leaving her emotions laid bare. She didn't like feeling vulnerable, not even with her sisters. She was supposed to be the big strong matriarch of the family, and yet, falling in love with Zach had left her feeling totally exposed.

Last night, comforting him had felt like the most natural and wonderful emotion in the world, but today, her sisters reminded her how tenuous the situation with Zach really was and that left her completely unprotected. Her chest ached at the thought of Zach and Simon.

"That's the problem. I think I've fallen in love with him." She sank down onto the bed. "Yesterday, we learned Simon is indeed a killer. Zach thought his brother was innocent up until Mrs. Lowell told him Simon had shot her husband in cold blood. Do you know how that must have hurt? It'd be like me having to turn one of you in. I don't know if I could take you to jail, knowing you were going to hang. You're my sisters. You're my family."

Annabelle clenched her fists like she wanted to hit something or someone. "You're getting soft. Love is turning our stubborn sister into a big softie. Before, you never would have let a bounty get away."

Meg's temper flashed hotter than a chicken frying in a skillet. "I didn't say I would let him get away. I just said he's Zach's brother. I didn't say anything about him getting off. Did I?"

Both girls looked at her chastised. Yet, she couldn't fuss at them too much; her insides were churning like a dust devil out in the prairie. She felt so torn about whether or not Zach would make the right choice. "Look,

I'm just as confused by all this as you are. I love Zach, but his brother's guilty. I've met his mother, and I feel sorry for her. She's going to lose another son. If I turn him in, then I could lose Zach. His mother could hate me forever."

"But he's wanted, Meg," Annabelle said.

"I understand. I'm trying to stand by Zach's side until he's made the decision as to what he's going to do." She prayed Zach would not let his love for his brother sway him in the wrong direction.

Ruby shook her head back and forth like she was reaffirming her position. "God, if this is what love does to you, then I think I'll pass."

Annabelle laughed. "I guess this means we have to be nice to Zach? I can't drag him down to a minister and make him marry you?"

God, no. There would be no hasty marriage. She wanted Zach to choose her this time because he truly loved and wanted her.

"If Zach loves me and wants to marry me, then we'll discuss a minister, but not before," Meg said, knowing she had to make certain Zach was the type of man who followed the law. Sure, he was a sheriff, but his brother had caused him to lose his way. Could he find his way back?

"What now?" Ruby asked, limping over to a chair in the room.

"We go to the restaurant and see if Zach wants us to help him find his brother. If not, well then we go home."

If he told her he was going to find Simon and help him escape, then she would hunt Simon down herself. If Zach planned on turning Simon in, she would stand by him and help him bring his brother to justice.

"That's horse hockey," Ruby exclaimed. "I'm not letting a good bounty get away."

Annabelle just shook her head. "He's wanted. The bounty should be ours."

"The bounty is not what's important. Zach is who is important," Meg said, knowing her love for Zach had influenced her decision.

"Maybe for you," Ruby said quietly.

*

Zach hurriedly dressed in the hallway of the hotel, knowing if anyone came out their door, he'd look like the biggest damn fool, also recognizing there was real danger in that bedroom. He'd known Ruby was injured and Annabelle took care of the farm, so what had caused the sisters to come looking for Meg?

They would have hurt him if he hadn't given them Meg. There was pure meanness oozing from those women who protected one another better than the southern cavalry. Wiley, tough sharpshooters, who were protective of one another, he was lucky he'd gotten out of there alive.

And the threat of a wedding…now that was one risk he didn't mind taking, but Meg had put a halt to that idea right away. He wanted to marry her, he wanted to spend the rest of his life with her, watching her create dresses and raising his children. But instead they were chasing after his brother while her sisters hunted them.

At this moment, he needed a cup of coffee, something to clear the cobwebs from his brain, and a chance to regroup before the sisters descended on him again. He needed a plan of action that would satisfy Meg's sisters and get her to the altar. And a plan of action to help save his brother.

He walked into the café, sat down at a table, and promptly ordered a cup of coffee. The waitress brought the hot steaming mug, and he'd taken his first sip, when in walked Simon. Stunned, Zach's brain flooded him with memories of Simon as a child, and his hands clenched trying to hold on to the goodness of that little boy.

Why had Simon chosen now to show his face? Did he think he was invincible?

"Hello, brother," he said with a smile as he walked right up to Zach's table.

Zach closed his eyes and shook his head with disbelief. "You have stupid timing."

"What are you talking about?" Simon asked, his eyes narrowing. "Last I saw, you were laying on the ground with a bullet in you."

"Yeah, thanks for thinking about me and checking to make certain I wasn't dead. That bullet was meant for you," Zach said, knowing he would never have ridden off if his brother had been lying on the ground. Why couldn't he just let the consequences catch up to this boy?

"Thanks. You're okay?" Simon questioned, standing before him. "Look at you. It must not have done too much damage."

The ache in Zach's shoulder reminded him of waking up with Meg bent over him, removing the bullet. She'd stayed behind to take care of him. She'd made certain he was healing. Not Simon.

"The McKenzie sisters are over at the hotel and should be arriving here any minute now for breakfast with me. They're hungry for the bounty on your head," Zach warned.

Simon looked back over his shoulder. "Those bitches are crazy."

No, they were three women who cared about one another, looked out for each other, and would die trying to protect one another. Unlike Simon.

Zach took another sip of his coffee. "Simon, if you weren't my brother, I'd hand you over to them." The image of his mother's distraught face caused his guts to cringe like he'd eaten bad food. "I'm probably going to regret this decision, but I better get you out of here."

It would mean going against Meg. It would mean going against his law career. It would mean helping his brother, but most of all, his mother. Though he'd sworn to uphold the law, Zach couldn't turn his brother in. Sometime last night in talking to Meg, he'd reached the conclusion that even though it meant giving up what he loved, he'd save his brother and keep the family together.

"They weren't at the hotel last night. How do you know they're over there now?" Simon asked.

A sigh escaped from Zach's lips. Sometimes this boy's head contained nothing but a bag of rocks. "Because I just left them arguing and wanting to fill my backside with buckshot. They were going to meet me here for breakfast. Do you want to stick around and have pancakes with us?"

Simon frowned. "Not with that bunch of crazy women. Ruby would just as soon shoot me as turn me in, and Meg..." he stopped and stared at Zach, his face tilting. "You and Meg..."

"What about us?" Zack asked, not liking the direction of Simon's thinking.

"You're sweet on her, aren't you? They're over there arguing about the two of you," he said, a frown drawing his dark brows together. "They're probably arguing over me, too, but I think this has something to do with the fact you and her were together last night."

"What makes you say that?" Zach asked.

"I saw you ride into town together."

He didn't want his brother even saying Meg's name, let alone talking about his suspicions of what had transpired last night. "Yeah, and we rented two rooms," Zach said, pulling change out of his pockets, not looking at Simon.

"No, you didn't. I tried to visit you last night, until I learned you weren't alone," Simon said, smiling at him.

Uneasiness filled Zach, clenching at his stomach with the realization that Simon knew he'd slept with Meg. It gave the younger man something he could hold over his older brother, and that couldn't be good. "I think you better stick to your own business if you want to survive," Zach said, throwing some change on the table. "Let's get out of here before the McKenzie sisters arrive and hog-tie you one more time."

"Damn, I think I hate those girls," Simon said as they walked out the door.

"So, what were you doing coming into the café?" Zach asked. He wanted to leave Meg a message. He wanted to let her know he'd be in touch. But right now, he had to get Simon off the streets before Meg and her sisters came out of the hotel and took Simon into custody once again.

"I wanted to talk to you. That's why I came to the hotel last night, and that's why I'm here now. I need your help," he said. "I think we visit Mama then go to Mexico."

*

When Meg walked into the restaurant, she glanced around searching for Zach. The homey café was filled with patrons who lived in the small town, the clientele sipping on coffee, eating their breakfast, and catching up on the local gossip. As she stared into the faces of the cowboys, she realized Zach wasn't here. Queasiness began to build in her stomach, quivering and rolling like a bad boat ride. Where was the man who'd spent most of the night wrapped in her arms, making her feel special and loved? Where was Zach?

Her sisters gave her stares that told her they believed he'd just left her high and dry in the desert without water. No, Zach wouldn't leave without speaking to her.

"Knowing Zach, he ran down to the sheriff's office. Let's just get some coffee and wait on him," Meg said, sinking down into a nearby chair. Zach Gillespie had better show his face in this restaurant in the next five minutes or have a really good excuse.

Annabelle and Ruby pulled out chairs and sat down to wait with her. Ruby began to drum her fingers on the table and glance about the restaurant. "Meg, Simon is his brother. He's going to help him. He's gone to warn him and let him know we're in town."

"Ruby, give Zach some time. He's the sheriff. He loves his job and knows what he has to do," Meg said, staring at her younger sister, while Annabelle didn't say a word. She just sat there taking notice of the café.

After a few minutes, she said, "The waitress must be on break. No one has offered us coffee."

"You know too much about how a café runs," Meg replied.

"And you're not looking at all the obvious things around you," Annabelle said. "You're in love…"

Ruby started to laugh. "I think we need to make you stay at home on the farm. At least until you get over this love sickness you've contracted. Annabelle can go with me, when I get well."

Like a volcano ready to spew at any moment, frustration rose inside Meg. She'd reached her limit of her sister's sassiness. Yes, so maybe she'd gone against what they'd been taught, but she was the oldest, and she was still in charge.

"Look you two. I kept going after Simon, even when I learned about his brother. That bounty will be enough so neither one of you will ever have to go bounty hunting again. Do you understand?"

"Then why are you considering giving it up?" Annabelle almost snarled.

"Because I'm waiting to see what Zach chooses," Meg snapped. If he'd left without her, it would show her he'd chosen to save his brother.

A frown drew the skin together on Ruby's forehead. "I kind of like being a bounty hunter. It's fun, it's exciting, and it's dangerous."

Annabelle shrugged. "I've only been once. So far it's been fascinating. We haven't caught a bounty, but I've learned a lot."

A man brought the coffee pot over to them. "Would you ladies like a cup of coffee?"

"Yes," Meg said, knowing she needed something while she waited, hoping Zach would show up, and her sisters would then know what she said wasn't a lie. Zach was going to help them capture Simon and turn him in. She'd given him her heart. He wouldn't stand her up now, would he? "Have you seen a tall man with dark hair and brown eyes, wearing a plaid shirt?"

The man gazed at her like she was crazy. "I'm sorry, but that describes half the men in this room. I'm the cook. I'm always in the back, unless Opal is taking a break like she is now. Give her a few minutes, and she'll be back. Ask her then."

He walked away, and she gazed at her sisters. "I bet Zach's at the sheriff's office. He'll come in here any minute and have a perfectly good excuse for being late." She would strangle him, the next time she saw him. If he'd stood her up, she would take her rope, and instead of it going around his wrists and ankles, he would find it around his throat. She'd never felt more on edge than she did right now, waiting for him to appear.

"Well, we know Zach Gillespie is good for his word, don't we?" Annabelle said, sarcasm dripping from every syllable.

"We know he's good at sweet-talking our dear sister," Ruby said. "Let's see, I had to clean the chicken coop for nearly a month after you caught me kissing boys. What kind of punishment are you going to receive for sleeping with him?"

"Shh," Meg said, glancing around at the other patrons in the café. "Could you keep that information to yourself?"

Ruby shrugged and smiled. "Maybe. But I think you owe me a month's worth of chicken coop cleaning."

If they hadn't been in the restaurant, Ruby would have received a tongue lashing that would have left bruises. "I'm not fifteen years old. In fact, most people would consider me an old maid. Keep up this conversation, and you may find yourself cleaning the chicken coop for years."

"Sorry, I have a bum ankle, and I'm not supposed to

be on it for long. So tell me how long you're going to give this guy?" Ruby asked.

Oh God, it was the question of the century. If she walked out, that would mean Zach had left her behind to go searching for Simon without her. That would mean last night had meant nothing to him if he could leave her behind without so much as a goodbye. The last words he'd said were "I'll meet you at the café". So where was he? Had something bad happened to him? "What if he's been hurt?" she asked.

Annabelle looked around the floor. "I don't see any blood splatters anywhere."

Meg gave a little shudder. "If something had happened, they would have cleaned it up right away."

"Not necessarily," Annabelle said. "Remember, I've worked in a restaurant before."

"Wouldn't the cook know if someone had gotten hurt?" Ruby reminded them.

The girls were growing restless. Fifteen minutes had passed with no sign of Zach. Meg didn't know how much longer she could hold them off, before they rushed out of here. Cozy restaurant or not, she hoped to never see this place again. It would always be remembered as the place where she didn't know what Zach would do. They were some of the worst minutes of her life.

"Okay, let's wait until the waitress comes back, and then we'll know what direction to take," Meg said and took a big gulp of coffee. She set her cup on the table. "You know when you guys first showed up this morning, I was ready to give Simon over to Zach and let him have him. But if he's stood me up...I'll go after him with a vengeance."

"We'll all go after him with a vengeance," Annabelle

said.

"He won't get away," Ruby affirmed.

The waitress came back on duty, and they waved her over. Meg felt like her heart had expanded, filling her throat, as she waited to learn the truth about Zach.

"Have you seen a dark-haired man with brown eyes wearing a plaid shirt this morning?"

She frowned. "There was a man who came in for coffee and then a second man joined him. They spoke for a few minutes. Then the two men got up abruptly and walked out the door. He left me a generous tip."

"Was the second man black-haired with deep dark eyes wearing his gun low on his hips?"

The waitress thought a minute. "I think so."

Annabelle pulled out the wanted poster from her pocket. "Did he look like this?"

"Oh yeah, that's him," the waitress said, refilling their coffee cups.

For a moment, Meg sat there in stunned silence. Anger rumbled through her chest, leaving her aching with hurt. She felt dizzy with the realization Zach had left with Simon. After everything they'd shared the night before, he'd gone off this morning, leaving her behind, to save his criminal brother.

He'd made his choice. His decision. And it didn't include Meg.

For a moment, her heart broke, and she felt tears swell in her eyes. But she refused to cry.

"Come on, girls, drink up," Annabelle said. "Remember, all we have to do is pick up the trail to Zach's horse. We know what it looks like."

"How?" Meg asked.

"His horse's right shoe is missing a couple of nails. It

has a distinctive pattern. It's how we found you."

Meg swallowed her tears and put on a smile. She pulled her little pot of color from her pocket, dipped her finger in, and smeared the lipstick across her lips. Showtime.

Time to find Simon and collect their bounty. "Come on, girls. Pay the bill and let's go. We've got a bounty to catch."

Chapter Thirteen

Dust swirled from their horses' hooves and the warm sunrays beat down on Meg. Sweat beaded on her forehead as she swayed in the saddle to the rhythm of her horse. Spring was coming to a close, and hot summer heat would soon fill the days. And yet, her life felt like a cold winter blizzard had frozen her in time.

She was sick of this life. She was tired of chasing bad guys for money, of being on the trail for days at a time without shelter, with boring food and risks everywhere. This life no longer held any appeal, if it ever had.

She wanted to go home, crawl in her bed, and sleep for days. Sleep until this sadness that pumped with each beat of her heart was gone. Sleep until her chest no longer throbbed with anguish at the memory of the two of them entwined together.

Zach had chosen to save his brother over having a life with her. That knowledge left her feeling hollow like all her blood had emptied out of her body, leaving her bereft and lacking. What she'd thought was love, he'd tossed aside then ridden out of town without so much as a backwards glance.

Now, they were following his trail, and she knew

exactly where he was going. He was headed back to his mother's with Simon in tow. Probably to say his goodbyes before he and Simon headed to Mexico.

Well, there was one little kink in their plans. Her sisters were out for blood. They were furious he'd slept with her and then left without so much as a goodbye. His *adios* to his mother had better be quick if he thought he was going to slip out of the country unnoticed.

The city of Zenith would need a new sheriff. Someone who upheld the oath he'd pledged when he took office.

She wouldn't kid herself into believing she could turn in her own sisters if they had disobeyed the law, but they would never murder a man in cold blood. They believed in justice. Their father had raised them to obey the edicts of the land. The only man in danger from them was Zach Gillespie, and while there was a pretty good chance they'd do him some harm, they'd never kill him.

Her sisters had given Meg hell when she'd stolen a ham to feed them. They would rather starve than be dishonest. Frankly, she admired that about her sisters. She would defend their honor with her last dying breath because she knew they were strong, law-abiding, upright ladies who deserved respect. Sure, they weren't your typical prairie women; they were better. They were stronger.

Still, she'd have thought after their last night together, Zach would have told her his decision. Maybe he'd been unable to face her once he'd made up his mind.

At the thought of Zach, her chest tightened like someone had stabbed her. And she wanted to ask him, how could he just ride away?

Deep down she'd never believed he would choose the wrong side of justice. She'd believed he was a good man who hated what he had to do and wanted to make it easy on his mother and his brother.

But riding off without saying anything, she had trouble accepting. Leaving her high and dry sitting in that café waiting on him, when he knew there were so many unresolved issues between them. When he knew she'd given him a piece of her heart last night.

With every ticking second, she'd felt like she was dying inside.

"Meg, I think we need to stop and make certain we're still following the right trail," Annabelle said, riding alongside her sister, glancing over at her with a worried expression on her beautiful face.

Meg pulled her horse to a stop, not saying a word. Since they'd left Vera Cruz, she'd uttered one-syllable responses, if she said anything at all. She'd concentrated on not bawling like a calf without its momma. Even now tears could spring a leak at any second. The slightest thing and she would break down and sob until there wasn't a drop of moisture left in her eyes.

And Meg never cried.

It would serve her well to bring out the anger. To look at everything bad Zach had ever done to her, to get enraged, and think enough is enough. Then she could take that blinding fury only Zach could cause and turn it into determination to end this hide and seek game. They'd been playing chase for weeks, and it was time to bring it to a conclusion.

One with her winning and Simon behind bars.

Annabelle walked along the path, searching for hoof prints from Zach's horse. "Here it is," she said, pointing to an area ahead of them. "We're still trailing them."

Meg glanced at the sun. "We can't be far behind them. We should catch up with them just after dark."

Ruby laughed, the sound cheerful like a warrior princess ready to rumble. "The sun will set, the moon will rise, and the McKenzie sisters will tarnish some hide."

"Cute," Annabelle said, swinging her leg over the back of her horse as she climbed on. "But what are we going to do to them? What's our plan for the attack?"

They started riding again, their horses moving at a steady pace through the countryside, following the trail back to Dyersville.

"I'm going to make Zach Gillespie wish he'd never spent the night in my arms. I'm going to make him sorry for every lying word that's come out of his mouth," Meg said, suddenly feeling energized. She deserved some vengeance for this one. She'd given him two chances, and he'd mucked up both times. There wouldn't be a third time.

Zach was about to have a face-off with Lady Justice, named Meg. Vengeance would be hers.

"What can we do to him?" Ruby asked.

"We could remove his clothes and tie him naked over an ant bed," Annabelle replied.

"What about dragging him behind our horses all the way into town," Ruby suggested. "You know, shame the sheriff in front of the whole town."

Bile rose up in Meg's stomach. The angry part of her wanted to hurt him while the sad part just wanted to cry. She knew she could never let anyone hurt Zach, no matter what he'd done. The trick was she would need to seal her heart from the danger. Seeing him again could be her undoing. The fragileness of her heart might not withstand an assault from Zach proclaiming his innocence. He was guilty. He was guilty of leaving her behind while he rescued his brother.

Annabelle laughed. "Or what about honey? We could tie him up and pour honey all over his naked body. Every fly, gnat, and bee would be overjoyed at the food we were providing. Makes me itch just thinking about it."

"I think you want to see him naked," Meg said quietly. "Too bad he has a very nice male physique."

Annabelle sighed. "I'd like to see any man naked at this point in my life."

"Annabelle," Ruby said, her voice light.

They were trying to make her smile, and for that she was grateful, but nothing could ease this heartache.

"It's true," Annabelle admitted. "I'm going to die and never know what the male body looks like."

"That's a little dramatic," Meg said quietly.

They rode along for a few minutes, passing a farmhouse that appeared empty, its door hanging off the frame at a cockeyed angle. They continued on down the trail, the sun sinking into the western sky.

"I know. We could pick some mushrooms to feed him that would make his stomach cramp and empty his bowels," Ruby replied.

"Aw, that's just nasty, Ruby," Annabelle replied.

Meg smiled at her sisters' antics, knowing their intentions were to make her feel better, yet suffering from the fear Zach could get hurt. No matter how much she hated him at this moment, last night she'd realized how deeply she felt for him. Loving someone meant that even when you were angry, you wanted them safe from harm. Safe from harm, even when they were causing such pain.

"Well, that's what Sarah Jane's mother did to her husband when she found out he was sleeping with the saloon girl."

With a tilt of her head, Annabelle replied, "I guess that's one way to keep your husband in line."

Meg shook her head at her sisters' tomfoolery. "Part of me says yes, let's do all those things, but the deeply angry and hurt part, says he's all mine. You girls are going to be busy getting Simon, while I deal with Zach. And I plan on making him a miserable human being."

But how could she make him a miserable human being? Did he care that he'd hurt her so badly?

"So, what do you want to do to him, Meg?"

Oh, the things she would do to him if she could. She could never physically injure him, but she'd dream about getting her retribution. "I want to strip him naked as the day he was born," she said, revenge bubbling within her like hot pot of chili. "Then I would arouse him until his pecker is standing at full attention."

"That wouldn't be too hard. From what we could see this morning, he burns pretty darn hot for you," Annabelle replied.

Meg smiled, enjoying this fantasy that was releasing all the anger that had built inside her like a thunderstorm about to burst with rain. "Then I'd carve my name on his stomach right above his hardened tallywhacker, so whenever another woman looked at his body, she'd see my name. She'd know I'd been there before her."

He'd worried about her stitching her initials in his shoulder. That would be nothing compared to how she'd inscribe her name across his abdomen.

Annabelle shook her head. "I'm starting to feel kind

of sorry for poor old Zach. He has no idea what's about to befall him."

"Oh, don't feel too sorry for him. He's chosen which bed he wants to lie in. And he's going to come up with fleas," Meg responded, wondering when he'd decided to take care of his brother.

At what point had Zach made the decision about leaving her behind last night? When they were cuddling or when they were having the best sex of either one of their lives? When had he decided he'd choose Simon over Meg?

"So, what else, Meg? Torture the man, he deserves it," Ruby said, clearly getting into the fantasy. After being almost raped at fifteen, she no longer had much use for men. Very little sent her over the edge, but when she did, she was known for coming out blasting her pistol. "He took your virginity."

"Ruby, there was no taking. It was something I wanted to give him," she admitted to her younger sister.

"Meg," Ruby said shocked.

"I know…and his *defection* is crushing," she whispered, barely able to get the words out.

Meg thought about everything they'd done to each other's bodies last night. How he'd had her screaming his name. She wanted to make him hurt even more for causing her to feel so loved, only to learn it was a lie. She pulled back her shoulders and lifted her head, resolving to make him pay for the way he'd treated her. "I want to shoot him. I want to put a bullet in a certain part of his anatomy, rendering it useless."

They all laughed. That would be one less pecker in the world to take advantage of women.

"Good grief, men should beware of dealing us a dirty

hand. We get even," Annabelle said, swaying in the saddle to the rhythm of her horse.

"You'd think they'd learn to treat women with respect and how it would get them so much more than treating us like we're idiots," Meg said, her resolve strengthening.

Zach Gillespie was a jackass. And yet her heart still swelled with love at the thought of him.

"How many times have we caught up with Zach and Simon in the last couple of weeks? How many times have we tied them up and rode off with Simon?" Ruby asked.

Meg nodded her head. If only her heart and head would come into agreement, then she could ride on and leave Zach behind for good. But her heart wanted Zach and her head wanted Simon to pay, not only for poor James Lowell's life, but also for Zach's treachery. "When will Zach learn that we will catch him and when we do there will be hell to pay? It seems like such a simple lesson that this smart man is having a hard time learning."

"Well, today's lesson needs to be a little different," Ruby said.

Ruby was right. This time when they took Simon, Meg needed to do something distinctive. Something that would surprise Zach and show him he wasn't following Meg. He wasn't getting Simon back.

"Oh, don't worry about that. This time he'll never forget how Meg McKenzie and her sisters got even with him for walking out. Some men need their lessons to be personal, and this one is going to be very intimate."

If Zach Gillespie lived to tell the story of how he lost Simon, he'd be doing well.

*

Within the first hour, Zach regretted his decision. Now five hours later, he was beginning to question his sanity.

"So, we're going to go say goodbye to Mom and then the two of us are heading to Mexico?" Simon asked, riding alongside his brother, his gray gelding setting the pace as they rode quickly toward his mother's.

"Yes. Day after tomorrow, we're heading out. I'm hoping the McKenzie sisters, if they're behind us, have lost our trail after we did that little switch back," Zach said, thinking this had seemed like a good solution to his dilemma this morning, but now he wondered what the hell was he thinking. God, he'd be leaving Meg behind, and when he returned, could she forgive him?

He had to remind himself he was doing this partially for his mother, partially because he wanted to give Simon a second chance, and partially because the thought of turning in his own brother was just too much.

He hoped in Mexico Simon would establish himself in a job or maybe a business. Something his brother enjoyed doing and in which he could make a decent living that didn't involve jails or hangings. Zach would be giving Simon a second chance to get his life on the right side of the law.

"So what kind of job do you want?" Zach asked. "How are you going to earn a living in Mexico?"

Simon laughed. "Sleep. Do they have jobs that pay you to sleep? I know they take siestas."

For a moment, Zach was kind of stunned, thinking surely Simon wasn't sincere. The day had already been long and tiring; he was being silly. Though his outlaw brother was never known for his humor.

"No, I'm serious. When we get to Mexico, how are you going to start your life over? What will you do different?" Zack asked.

Simon shrugged his shoulders. "What do you mean? The only thing different will be that I don't have a bounty on my head and the McKenzie sisters chasing me. Those girls are crazy. Thank God, I got you away from Meg. She's the worst. That woman is loco."

Zack ignored Simon's comments about Meg, though the very thought of her made his chest tighten as sadness gripped him. Last night Meg had wrung him clean out and left him more satisfied than he'd ever experienced. They had lit up the stars in the night sky with their lovemaking. He'd never expressed his desire for a woman in such an open way. This morning, he'd planned on asking her to marry him until her sisters had arrived and changed the direction of this day and his life forever. Now she would never know.

Could he be making a mistake throwing everything away for Simon? Was his brother conning him to keep from hanging?

"Yeah, but you've got to earn a living so you can eat. No money, no food, no rent," Zack said, swaying in the saddle of his horse.

Simon laughed, the sound confident. "I always find a way. I'm not too worried. I'm sure they have lovely senoritas in Mexico who need help with their ranches. I'm always willing to lighten their load."

And their pocketbooks, Zack couldn't help but think. A cringe traveled from his head to his toes, making him feel even worse. "But you got in trouble here in the States," he reminded Simon.

"That was Frank's fault," he said. "And he won't be

going with us."

"Why not?" Zach said, immediately becoming suspicious. Had something happened to the renowned gunslinger whose checkered past, hopefully, had caught up with him? Simon didn't need to be hanging around that outlaw.

"Oh, he got some girl pregnant, and her papa gave me the option of staying and dying with Frank or leaving and never looking back. So I left."

Revulsion swept through Zach at the idea of just walking away while your friend was murdered. How could Simon be so cold? "Why didn't you help him? Or at least get help?"

"He should have kept his tallywhacker in his pants. It was five guns to two. I considered the odds and decided he was on his own," Simon said defiantly. "Dumb. Save it for the whores."

Zach sat stunned. Why had he assumed his brother would want to make his life better? Why did he think Simon was going to be a different man with changed values? Why did Zach think Simon was going to assume responsibility for his actions?

Nothing had changed, except that Zach was going to lose the woman he loved and a job he enjoyed in order to give his brother a second chance. A second chance Simon was going to piss away.

Zach swallowed the bitter pill of disappointment suddenly filling his throat and choking him. His body grew numb with the realization Simon didn't intend to become a good man. "Simon, you can't go to Mexico and keep living the same way. Sooner or later it's going to catch up to you. I'm only staying long enough to get you settled, then I'm coming home."

Simon shrugged. "It'll be fun just you and me, starting over together. I'm sure that sheriff job was toilsome. Not to mention dangerous. You might change your mind and stay."

Doubtful. Very doubtful, but Zach wouldn't tell Simon that.

Zach's chest tightened and a feeling of dread filled him at the mention of his job. It had been a fulfilling line of work for him. He'd enjoyed bringing in bad guys and keeping the town orderly. And now he was giving it up for his brother who didn't want to change his life.

Why did it feel like he was sacrificing everything and Simon nothing?

The image of Meg came to Zach and sadness overwhelmed him, nearly knocking him off his saddle. No chance to tell her goodbye. No way to get word to her. Maybe once this was all over, he'd send her a telegraph and tell her he was sorry. But that didn't seem like enough. In fact, it seemed cold. Leaving this morning had seemed wrong, especially after last night.

Last night had been amazing. The best night of his life and he'd walked away from Meg. All in the hopes of helping his brother get a second chance. It had been a spur of the moment choice, and one he was starting to regret.

He'd give his mother the green dress and ask her to deliver it to Meg, along with his apology for not saying goodbye.

"You're going to have to find a job," Zach responded to his brother.

"Fuck that. I'm not working a job where some hombre tells me what to do. If we hit a couple of banks before we cross the border, we could get us some cash and live the good life," Simon shouted. "You know, build up the nest egg before we cross the border and clean my slate."

Anger roiled through Zach at the thought of stealing from people who worked hard and didn't deserve the misfortune that cleaning out a bank brought to a town. Taking farmers, storeowners, and just ordinary peoples' life savings was wrong. But then, maybe keeping a man from justice could be wrong as well.

Even your own brother.

The thought almost paralyzed him.

"No banks. I'll turn you in myself if you rob a bank."

"Whoa there, brother, we're supposed to be partners."

"Why do you always think other people have to take care of you? Why can't you learn to take care of yourself?" Zach asked.

The air fairly crackled with tension as they made their way down the trail toward their mother's farm. She would be glad to know Zach had taken an interest in Simon, but saddened he was leaving Texas. If they made it to Mexico without killing each other, then Zach would return home without his job. No more Sheriff Gillespie.

He'd have to give up the badge because he'd always know he helped his brother escape. He'd helped a known murderer leave the country, and that would make him dishonorable. He'd helped a man who had killed another man for simply raising sheep.

"You're starting to sound like our mother. I'm not going to have to listen to you harping all the way to the Rio Grande, am I?" Simon finally said.

Maybe some people just couldn't be saved. Maybe they didn't want help, believing that not obeying the law, stealing, and killing were the way they were supposed to live. Maybe they thought family was supposed to take care of them, even when they'd done wrong.

"All of our brothers listened to our mother, and they turned out all right." All except for Simon, who Zach was quickly grasping didn't learn very fast or care if he was living irreverently.

"They didn't see their father gunned down in the street," Simon replied, his voice tense. He glared at Zach as if he just didn't understand and he didn't. His own father had died plowing a field. Yet, he didn't use that as an excuse, did he?

God, no. His father would have smacked him from now into the next life if he'd found out Zach was doing wrong. His father had attended church each Sunday, prayed over the dinner table, and loved his wife with a passion. He'd never be found in a saloon cheating at cards or smelling of a whore.

"No, they didn't, but how long are you going to use that as an excuse for your own life? I'm not saying it wasn't bad; it was horrible. But it's time to move past your father's death and show what kind of man you're going to be. The choice is up to you. You're being given a second chance. Use it wisely."

Another awkward silence filled the trail, and Zach realized that Mexico might be a quiet trip—a trip that either killed him or Simon.

"If this is going to work, then you have to let me be myself," Simon said.

"I agree," Zach replied, thinking they hadn't even made it one day and already they were at odds. What would the next month be like? "But I'm not living my life the way you're living now. Why should my morals become like yours when you've done nothing but get into trouble? Are you going to change?"

Simon shrugged. "I could, but I don't like to work. It's labor and drudgery. I could be playing cards or drinking. Maybe we should open a whorehouse? You know run a brothel where cowboys can come across the border for their pleasures. We'd have girls always available for a randy cowboy. The girls would do the work, and we'd be making the money."

Zach shook his head. The boy told him what he wanted to hear, but gave it his own twist at the end that left Zach wary of what his intentions really were. Before the words left Zach's mouth, Simon was already thinking of his response and how to make it fit his needs so he got his way. Why did Zach think Simon would ever change? "I don't want to run a whorehouse."

"I don't want to work," Simon replied.

With every mile, Zach realized more and more what he'd given up. With every word out of Simon's mouth, he understood what he'd gotten himself into. How had he been so blind to his brother's faults? Had he just wanted to remember the loving little boy Simon had once been? Was there a chance he would never change? Would he drag Zach down with him?

"I need to tell you I spoke to the widow Lowell."

Simon turned in his saddle and frowned at Zach. "I should have killed that bitch."

Zach flinched at the venom in his brother's words. "She told me the truth."

Simon shrugged, clearly not caring that he'd left a woman and her kids without their husband and father. "Her truth and my truth probably don't agree."

"You killed that man, Simon." There, it was out in

the open. Now there was no more skirting around the issue that was sending them to Mexico.

"We're going to Mexico so we can start again. Leave the past in Texas," Simon said, his voice cold, his eyes deadly.

A chill spiraled down Zach's spine and he shuddered. Simon's attitude seemed careless, like he felt no responsibility for taking another person's life. That he'd robbed this man of watching his children mature into adults, grandchildren, birthdays, holidays, and the years of growing old.

"Is this the first man you've killed?"

Simon shook his head, but didn't look at Zach. He stared straight ahead. "Why all the questions? What does it matter how many men I may have killed? We're going to Mexico to start over. Again, I recommend you leave the past here in Texas."

With startling clarity, Zach realized James Lowell was not the first man his brother had killed. There had been others Simon had gotten away with murdering. The shocker for Simon was that this widow had shouted from the rooftops the name of the man who'd murdered her husband. She'd stood up and drawn attention, until the law had been forced to charge Simon with killing her man.

How many other widows were there who had quietly shrunk away letting the young man get away with the sacrifice of their husband and fathers?

The sun was beginning to descend in the west, and Zach felt like the clouds in his mind were being burned away with the setting rays. Suddenly, he was beginning to see what the future would look like with Simon, and frankly, it wasn't as rosy as it had first appeared.

Some people didn't deserve a second chance.

"I think it's time we stopped and setup camp."

Simon glanced at him. "But it's just now getting dark. We could probably continue riding and make it to Mom's."

Zach was worn out. The day had drained him, and he couldn't let Simon arrive at their mother's.

"No way. We're still a good three hours away, and besides, we could use the rest. The horses are beginning to tire, and we're going to need to take good care of them to reach Mexico."

Simon shrugged and started to look around. "There's a place under that tree that's off the trail. Let's set up there."

Part of Zach knew exactly what he was doing, and some part of him still refused to acknowledge what his subconscious was screaming at him.

Chapter Fourteen

"They're not moving. It looks like they're asleep," Annabelle whispered in the darkness. The sisters had caught up with Zach and Simon's camp over an hour ago, and Meg was just waiting for them to fall into a deep, deep sleep before they attacked.

Their trail had been obvious, and Zach hadn't tried to hide their camp. He'd had a blazing fire you could smell for over a mile, and the glow had been easy to locate. In some ways, it felt like he wanted them to find him.

Meg pulled her hat down over her eyes and leaned back against her saddle, which was propped on the ground. "It's not time, Annabelle. Close your eyes and get some rest. We'll attack before dawn."

"I can't sleep. I'm wound up tighter than a bucket in a well," she said. "I just don't want them to get away."

Though Meg was having the same problem, Annabelle wouldn't get any sympathy from her. Her instincts were telling her to wait, and that's what she was going to do.

"They're not going anywhere. Deep slow breaths," Meg said, closing her eyes again.

"How do you do this all the time? How do you stay

so calm? Aren't you afraid of being shot?" Annabelle asked.

"Right now, I'm afraid you're going to wear my ears out with your yammering."

Annabelle sighed and leaned her head against her knees. "Hmph. Sorry, but it's my first time. Even Ruby is all laid out resting."

"She knows that it's going to be a long day. And no, I don't fear being shot. But I'm ready to end this career. It's tiring."

At times like this, Meg thought about her dreams. Her dress shop. A husband and family of her own. Her wants and desires weren't excessive. Just a chance for happiness doing something she loved. She feared she'd never have the opportunity.

Annabelle stretched out beside Meg. "Do you remember Mom?"

The question took Meg by surprise. She pushed back her hat and glanced at her sister in the dark. What had sparked this question?

"Of course, I do," Meg replied. "Why?"

"I just keep thinking about the three of us and wondering when one of us is going to get married. We're in our twenties. Most girls are married by now. Don't you worry about never meeting the right man?"

Zach's face swam before her eyes, and Meg's chest ached with a longing she'd never felt before. She'd given him every opportunity to show her he loved her and wanted her to be his wife. She was done. Seriously done, as in *no more*.

"Are you worried about being alone?" Meg asked, wondering what had prompted Annabelle's concern. She'd never been the one who openly wanted romance, but she was a woman.

"Kind of."

Now more than ever, Meg could see the importance of finding the right man. The one who she dreamed about, who had the same wants and desires as her. Who woke up each morning and was happy she was there.

"Don't be. How many women get to live the life they want without a man telling them what to do? How many women our age don't already have babies? We have to hang tough and find men who will love us for who we are. Not expect us to be wives they can boss around."

They lived their lives their way on their terms. Meg could never see herself bowing down to a man's wants. She hoped her sisters would never settle for anyone, unless they were absolutely certain he was the right man. And that advice went to her as well. Right now, she was certain Zach was not the man for her.

"Don't you want kids, Meg?" Annabelle asked.

The thought of being pregnant right now with Zach's baby thrilled and frightened her at the same time, even though now was not the time for children. "Someday. But first, I have to find a man who I would consider marrying."

With each beat of her heart, sorrow paralyzed her at the thought of Zach. There had never been another man she'd ever even considered besides Zach Gillespie. Once she opened her dress shop, maybe then she'd look around and see who else might be available. Or maybe she'd just send off for a mail-order husband. That's what she could do. *Man needed, please come, don't expect to boss me around.*

But then again, who would want an independent thinking woman who wasn't afraid to stand up for what she believed in. Even a mail-order husband would have to learn, they were either a team or he was going home.

Annabelle was quiet for a moment. "You're done with Zach?"

Meg thought about Zach and knew with certainty there was little hope for the two of them. He'd chosen what he wanted, and it wasn't her. "I'd never marry a man who wasn't on the right side of the law. Zach hasn't proven to me he's one of the good guys. He's shown he could be persuaded to do wrong."

"But it's his brother," Annabelle said quietly.

Yes, but family didn't protect family forever. In order to belong to the clan, you needed to do what was right for the clan. "Remember that ham I stole when we were starving. How did you girls react? I think the only reason you didn't turn me into the law was because Zach paid for the meat. I have no doubts neither one of you would ever be on the wrong side of the law. I need to know that about Zach."

Sadness crept over Meg, filling her with a feeling of ineptitude. Like a silly girl drunk on love, she'd believed in Zach right up until he'd disappeared with Simon. Then she'd known he would choose his brother over her. That was completely unacceptable.

She pushed the pain deep inside her, closed her eyes, and tried to sleep.

"This morning when we found the two of you together, he acted like he had every intention of meeting you in the café. With the way he looked at you, I believed he was in love with you. I should have made him marry you."

"No," Meg said, shaking her head, her throat closing up tight. "I'd never force a man to marry me. Never."

Annabelle's statement had hurt, rising up inside of Meg, crushing her chest, and making her breathing painful. Never had she ever felt so betrayed. So lost and alone. "Well, he certainly doesn't appear forced or held hostage by his brother, does he?" Meg said, bitterness almost closing her throat.

"No, but sometimes we make rash, foolish decisions and then regret them," Annabelle whispered in the dark. "I'm not standing up for what he did. I'm just trying to understand him."

"Go to sleep, Annabelle," Meg said sternly. She didn't want to consider that Zach was regretting his decision. She didn't want to feel any sympathy when she rode into his camp in the next few hours. She wanted to ride in with her heart filled with hatred, her soul seeking vengeance. She wanted him to feel busted up inside like she did.

The moon rose high in the sky, and she slept fitfully until a coyote howled, the loneliness in his voice echoing through the prairie. Meg's eyes popped open, and she knew the time had come for them to attack. Time to show Zach that he couldn't deceive her and get away with the reckless abandon he'd discarded her heart.

She shook Annabelle awake and then Ruby. Quietly, they packed up their bedrolls and saddled their horses.

Meg checked her guns, found her rope, and nodded at Ruby. She was ready.

"Ruby, you take Simon. Annabelle, you get his horse and saddle the animal. Zach is mine."

"Don't do anything you'll regret, Meg," Ruby said quietly. "You still care about him even if he's hurt you."

Shaking her head, Meg knew her sister was right, but there was still that part of her that burned with the need to retaliate. To get retribution. "You're right. Never will I regret my actions of tonight."

They walked their horses the short distance to the men's camp and staked them. Quiet as church mice, they crept in, their guns drawn and their ropes ready. Meg watched as Ruby, once again, put a gun to Simon's head while she stood over Zach. He lay sleeping peacefully, his chest rising and falling in slumber. She picked up his gun that lay near his head. She stared at him for a moment longer. Then she pointed her gun at his privates.

"Zach!" Simon screamed in the night.

Ruby shoved her pistol in his ribs and yanked his arm behind his back, pulling the man roughly to his feet. "Shut up and get on your horse."

Zach sat up groggily, and Meg cocked her pistol. "One wrong move and I promise you, you'll be a eunuch for the rest of your short life."

The way she felt right now, his life could end this very night. She should put a bullet in him, but she never would.

He rubbed the sleep from his eyes. "We're back to this."

"You choose this path, cowboy, not me."

His eyes darted from her to Simon.

"One wrong move and this time, I swear I will shoot you and walk away. I won't stick around to play your nursemaid," she threatened, her hands shaking with anger.

He stretched and reached for his gun.

"It's not there. I have it, and no, you're not getting it back."

"I don't need my gun," he said, slowly standing. "I guess you're taking Simon."

"The girls have him on his horse and ready to go. Annabelle is tying him up even as we speak," Meg said, her voice cold, her heart almost frozen. Her finger felt twitchy on the trigger.

A laugh escaped from Zach's throat. "We're not making up?"

"You know the answer to that one, cowboy. You owe me some answers to my questions. Careful how you answer as I've yet to decide if I'm going to let you live." Her heart called out *liar*, but her head ignored the damaged organ.

"Ask away. I've got nothing to hide."

"Why did you tell me you'd meet me at the restaurant and then leave before I got there?" Of all the things he'd done, this one hurt the most. He'd been so caring, so loving the night before and then he'd just left her waiting for him to show up. Waiting for them to find Simon together.

"Honestly, Meg, I had no intentions on leaving you this morning. Hell, I never wanted to pull out without you. But then Simon walked into the restaurant, and I knew if I was going to save him, it had to be right then. Because once your sisters arrived, he'd be in the county jail."

She didn't say a word. He was right. Her sisters would have hauled Simon's ass over to the sheriff. And in fact, she would have helped them.

Zach took a step toward her. "I've been eaten up with guilt since I made that hasty decision to run out on you. All day, I've called myself every kind of fool for making the wrong decision."

She fired her gun right above his head, the sound echoing in the night air.

Ruby came running toward her. "Is everything okay?"

"Go away," she said. How could he lie to her with such a sincere tone in his voice? It infuriated her since she was certain he didn't mean a word of what he was saying.

"Damn it, Meg. If you're going to kill me, just get it over with. I feel bad enough as it is."

"Oh no, I want you to suffer the same way I've been hurting. I want you to know how it feels to think someone cares about you, and then he disappears. Do you know how badly my chest was aching from thinking our night together meant nothing to you? I have been a complete and utter fool to have trusted my heart with you, Zach Gillespie."

She watched as he ducked his head, his eyes closing before he raised them up and stared her straight in the face. "I've been confused. He's my brother and I know he's guilty. Worst of all, I threw away what we had together for a man who doesn't know right from wrong. And I do. He wasn't worth losing you over. I don't blame you for being angry. I've been wrong."

Meg stopped and stared at him. This wasn't what she expected, but could this just be another way Zach was manipulating her? Oh no, he wasn't getting off this easy. His bailing on her had broken her trust, damaged her heart, and left her reeling. She'd fallen deeply in love with him, and he'd betrayed her.

"Go ahead, he's guilty. I won't follow you. I won't come and take him back. You're actually doing me a huge favor by taking him in." He reached down and picked up the rope and threw it to her. Then he held out his hands.

She felt like he'd slapped her. He was telling her to take Simon. It seemed way too easy. Reaching down, she picked up the rope and wrapped it around his wrist, not tying the rope so tight that he couldn't get out of it. For once, she wanted him to follow her. She wanted to see if he was lying to her yet again. All the fight seemed drained from Zach, like he'd given up.

Stepping back, she admired her handiwork. It would take him a while to get out of the knots, but it was doable. "We're leaving."

"I'll see you back in Zenith," he said.

"Don't come looking for me," she replied, her heart breaking, tears threatening to spill. She turned and walked away. Zach seemed defeated. It seemed as if he were truly handing Simon over to her. And yet, that didn't set well with her either.

She crawled on her horse and gave the command. "Let's ride."

*

As the sun began to rise, Simon started singing to them. At first it was ballads, and then he broke out into religious hymns. Maybe he knew he was getting closer and closer to when he would spend some time with God and he wanted to start practicing his religion now. But whatever it was, he was driving them crazy.

"Simon! Enough," Meg finally said as the sun burned away the clouds, warming up the sky.

"You don't enjoy a good gospel hymn?" he asked.

"Not after the tenth time you sang it."

The man was deliberately trying to irritate them or make sure Zach heard his singing and located him. If Zach were coming, he'd better hurry. They were getting close to town, and Meg would be turning Simon over to a lawman.

"My knowledge is limited in music. It's been a day or two since I've spent time in church."

Meg shook her head and refused to look at the hardened criminal. "I just bet it has."

"I'm sure you'll get plenty of time to reacquaint yourself with gospel music before they hang you," Ruby said.

He laughed. "You'll bring me a pie in jail, won't you?"

"I don't cook, and even if I did, I wouldn't waste it on you," Ruby acknowledged.

"Wow, you girls are harsh. What about you, Annabelle? Any pity for a man who misses his momma's apple pie?"

She brushed back her golden red tresses and gave him a brilliant smile. "The only pie you'll get from me will give you the trots. When would you like for me to bring it to you?"

"Harsh, really harsh," Simon said, staring at Annabelle. "Have you no pity?"

The man was a charmer, and Meg felt proud her sisters hadn't fallen for his deceptive charisma.

"Oh yeah, I have pity for your mother for having to watch her son die," Meg said, bouncing in the saddle as her horse stepped around some cactus.

Simon rode along for several minutes, his backside swaying side to side in the saddle. He stared at each woman. "You girls know the bond between sisters. Don't you think brothers have that same kinship? Don't you think that Zach, even now, is probably not far behind us?"

"He said he wasn't going to follow us," Meg replied,

wondering if it was true. She'd been surprised he hadn't shown up already. She half expected Zach to ride up on them at any moment. But so far, she'd not seen him, and she'd been keeping watch.

Simon glanced over at her, dismay filling his brown eyes. "What do you mean?"

"That's what he said. Said I was doing him a favor taking you in," she responded.

Simon was silent for a moment, and then he smiled and acted relieved. "He's just luring you in. Letting you feel safe before he ambushes you, and we ride to Mexico together."

"Hmmm," she replied. "He said he'd made a mistake. I wonder if that mistake was taking a chance on you?"

A frown appeared between his brows as he considered her words. But then he smiled and shook his head. "You'd do the same for your sisters. You know how it is. You look after family members. You help each other out. Family protects family."

Meg laughed. "No. Not when they cross the line. My sisters would never kill a man in cold blood. They gave me hell when I stole a ham when we were starving. They refused to eat it. So no, family does not always protect family. Sometimes family helps other members face the consequences of their actions."

The girls snickered. "She's right," Annabelle said. "We told her we'd turn her in ourselves."

A frown grew on Simon's face as he contemplated her words. She could see him dissecting what they'd told him about Zach.

"Your sisters don't love you," he said. "They should protect you. Blood is blood, regardless of what they do."

"My sisters love me enough to warn me and keep me

following the right path. So help me God, they would haul me off to jail if I did anything they felt was wrong. I know because they've almost done it before." Suddenly Meg felt even more grateful for her sisters. They were honest and kept her in line. She could always count on them to tell her the things she didn't want to hear, but needed to know the most.

"Still, this is Zach, the sheriff. You care about him. You two have been sweet lovebirds for the last few weeks, and you're not going to do something my family would never forgive you for. You're not going to be the one to turn me in and lose my brother over it," Simon said, giving Meg a smile that set her teeth on edge and left her feeling dirty. The man could lure a nun into sin.

"I'm a good woman. I deserve a good man who is honest and trustworthy. Zach hasn't shown me he's worthy of me. And by leaving me, he's proven just the opposite. So I don't think you're going to have to worry about me and your family."

Simon opened his mouth to speak, and Meg took the opportunity to shove a rag in between his lips. He made strange mumbling noises.

"Thank God," Ruby said. "His off key singing was driving me crazy."

"Oh, my God, that mouth either had to be stuffed full of something that would quiet him down or get covered," Annabelle confirmed. "I'd heard enough."

"How far are we from town?" Ruby asked.

Meg heard her sisters talking, but Simon's words and Zach's words were bouncing inside her brain, like a bullet in the dirt. What was he doing? Was he actually letting her take Zach in, so he didn't have to make that very hard choice himself?

Is that why he said he wouldn't be following her? This way Simon was in jail, and he could always say Zach never turned him in. Zach didn't have to make that hard decision to show he stood by the law he'd sworn to protect.

She pulled her horse to a halt, anger spreading like a prairie fire through her. Damn him! Damn him for manipulating her into making his choice easy, for giving him an easy way out.

"We're going back," Meg said, turning around.

"What?" Annabelle questioned.

Ruby dropped her head in her hands. "Why are we taking him back? We've been trying to capture him for months?"

Meg took a breath and hoped like hell her sisters would understand what she had just realized. "I know this is damn frustrating. I know I've said all along he was our last bounty, but we're making this way too easy on Zach. He needs to make the hard decision about whether or not to turn his brother in. He should be the one who brings Simon to justice. Sooner or later, he will regret he didn't make this decision, and I took care of it for him. This is his opportunity to prove he's a good man who can make hard choices."

She refused to let Zach ride into town like he hadn't been chasing his brother all these weeks. No, Zach was going to make the life altering decision about his brother. Either he chose to put Simon behind bars and be the honorable man she loved, or Zach took him to Mexico and gave up being a lawman and Meg.

"Hogwash," Ruby replied.

"Who cares," Annabelle said. "Who cares who brings him in, as long as we're paid our money?"

Oh, how could she show them it wasn't the money? It was the principle. If Zach didn't make this choice, he would forever have doubts about his own integrity, and he would come to resent Meg for being the one who took the judgment from his hands.

While they probably could never recover from this event, she loved him enough to show him she believed he was a law-abiding man who would do what was right.

"I care," Meg said. "I've just made this very easy for Zach. He needs to be the one to decide the fate of his brother. Not me. Not you. Zach."

"But we're close to Dyersville. He can get Simon there," Ruby said.

"No. I'm taking Simon back to Zach, and I'm going alone. You girls go home, and I'll meet you there," Meg said, knowing she'd never make it to Dyersville before dark, weary of the trail and of having to see Zach yet again. She wanted this over. It was time for this chase to end, and there was only one way it could have a satisfactory ending.

"No, we do this together," Ruby said. "We worry about you when you're alone."

"I understand, but I have to do this on my own. I have to return Simon and give him back to his brother. Then I'll come home."

"Damn it, Meg," Ruby said. "We've worked hard for this bounty."

"I'm sorry, Ruby, but unless I do this, I'll never know for certain what kind of man Zach Gillespie really is."

Annabelle, who had been quiet the entire time, rode her horse over close to Meg. She reached out, leaned across her horse, and gave Meg a hug. "I understand. You do what you have to Meg. I'll make certain Ruby gets home."

"Thanks, Annabelle," Meg said quietly.

Ruby shook her head; there were tears in her eyes. "Be safe, Meg. Please don't let this man get loose. He's dangerous. He'll kill you."

"I know, Ruby. I'll be careful. Get home and rest that ankle. I'll see you soon."

"Love you," Ruby said as she kicked her horse and rode away.

Tears formed in Meg's eyes at Ruby's words. There were times her sisters drove her crazy, but then they did and said the most loving things to her. And though she was taking money away from the family farm, they were accepting her decision.

She glanced over at Simon and could see the laughter shining from his eyes. He thought she had just set him free.

And maybe she had, but she'd soon find out.

Chapter Fifteen

Zach wasn't proud of the way things between him and Meg had ended, and he couldn't blame her for being as mad as a yellow jacket at a picnic. Nothing Zach had done with Simon had been honorable. And yet, she'd taken the burden of turning his brother in to the law off Zach's shoulders.

This morning at the first snap of a twig, his eyes had popped open. He'd actually watched as Ruby and Annabelle, as stealthy as thieves, had trussed up Simon like a Christmas turkey. Quickly, he'd closed his eyes and feigned sleep, so they would appear to have gotten the upper hand.

It'd been the coward's way out, and that's what bothered him the most.

Meg had taken Simon off his hands. The choice was no longer his to make, and now he could simply go back to work as if nothing out of the ordinary had happened. As if he'd been gone for the last two weeks scurrying across the countryside searching for a criminal that had once again gotten away. Simon would be hauled in to a sheriff's office in a neighboring community, where Zach wouldn't have to deal with as much humiliation that his brother was a wanted murderer.

Part of him screamed *coward,* and the other part, the more rational, claimed the problem had been secured, and yet a third part was relieved. No more grandiose ideas of taking Simon to Mexico to save him.

My brother is a murderer who doesn't deserve to be saved.

But he would wonder to the day he died, if he could have actually turned in his brother to the law. He'd planned on riding to Mexico, but once Simon had started talking, Zach had known there was no future in saving his brother. But would he have actually taken him in to a sheriff at gunpoint and turned him in? Could he have done that to the brother he loved?

Could he have given up everything, his life, Meg, and even his job as sheriff, to save a brother who didn't seem to want to change?

Thank goodness that was no longer a question. Now he was headed home and ready to get his life back to normal.

Still loneliness filled his chest when he thought of Meg. He wanted to tell her he loved her. He wanted to tell her thank you for taking care of Simon. For taking the burden off of him.

Why did everything feel so wrong? Why did he feel like he'd just made the biggest mistake of his life by letting Simon go with Meg? Why did he feel like a coward for not taking his brother's life into his own hands and making certain he was turned into the law?

Because he didn't think he could do it.

On the road ahead, he saw two riders approaching him. The sun was up almost halfway in the nearly noon sky, and already he was tired of being out under the

Texas sun. He was ready to get home. He wanted time to think of Meg...

Peeking out from beneath a black hat, a glint of red hair glistened in the sun. The hat was much like the one Meg wore. He suddenly realized Meg was sitting astride that gelding, and she was pulling a man's horse behind hers, carrying Simon.

A groan slipped from between his lips and filled the air.

Dear God, Meg was bringing Simon back to Zach. His heart raced at the sight of her, so beautiful and tall sitting so proudly on her horse. His soul screamed at him, *look what you gave up! Look what you'll never have!*

Zach pulled his horse to a stop and glanced around the countryside, searching for the other McKenzie sisters, feeling certain this was a trick. But he saw no one. Nothing moved.

She came to a halt in front of him. "I'm returning your brother." No hello. Nothing.

"Why?" Zach asked, feeling uncertain, yet so enjoying the sight of Meg's green eyes and auburn hair. She looked so damn gorgeous he wanted to grab her and say to hell with Simon, but he knew she wouldn't listen.

"By capturing Simon, I've taken the choice away from you of choosing what kind of man you want to be. You've said all along you didn't know if you could turn your brother in for his crimes. If I turn him in, you'll never know." Her emerald eyes stared at him with a coldness in their depths. He so wanted her to look at him with warmth and love.

"Meg," he said, shaking his head and sighing, the sound empty and lonely like he felt. "God, Meg, you're not making this easy for me. I was awake this morning when you came into camp. I was relieved you took Simon."

His brothers' eyes widened at Zach's acknowledgement.

"I'm not going to make your decision. You need to know what kind of man you are, so you can live with your actions the rest of your life. I'm not turning him into the law for you," she said, her emerald eyes flashing with anger.

"What if I don't take him in?" Zach asked.

"That's your choice," she said softly. "From this moment on, what happens to Simon is your decision. Not mine."

He clenched his fists as anger at Simon raged inside him like a tornado destroying everything in its path. Only fifteen minutes ago, things had been looking up. But now...now he didn't know what to do. His head told him turn Simon in, he was a murderer, but Zach's heart remembered that little boy he'd saved in the river. Could he save Simon one more time?

"You can let Simon go and continue on like before, you can continue on to Mexico with your brother in tow, or you can turn him in and be the lawman I thought you were. Whatever you decide, it's your choice," she said and handed over Simon's horse's reins to Zach.

He took the reins and stared at his younger brother, with a rag shoved in his mouth. "Looks like he got mouthy."

"He was having a revival with a true come to Jesus moment," she said. "We grew weary of his singing."

Simon winked at Zach, and with startling clarity, he realized Simon thought he was home free—that as soon as Meg was gone, he and Zach would once again start their quest for Mexico.

But suddenly all Zach could think about was Meg.

She gave him a long look, and he knew she wanted him to say something, but he had nothing he could give her at the moment. Nothing. She was making him decide his brother's fate, and it stung like a thousand bees swarming inside his gut.

"I've got to get home," she stated, resigned and colder than a blizzard in Texas.

"What about the bounty?"

"We don't expect the bounty from Simon. We don't expect anything."

"What about us?" Zach said quietly, wanting her so bad he could barely breathe.

Meg shook her head, turned her horse and rode away, leaving him in the dust.

He watched her ride away and felt like she was taking his soul with her. Emptiness filled the cavity of his chest, causing his heart to echo in the destitute chamber. Meg made him a better man. She was strong and steadfast and caring and stood by the people she loved. When she'd shot him, she'd made certain he lived. She stayed by his side, not the brother he'd taken the bullet for. Simon hadn't even said thank you.

Meg wanted nothing in return, and Simon just knew Zach would set him free. Simon demanded Zach sacrifice everything for him, while Meg just required a good man—a man who was on the right side of the law. And now she was riding away from him. Leaving him behind.

So what did he do? Did he continue on to Mexico with Simon, or did he take his brother back to Dyersville and possibly a hanging? What should he do?

*

Zach pulled up in front of the sheriff's office in Dyersville. He knew the man; he was a good friend who would make this as easy as possible.

Inside, his heart was breaking, his soul empty. But it was the only way he could make certain his brother paid for his crimes and didn't inflict any more harm on another unsuspecting family.

No one should lose a family member to murder.

For the last block in to town, Simon screamed at Zach through the rag in his mouth, and every sound ripped through Zach's soul.

He tied the horses' reins to the hitching post then stepped around to help Simon get off his horse. His brother swung his tied hands at him, knocking Zach in the face as Simon fell off the horse, slamming them both to the ground, where Simon landed with a thud on top of Zach. All the air left his lungs in a swoosh, and for a moment, he lay there as Simon raised his fists in the air to hit him again.

Zach reached up and grabbed Simon by the rope. He threw him off then slowly stood.

Simon made a move to run, and Zach tripped him. When he could get his breath back, he reached down and lifted his brother up off the ground. "That certainly didn't change my mind."

Zach wrapped his hands around the rope and pulled Simon toward the jail. Opening the door, he pushed his brother inside.

The sheriff glanced up. "Zach," he said. "You okay?"

"Yeah," he replied, his breathing still not back to normal. "Simon Trudeau to be booked into jail for the murder of John Lowell."

His brothers' eyes scalded him with their hate, and

Zach sighed.

"I know you don't understand, Simon. But I couldn't take a chance on you killing anyone else. You know what murder did to your life. Why would make other people experience loss? I don't understand." He reached over and pulled Simon's rag out of his mouth.

"You son of a bitch, you've always had it easy. When you double-cross me, you die. My papa was stupid enough to get caught cheating, he died. You better hope like hell I hang because you're just as good as dead if I get out."

Zach smiled. "So much hate, Simon. Now I'm glad I didn't give up my life to try to save yours."

Simon spat at Zach's feet. "I'd have killed you before we made it to Mexico."

"Sheriff, lock him up. I don't want to have to kill my own brother."

*

Two weeks later, Annabelle walked into the house and sat down at the table; she'd called a family meeting. Since Meg had returned, she'd wandered around the house in a daze. She'd been quiet, reserved, and so damn sad Annabelle was ready to hunt Zach down and shoot him herself.

Maybe it was time to get back on the hunt. At least on the road, Meg would have something to focus on besides Zach Gillespie. Annabelle had been waiting and hoping one of them would come to their senses and realize they were meant to be together, but so far they were both more stubborn than any mule she'd ever had the misfortune to come across.

Meg refused to go into town and sat in the house, drawing what appeared to be women in dresses. It was the strangest thing Annabelle had ever seen her robust, take-charge sister ever do. She was worried sick about Meg and hoped to spur her into action.

Meg and Ruby sat down at the table, where the family had always gathered for important decisions. Annabelle looked at these women and realized how lucky she was to have them in her life. She loved them and wanted the best for them.

"I just wanted to give you an update on our loan at the bank. We've paid it down to a mere six hundred dollars. A couple more bounties and we should be able to end our hunting days," Annabelle said. "I'm going in to town tomorrow to pick up some more wanted posters. Maybe get some new ideas as to who we should chase."

Ruby shook her head. "I'm not certain I'm ready to give this up. In fact, I've been talking to our cousin Caroline about joining me and Meg."

A heavy sigh came from Meg and she stiffened. "No. Once the loan is paid off, I'll not be continuing to hunt for bad guys. I'm done with this type of life. And Ruby you should be as well."

Ruby raised her head and stared at Meg, her eyes darting with anger, a stubborn set to her chin. Annabelle could feel the tension radiating off her younger sister.

"No. I enjoy chasing bad guys. I enjoy the thrill of the hunt."

"Well, I don't, and I won't be continuing. I've got plans of my own."

Annabelle stared at the women around the table. This was totally unexpected. Meg wanted to quit, and Ruby was determined to continue their pursuit of nefarious criminals for cash.

"We'd only planned on doing this until we had the

loan paid off. Ruby, you can't mean to continue," Annabelle said, worry filling her at the danger her younger sister was willing to risk. Ruby seemed to have a vendetta. A need to prove she could take care of herself.

"Why not? What is there around this boring farmhouse to do, other than watch the crops grow? I like the life. I like the thrill of the chase, and I'm not giving it up," she said, raising her voice defiantly. "I like being seen as a strong woman."

"Yes, you will give it up. You got hurt on the last trip. I'm not going to worry about you, and I'm not going," Meg informed their youngest sister.

Tension sparkled around the table like candlewicks sputtering in the wind.

Ruby smiled. "I don't need your approval. I'm plenty old enough to decide what I'm doing with my life, and if I want to continue to bounty hunt, I will. You can't stop me."

Meg shook her head. "I'm too tired to argue with you. I'll continue only until the loan is paid off, but once it's gone, I'm done. If you want to hunt until someone shoots you dead, then that's your business."

"Meg," Annabelle said, her eyes widening at what her sister had said.

Ruby shrugged her shoulders. "Suit yourself."

Annabelle glanced between the two women, surprised at how they'd changed. Meg had once been the defiant one, and Ruby had been a temptress. But now it seemed Meg was more subdued, and Ruby was the defiant one, ready for a challenge. Where did that leave Annabelle?

"Ladies, this was not meant to start an argument, but rather to show you we are close to having the loan paid off. This was just to give you an update and have you start to prepare for our next outing."

Meg glanced at Annabelle and frowned. "You're not going," she said. "You're staying home and working the farm."

Annabelle felt her forehead pucker into a frown. She liked being included. She had enjoyed getting out. "I'm not so certain. Maybe you should stay home and Ruby and I should go out."

"No," Meg replied. "I'm in charge."

"No, you're not," Ruby said.

"You're the oldest, but I think we should consider holding a vote," Annabelle said.

"I'm not discussing this any further," Meg said, rising from the table. "Tomorrow, when you go in to town, get us new posters that we can make some decisions over. Things stay the same. Ruby and I will chase the bad guys. You handle the farm."

A spark of anger zipped along Annabelle's spine, at the way her older sister just assumed she would be going on the hunt for the next bounty while leaving Annabelle at home.

"I'll get the posters, but I want to be included," Annabelle said, standing.

"And I will continue," Ruby said, getting up from the table.

Meg ignored their comments and walked out the door. Sometimes she could be more stubborn than a three-year-old with a doll. Just try to get her back to discuss their new situation. Just try to take a doll from a baby.

Annabelle shook her head. Well, that had certainly not gone as smoothly as she'd planned. But since her return, Meg had been difficult. She had been irritable, moody and downright sad. Men could be so stupid when it came to women, and Annabelle knew Zach had shattered Meg's heart into a thousand pieces. After all, she'd given Zach Gillespie her heart and her virtue.

And all he'd done was left her to save his criminal brother.

Tomorrow, when she was in town, she'd find out what had happened to the sheriff. Had he chosen Simon and Mexico or was he once again back in his office, chasing drunks and thieves. If he was in town, she'd give him a small piece of her mind for how he'd treated her sister.

She walked out the door and watched the sun descend behind the prairie. Somewhere out there was a man for Annabelle. A sweet man who would love her, take care of her, and give her children—a man who would love her, in spite of her faults.

*

The next day, Zach rode his horse in to the yard of the McKenzie's farm. He hoped Meg was home. He'd been waiting for the last two weeks for her to come in to town, and finally, he'd given up. The time was now. If she didn't come to him, he'd come and get her.

He pulled up in to the yard and noticed it seemed quiet. No one greeted him. No dogs came out of the door, running and barking. It was silent and peaceful, except for the violent vision of the shotgun nozzle poking out an open window.

That was a welcoming sign, if ever he'd seen one.

"What do you want?" Meg called.

Thank God, it was her and not Ruby or Annabelle. He'd be laying on the ground and bleeding if one of them had pulled the shotgun.

"Put the damn gun down and come outside," he said.

"Why should I?" she replied. "I'm not talking to you. We're done."

"We need to talk."

"Are you stupid? I'm not talking to you."

He had to entice her outside. "Don't you want to know what happened to Simon?" he asked.

"Not really. You're here and not in Mexico."

He laughed. "Don't you want to know what happened to the bounty money?"

There was silence for a moment. He knew she was thinking it over. "Come outside." He really didn't think she would listen, but finally, she came to the door, the shotgun still in her hand.

"All right, I'm here. Make it quick."

"Where are your sisters?" he asked, feeling vulnerable, expecting an attack at any moment.

She frowned. "Why?"

"Because I want you to come to town with me."

"Is that why you brought two horses? You wasted your time. I'm not leaving here with you. Must I keep repeating, we're done."

The only way to lure her out the door was to entice her, but he wasn't ready to reveal the big surprise just yet. "If you want to know about the bounty money, you have to go to town with me."

"I'm going back inside now. I don't have to know what happened to the money."

She was absolutely the hardest headed woman he'd ever met. She would drive a saint to drink. She would drive a nun to curse and a preacher to kill.

He took a deep breath and reached for the lariat he

had at the ready, prepared just in case of this very reaction. Deep down he'd know she wouldn't make this easy, and he couldn't blame her. He was to blame for her reaction, and for that he felt sad. "Damn woman, you would try the patience of a saint."

She smiled and crossed her arms. "I aim to please."

He pulled the rope off his saddle and her eyes widened.

"Oh, no. We're not doing this again." She turned to go back into the house just about the time the rope whirled over her head, wrapping around her middle, trapping her arms. With a clang, the shotgun fell to the ground.

Zach pulled the rope tight, effectively pinning her arms to her sides. He jumped off his horse and quickly tied the knots.

Curses flew from her mouth. She was using cuss words he'd never heard before. Naughty words he didn't even know existed.

"Damn it, Zach. Enough. We're finished. I'd turn you in to the law, but…"

The laugh escaped, and he knew if she could have, she would have belted him one by now. "Yeah, I know I'm the law. Now, honey, if we ever have children together, I'm going to insist you clean up your language."

"There is no chance of that, cowboy," she screamed. "In fact…" She started cursing at him again.

"Language, sweetie, language. You wouldn't do this the easy way. But we are going to Zenith. At least when I take you to town, you'll have your clothes on. That's more than what you did for me."

"You brought that on yourself. I will kill you, Zach

Gillespie. I will tie you up and then slowly peel your skin off, until you are begging me to put a bullet in your brain. Gladly, I will say no."

He grinned at her. "Vindictive, aren't we? If you would just listen to reason without me having to tie you up, we'd already be on our way. But, oh no, I can see there is probably going to be a lot of rope in our future."

"What are you talking about? Have you lost your mind?" she asked. "The heat must be getting to you."

He shook his head, wanting to say so much, but knowing he should wait. "Do you want to ride in the saddle the correct way or do you want me to just throw you over the top of the horse?"

"I don't want to go anywhere with you," she spat out. "In fact, if you untie me, I'll forget this ever happened, but if not…"

He ignored her, not afraid of her in the least. "Choose now, or I will throw you over the back of the horse. We are going to town. Together. Today."

Her green eyes flashed with enough anger he knew he needed to keep away from her, or she'd take him down any way she could.

"Oh, all right. I want to sit in the saddle the correct way. Why are we going to town?"

"You'll see." He helped her into the saddle then took the reins from her and led the horse over to his own. After climbing on, he gave his horse a kick, and they started down the lane into town.

"I have waited for you to come in to town for two weeks. Where have you been?" he asked, knowing he couldn't have waited another day. He'd missed her.

"I've been at home, cowboy. I'm a farmer, when I'm not out chasing criminals."

"Yes, but even farmers come to town sooner or later."

Their horses plodded along the road, and for a moment, he thought they were going to have a nice, pleasant conversation.

"I didn't want to see you," she said softly.

"God, I could hardly wait to see you. I've missed you, Meg. I lay awake at night remembering then fall asleep dreaming of you."

Her brows drew together in a frown. "You can stop sweet-talking me. We're done."

"You have every right to be done with me. You've been a patient woman who has put up with more than her share of stupidity from this cowboy. But the day you rode down that dusty road and out of my life, I woke up," he said softly. "I realized what I'd lost when I chose Simon over you."

Watching her leave had ripped whatever was left of his heart completely out of his chest. Realizing he had to save his self-worth and integrity if he wanted to live with himself and have Meg in his life, he would have to turn his brother in.

Their horses clopped along the road into town.

"Did some bird come down and wallop you in the head? Did lightening strike and give you a jolt? Or maybe some outlaw finally beat the crap out of your brains and cleared your thinking?"

He laughed. "God, woman, our life will never be boring, will it?"

"What do you mean our life? You're assuming a lot."

Yes, most definitely he was assuming she would forgive him. He needed that like he needed his next breath. "By the way, my brother Simon is in jail."

She didn't respond, and he couldn't help but think he'd ruined their chances of being together.

There was silence for a long time as they rode along the dusty trail into town, their horses moving slowly in the heat.

"Did he get caught on his way to Mexico?"

"No, I hauled his ass in to the next town and turned him in. It was the hardest thing I've ever done, but it was right."

Meg didn't say a word. The only sound the rest of the way into town was the clip-clop of their horses' hooves.

When they got to the edge of town, he stopped. "If you will ride the rest of the way with me, I'll take the rope off. But you have to ride into town with me."

She frowned at him. "What have you done, Zach? What do you want to show me?"

He smiled. "I've got your curiosity up now. You'll have to come into town to see." He untied the knots from around her wrists, her body, and even her arms. He handed her the reins. "You double cross me and I will bring you back in to town in your bloomers."

Meg smiled, her green eyes lighting up. "You'd have to catch me first, cowboy."

"Be careful or I'll take you up on that offer."

Maybe he was finally starting to tear down that fort she'd built around her heart. Maybe she was starting to see he'd done what he said he was going to do. He'd taken his brother to the sheriff.

She clucked to her horse, and together, the two of them rode side by side. He was watching her face when they turned the corner and she saw the sign. She let out a gasp.

"Oh, my God," she cried. "My dress shop, Meg's

Creations. You remembered."

They pulled up in front of the store, and for a moment, she sat there staring at the sign, her eyes wide, her mouth open. Finally, he helped her alight from her horse. The feel of her waist between his palms had his heart racing. He took her by the hand and led her up the few stairs, tears welling up in the corner of her eyes. When he opened the door, the green dress she'd worn that night so long ago was hanging on a chair in the corner.

"My dress," she cried and ran to the garment, touching the fabric lovingly.

He watched her face and could see the happiness glowing on her cheeks. It made him feel good that he'd made her happy.

Slowly, she turned to face him, confusion reflected in her gaze. "Zach, I don't know what to say," she said, glancing around the room.

He walked over to her and dropped down on one knee. She gasped, her eyes widening. "Meg, the last few weeks with us together on the trail has made me realize you make me a better man. You help me see my weaknesses. You make me stronger. You support me and prop me up when I need strength. But most of all, you've captured my heart. I've fallen madly, deeply, in love with you, and I can't imagine spending another day on earth without you by my side as my wife."

Tears rolled down her cheeks as she stared at him. Her green eyes were glistening with what looked like happiness.

"To show you my love, I wanted to give you your dream. This building is ours, if we want to rent it. You can have your dress shop down below, and upstairs are living quarters for us and the family I hope we someday will have. If you love me, then please be my wife. Spend the rest of your life with me by your side."

She pulled him to his feet and fell into his arms. "I love you, Zach. I've been miserable these last few weeks without you, not knowing what you'd done. I believed you would make the right choice, but then I heard nothing. I never doubted you were a good man, but I knew you loved your brother."

"You believed in me, when I didn't believe in myself. You knew I would make the right choice." As much as he loved his brother, the decision she'd forced him to make was the best one for Zach and for Simon.

"I love you, Zach. I want more than anything to be your wife."

His mouth covered hers in a kiss that swept her up off her feet and pressed her body tight against his. Oh God, this was what he'd missed—her love, her strength of character, and her love of family. Zach knew that without Meg's love, he would never be as strong a man. This woman had made him tough, and he could only hope he would prove as good a husband to her as he knew she would be a wife to him.

Their lips came apart.

"The bounty money," he said.

She frowned. "We didn't expect any money."

He reached in his pocket and pulled out the cash. "It's yours. You caught Simon. You deserve the bounty."

"It'll almost pay off the note," she gasped.

He smiled. "I know."

She rained kisses on his face, and he laughed with pleasure. "One small request."

"What, cowboy?"

"I tied you up last. Can we end it there?"

She laughed. "As long as you don't give me a reason to tie you up, then we're good."

"Boy, if there isn't a threat in there, I'm not sheriff."

She whispered in his ear, "Maybe I'll let you tie me up in the bedroom."

"No way, I want your hands free and on me."

Their lips met again, and Zach knew he'd made the right decision. He'd chosen love over family.

The End

Thank You For Reading!

Dear Reader,

I hope you enjoyed *Deadly* as much as I loved writing this story. Westerns have always been one of my favorite stories and I wanted to portray strong women taking charge of their life. The idea of a woman who enjoyed lipstick back in this time period intrigued me and I wanted to make it challenging for her, so she's a bounty hunter. Annabelle's story, Dangerous will soon be available.

I have one small request. If you're inclined, please leave a review. Whether or not you loved the book or hated, it-I'd enjoy your feedback.

Reviews are difficult to obtain and have the power to make or break a book. If you'd like to learn about my new releases as soon as possible, please sign up for my newsletter at:

http://www.sylviamcdaniel.com/newsletter/

Reading one of my books is like spending time with me, and I just want to say Thank you from the bottom of my heart.

Sincerely,

Sylvia McDaniel

Author Bio

Sylvia McDaniel

Sylvia McDaniel is a best-selling, award-winning author of western historical romance and contemporary romance novels. Known for her sweet, funny, family-oriented romances, Sylvia is the author of The Burnett Brides a western historical western series, The Cuvier Widows, a Louisiana historical series, and several short contemporary romances.

Former President of the Dallas Area Romance Authors, a member of the Romance Writers of America®, and a member of Novelists Inc, her novel, A Hero's Heart was a 1996 Golden Heart Finalist. Several other books have placed or won in the San Antonio Romance Authors Contest, LERA Contest, Golden Network Finalist and a Carolyn Readers Finalist.

Married for nearly twenty years to her best friend, they have one dachshund that reigns as Queen Supreme Dog and a good-looking, grown son who thinks there's no place like home. Sylvia loves gardening, shopping, knitting and football (Cowboys and Bronco's fan), but not necessarily in that order.

Currently she's written eighteen novels and is hard at work on number nineteen. Be sure to sign up for her newsletter to learn about new releases, contests and every month a new subscriber is entered into a drawing for a free book.

You can write to Sylvia at P.O. Box 2542, Coppell, TX 75019 or visit her website.

Dangerous

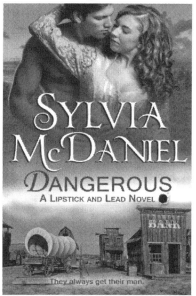

Chapter One

Annabelle McKenzie strode down the wooden sidewalk on her way to the bank. As the family bookkeeper for their bounty hunting business, Lipstick and Lead, it was her responsibility to make certain the bank loan was paid, the farm continued to operate, and supplies were bought, while her sisters had all the fun chasing bad guys and bringing them to justice. Her sisters earned the money, and Annabelle made certain they had a home to return to.

After their father died, they'd learned his profession

out of desperation and become bounty hunters. The job paid better than being a waitress or a seamstress or even a housekeeper. And you only had to answer to the men captured and brought to justice.

Not the randy hands of the owner of a business or his employees.

Living on a farm alone, taking care of cattle and chickens and gardening, was enough to make any person question her sanity. In the last year, Annabelle had begun to regret agreeing to take care of their land, while her sisters did the hunting.

She longed for adventure, excitement, danger. Something more challenging than shoveling manure. Only, her sisters disagreed. Meg and Ruby wanted her to remain on the farm.

Hogwash! It was someone else's turn to babysit the chickens, harvest the garden, and chase the stray cows.

This morning, she'd stopped at the sheriff's office and picked up the latest wanted posters. Tonight, when she got home, she was going to make her sisters understand she needed to get away from the braying of cattle and the collecting of eggs.

Slap her silly, but she was done!

Deep in thought about how she would explain to them she craved adventure and longed for excitement, she rounded the corner to enter the bank and slammed into the hard chest muscles of a large dark-haired man. The scent of soap and campfire smoke spiraled through her straight to her center. This was a manly man and Lord knew, they were scarce in Zenith, Texas. Where had he come from?

His hat was pulled low over his face, and he grabbed her by the arms, halting her progress. Her head fit just below his chin. She looked up at his strong, rugged jaw, and serious face.

Long black lashes blinked over emerald eyes as he gripped her arms. "Slow down," he said in a deep husky drawl. He kept his head down, barely looking at her. "There's still plenty of cash left in the bank."

What a condescending, egotistical, handsome renegade. Not an "I'm sorry" or "Excuse me", but rather a crass remark about the money in the bank. "Maybe you should watch where you're going."

She tilted her head and stared into those dark forest eyes. There was something about him that seemed familiar, yet she couldn't place him. She'd seen his face. She stared up at him. "You're tall enough you should be able to see a woman coming."

He nodded, and she stared at the way his shirt fit his strong shoulders and muscled arms. And his lips were full and tempting, made for kissing.

"You're right, ma'am. I should see a small package like you, barreling around a blind corner. Maybe I need to replace my spectacles with a pair that can see through walls," he said, releasing her arms.

"Maybe you do," she said, knowing the oversized giant was smarting off to her. He wasn't wearing spectacles. Where had she seen him before? "What's your name?"

A sly smile turned up the corners of his full, luscious lips. "Why? You plan on having me arrested for running into you?"

The man had an ornery mouth, and she was just the woman to give it right back.

"Maybe," she said. "I know the sheriff well. It would serve you right for being belligerent and disrespectful."

He smiled a wickedly sly grin that sent tingles through her. "You have a really *nice* day."

His voice was dripping with sweet sarcasm that made her feel like she'd eaten too many cookies. Tipping his black hat at her, he sauntered out the door.

Like a kick from a bull, it hit her.

He was on one of the wanted posters she had out in her saddle bags.

For a moment, she stood there stunned, wanting to grab him by the arm and haul him down to the sheriff's office. He was getting away, and yet, part of her wasn't certain he really was a criminal. What if her imagination was stampeding with ideas, trying to get her out of this one horse town?

But what if this was her chance. Her opportunity to show her sisters she could do more than just watch the cows munch grass. She had bounty hunter blood flowing in her veins. She could catch criminals just as well as they could.

Two hundred dollars lay in her satchel that she'd been going to deposit into their account. One more payment toward paying off the bank note. They only needed a little more, and then the old place would be theirs.

But she didn't have time to make a deposit. She had a criminal to catch.

She hurried out the door and watched as the man walked down the street toward the mercantile. She hurried to her horse that she'd left tied up on Main Street. Opening the leather bags, she thumbed through the papers. The third one she came to had a picture of her man. *Beau Samuel – Wanted for Bank Robbery. Five Hundred Dollar Reward.*

Oh, my God, she'd just run into him at the bank. He was planning on robbing the Zenith Savings & Loan.

She checked her purse, finding her six-shooter resting beside her little pot of lipstick. The bounty was more than enough to pay off the bank. Meg could start her dress shop. And Annabelle would have a little adventure in her dull, boring life.

Excitement tingled down her spine and flooded her nerves like a welcome ray of sunshine. A wide smile spread across her face. This was going to be so much fun. She'd follow Mr. Samuel, and before he left town, he'd be in her custody, and she'd be the heroine who saved the day.

In one afternoon, she would accomplish what Meg and Ruby had taken all year trying to do.

He'd disappeared inside the mercantile. She'd be waiting for him when he came out.

*

Beau Samuel looked around the mercantile. Quickly he replenished his supplies and headed out the door. The faster he got out of this one horse town and to Fort Worth the better. Hopefully, without any run-ins with the law. That wanted poster was like a rock hanging around his neck. Dangerous and deadly.

One wrong move and he'd find himself in the calaboose.

Opening the door, he stepped around to the back of the building where he'd tied his horse. The sound of a gun clicking had his breath freezing in his lungs, his fingers twitching near his sidearm.

"Beau Samuel, you're wanted for robbery."

That same aggravating female he'd met at the bank stood behind him with a gun cocked and loaded. He whirled around, grabbed her hand holding the gun, and wrapped his other arm around her, bringing her into his side. "Now, sugar, you know better than to point a gun at a man."

They had a silent tug of war over the gun, and finally, he wrenched the weapon free of her fingers. The sweet scent of roses surrounded the beauty. Her red-gold curls were the type that a man would love to run his hands through, but instead, here he was wrestling her for a gun.

What kind of woman was she?

"Damn it," she said. "I'm going to scream my head off, if you don't let go of me and give me my weapon back."

He shoved the gun into his pocket on the other side of his pants, out of her reach. "I wouldn't recommend doing that unless you want me to silence you with a kiss."

Her blue eyes widened, and she tried to take a step away from him, but he held her firmly in place.

"Besides, I'm not the Beau Samuel that's wanted."

"Your face is on the wanted poster."

"It's a mistake," he said, enjoying the feel of her body against his.

"Yeah, and you're a rich cattleman who owns half of Texas. Believe me, I've heard enough tall tales to know when someone's talking out the corner of his mouth. You, sir, are a liar and a thief."

He laughed, gazing down at her, enjoying her pert little nose turned up in a scornful snit. "You get up this morning and have a dose of vinegar to begin your day?"

"Actually, I had two. One is Meg and the other is Ruby."

"Oh, your vinegar has names," he said, walking her away from the mercantile toward his horse. If he could get to his horse, he'd leave this sassy miss behind after he emptied the chamber of her six-shooter. There was no need for her to put a bullet in him. This could be handled quickly once he reached Sadie.

"No, they're my bounty hunter sisters, and you're being served up next."

He laughed. "Sugar, if they are as easy to disarm as you, then you tell them to come on and we'll have a party."

"Oh, it's going to be a party all right." She slapped his hand off her shoulder and wrapped it behind his back, tugging upwards.

He knew she thought she had him in a hold, and he decided to let her think she could get away with it until they reached his horse. Glancing around, he spotted Sadie.

"Hey, that hurts," he said, as the woman tugged on the hold she thought she had him in. It was then that he noticed they were two doors down from the sheriff's office. Dang, now was not the time or the place to draw attention.

Oh no, this wasn't going to happen like she wanted. He had business to attend to that didn't include a stay in the calaboose.

Quickly, he twirled her around, releasing his pent-up arm then slammed her against the wall of the bank. Her sapphire eyes widened, and she gazed at him as he leaned into her, not caring that anyone could see them. In fact, he hoped it looked like a lovers' embrace.

"You know your smart mouth has tempted me all morning. First in the bank and now out on the street. I've taken your gun away. I'm not going to the sheriff's office with you. Now unless you want me to kiss you senseless here in a back alley off Main Street, then I think we need to have a parting of the ways."

She raised her knee and jammed it into his groin, knocking the breath out of him as the world spun crazily, his privates slamming him with pain as his lungs gasped for air.

"Damn it," he groaned, slumping over. The woman packed a nasty punch in that knee.

While he leaned against the wall, gasping for breath, she whispered, "Why would I kiss a man like you, wanted by the law?"

Grabbing his hand, she tried to pull him down the wooden sidewalk. She stopped and considered him. "You're looking a mite peaked."

"Give me a moment, I can't move. You knocked my man parts into next week."

She smiled at him sweetly, and he just shook his head. Where in the world had this woman come from and how did he get rid of her? She was trouble and he didn't need the aggravation. He should have already been on the road by now.

"You go get the sheriff. I'll wait right here."

"There you go telling tall tales again."

"Does it look like I'm capable of walking right now? Do you think I could get away if I wanted to?" He leaned over and moaned more for effect. The time to leave this town with the hair on was now. He'd be up and on his horse before she could get the sheriff out the door.

Her sapphire blue eyes drew together in a frown. She was a beautiful woman, but he didn't have time to play parlor games. There was a gang hot on his trail. But she appeared to be taking the bait. Just a little bit more and he'd have her on the hook.

"You might have to get me a doctor. I think you broke something."

"Oh, good grief. Stay here and I'll get the sheriff. He can determine if you need a doctor."

He watched her hurry down the wooden sidewalk. When she got to the door, she stood there for a moment and called into the office.

He didn't waste any time. He rose, took the three steps to his horse, and jumped on—pain radiating through him when his crotch met the saddle. Quickly, he pulled out the woman's gun, emptied the chamber and threw the weapon in the dirt where it landed with a thunk.

Good riddance!

Backing up his horse, he turned and galloped down the street, making a right at the first street he came too. He'd meander his way through town before taking the road that would get him out of this hellhole town.

No wonder that beautiful woman was alone. That sweet face had a tongue that could lash a man into submission or charm him into giving her what she wanted. He needed to put as much distance as possible between them.

Finally, on the edge of town, he kicked Sadie in the sides.

Somehow, he had to reach Fort Worth. He could only hope the Harris gang and him didn't meet up along the road or he would be a dead man.

Kicking his horse, he rode at a fast-paced trot. He wanted to put a lot of distance between him and Zenith, Texas, before the moon rose.

An hour later, shadows fell across the road, and he knew nightfall would soon arrive. He could continue on, but now a gray horse with a woman rode behind him. She'd been back there for over an hour. and every time he glanced back, she appeared a little closer. Could she be following him on purpose or was it happenstance that they were going the same direction? He turned off the trail behind some trees and waited.

He watched as she turned into the trees. Oh yeah, she was following him. Had that shewitch he'd just dumped in town not given up? That woman had been nothing but trouble. His nuts still ached from the power of her knee.

*

Annabelle meandered through the trees, leading her horse in the general direction of the ruthless outlaw. What made him decide to get off the trail just as the sun set? Was he making camp for the night or had he spotted her?

She rode along trying to catch a glimpse of him, but darkness was quickly falling and the idea of sitting in the dark without a fire was not conducive to sleep. Finding Beau Samuel would have to wait until morning.

Pulling her horse to a stop, she slid off the animal and tied him to a tree. In the darkness, she gathered enough wood to last her until morning and set about making a fire.

Their Papa had taught them to always carry flint, a few rations and a canteen of water, but that was all she had. She needed to catch this criminal and get back to town. She wasn't prepared for a lengthy trip.

And Beau certainly hadn't proved to be as easy as she'd thought. She hoped by now she would be home, sitting at the table telling her sisters all about catching her first bounty. But oh no, they would be worried and angry and frustrated that she hadn't let them know where she was going.

She built up twigs and dried leaves and struck her flint to the material. Soon, she had a roaring fire blazing, casting light. For a moment, she just sat and contemplated her situation.

Maybe she'd left a little too hasty. She was without rations, she had enough money on her to be considered dangerous, and she was following a wanted criminal alone. A dangerous man. A bank robber.

Wouldn't he just love to rob her and leave her dead along the trail?

The brush rustled behind her and she froze. Her heart pounded in her chest, her blood rushing through her. Of all the stupid, rookie mistakes, she realized she'd left her gun in her saddle. No protection, except the small pistol strapped to her pantaloons.

Rising slowly from the ground, she turned and watched as a cotton-tailed rabbit hopped from one bush to the next, hurrying when he saw her standing there.

She breathed a sigh of relief and shook her head. Relaxing would be difficult, but she could expect animal sounds all night long. There was nothing to fear, but she'd get her gun just the same.

Just as she relaxed, the sound of a gun hammer being drawn back sent terror freezing her lungs as panic pumped her blood.

"You planning on arresting me while I sleep?" a deep voice drawled.

Beau Samuel, bank robber, handsome hunk, breathed in her ear, sending a trickle of awareness through her. Sometimes the best offense was to act dumb.

She whirled around and came face-to-face with the man from the bank. "What are you doing?"

"I'm trying to find out why you're following me. You think you can tie me up and haul me back to town?"

"I didn't know you were out here."

"Liar," he said his lips turned up in a smile that any other time she might have found attractive.

"Where's your good friend the sheriff?"

"We spread out. He should be along any minute now."

"Liar."

"Do you like that word?" She shrugged. "Don't be surprised when he comes riding in here."

"I just call it like I see it. You're lying. You just don't give up, do you?"

"Why should I?" Annabelle said, staring at him trying to muster courage.

"What's your name Miss Smart Mouth?"

"Annabelle McKenzie, bounty hunter."

He threw back his head and roared with laughter.

"I'm taking you in," she said incensed that he would laugh at her.

"I outweigh you, I have a gun pointed on you, and I'm stronger than you. Sugar, this is a battle you're not going to win."

"And I'm smarter than you."

He shook his head. "You keep thinking that."

Glancing down at his gun, she looked up at him. "You really think a big strong man like you needs that gun pointed at me?"

"Yeah, I do," he said. "You're dangerous."

"Are you headed to Mineral Wells?" she asked, wanting to know where he was headed in case she lost him. Because she had no intentions of letting him get away a second time.

"No."

"Then why are you on this road?"

"Lady, it's none of your business why I'm on this road." He shook his head. "Wait a minute. I'm asking the questions, not you."

She smiled at him.

"I'll just have to go through your saddlebags to see what I can learn about you."

Thank God, she'd strapped the money in a secret pouch inside her skirt. He couldn't find it. If he did, he'd steal it, and then Meg and Ruby would be furious that she'd lost some of their bounty money. And she couldn't blame them.

"Let me tell you what you're going to find," she said. "Empty bags."

"Liar." He frowned at her.

She shrugged. "Believe what you want. I'd gone into town to buy some supplies. There's nothing in those saddlebags, except for some feminine things I need. Do you understand?"

Come on, she thought, he didn't appear to be that dense.

His eyes widened. "Oh."

"Yes, I thought you wouldn't want to embarrass yourself by going through those rags."

His brow drew together. "Lady, for some reason I think you couldn't tell the truth if it slapped you upside the head."

In two long strides, he reached her horse and drew open the first saddlebag. It contained the wanted posters. *Dang! Dang! Dang!*

Why had she thought this would be so easy?

He pulled them out and his was on top. He held it up.

"You know, I don't think the artist caught my best side? Do you?"

She frowned. "He left off your horns."

A smile spread across his face as he laughed and shook his head. "Woman, you have a smart mouth, and it's going to get you killed," he said. "I was hoping you'd learned a lesson this afternoon and wouldn't follow me."

"There's five hundred dollars riding on your head. I'd follow you a long ways trying to earn that cash."

"Are you hungry? Do you need the money?"

"No," she said, surprised.

"Then why are you out chasing outlaws for money? It seems to me a woman like you would have a husband and a passel of kids by now."

The gun in his hand was pointed at her midsection and that made her uneasy. It could so very easily go off.

"Who says I don't?"

He considered her comment, staring at her like he wasn't certain if she was telling the truth or yet another lie. "Maybe your husband is waiting somewhere up the road and together the two of you were going to make some extra cash."

"Oh, he's waiting somewhere up the road, that's for certain."

The idea sounded good, and if he were stupid enough to believe it, then she'd let him. So far her luck with men hadn't been good. One wife-cheating restaurant owner and nothing else. Was she ugly as sin or unappealing in some way?

He shook his head. "Why would a man send a woman alone to capture me? None of this is making sense."

She smiled and cocked her head. "Maybe I'm just a

lonely woman trying to get home. Maybe I'd forgotten all about our little run-in behind the sheriff's office."

"Liar." He gazed at her, his eyes a deep dark green that shone brightly in the firelight. And those dark lashes, they could flutter and set a girl's heart quivering. "And you're not too good at it."

"Why thank you. I've never wanted to be known as a woman who could lie well."

God, if she could just get out of this. If she could somehow turn the guns on him, tie him up, then drag him back to Zenith and collect her bounty, she'd never do this again. She'd leave bounty hunting to Meg and Ruby and go back to taking care of cows. Smelly, stinking, mooing cattle, which didn't have the sense to get out of the rain.

"So, what's it going to be, sweetheart? Are you going to tell me the truth or am I going to have to beat it out of you?"

Beat it out of her? Really? Of course, he was a wanted outlaw. A dangerous man who could hurt her. But then again, was he just trying to scare her?

"Tell me about the beating. What exactly would you do to me? Not that I'm lying to you, but I'm just considering all my options here," she said, hoping he was trying to intimidate her and wasn't serious about harming her. From their interaction, he seemed more of a smart aleck than a truly evil man.

He frowned at her and shook his head. Taking a step toward her, he stood close enough she was forced to look up. "Lady, I should have known you were going to be trouble when I ran into you at the bank."

"Did you rob that bank?" she asked.

"Hell, no."

"Are you planning on robbing the bank?"

"There you go again, asking the questions. I'm in charge here. I'm the one with a gun pointed at you. I'm threatening to beat you."

She shrugged. "I just wanted to know the answer to my questions. I mean, you're wanted for robbing a bank. You could have been scouting out our little bank. I have money in there. I may need to withdraw it all before I see you in town again."

He shook his head. "Answer my question."

"Could you repeat the question? I've forgotten it since we started talking."

"Why are you following me?"

"Simple. Five hundred dollars. You're my bounty."

He didn't respond, but grabbed her arm and then dragged her over to his waiting horse. With the gun still pointed on her, he reached inside and pulled out some rope.

"What are you doing?"

He didn't say a word, but shoved his gun into his holster and spun her around like she was a spindle top, tugged her arms behind her back, and tied her wrists together.

"Why are you tying my hands? It's very uncomfortable." This wasn't good. This wasn't good at all. She needed her hands available to fight him off. To get her gun. To escape and come back with her sisters. She should have gotten Ruby and Meg before coming out on this trip.

"I'm not interested in your comfort."

"Why are you so mean? Are you proving to me that you can be a bad guy?"

Beau stopped and looked at her. A smile lifted one corner of his mouth. "Sugar, I don't have to prove anything to you. I know I'm one mean son of a bitch. And you want to take me in to the sheriff. Did you think I was going to faint and say please take me to my hanging?"

She shook her head. "A girl can hope."

He chuckled then reached down and traced his finger along her mouth. "You've got one smart mouth."

A shiver trickled down her spine, igniting areas of her body she'd not experienced before. She didn't know if it was fear or some other emotion that she hadn't yet been able to identify.

How was she going to get out of this while she was tied up? She'd left a note in the sheriff's office when she'd gone in to get Zach, but he was long gone and the office was empty. Hopefully, the sheriff would be on their way in the morning. She would do her best to ride this out until then.

Beau didn't say a word but marched her back to the campfire. "Get comfortable. It's going to be a long night."

"I need a bedroll."

He glanced over at her horse. "You don't have one?"

"No, but you do," she said with a smile.

"Who rides out without a bedroll? Do you have any supplies? Anything?" he asked, staring at her like she was crazy.

"Yes, I've got a few supplies."

"You followed me on a whim. Greenhorn mistakes like that can cost you your life."

"I'm not a greenhorn," she spit out.

"Well then, you're not very smart."

Annabelle had to bite her lip to keep from saying anything. She'd followed him without much thought as to her actions. Maybe it wasn't the smartest thing she'd ever done, but he'd have to torture her before she'd ever admit to her error.

He got up and marched over to his horse and pulled off his bedroll. He came back to the fire and spread it out. "We'll share."

"No. We won't."

"Your husband wouldn't approve?"

"Lay a hand on me and my husband will beat you until you're talking out of the other side of your mouth." She turned her back on him. "You're sleeping on the ground, and I'm taking the bedroll."

He stared off into the night, a frown on his forehead, like he was deep in thought. Suddenly he grabbed her hand and held it up to the firelight. She watched with trepidation as his lips curled up in a smile. "I don't think you're married. There's no ring. No shadow of a former ring. There's no man waiting down the road for you. You're alone."

"Not for long. My sisters are on their way, and they'll be bringing the law."

"Well then, I'll be sure to leave you tied up where they can find you."

"You wouldn't."

"I would." He leaned back against his saddle, closed his eyes and pulled his hat low. "Good night, bounty hunter."

"You bastard."

He chuckled. "Such a nasty, sassy mouth. Makes me want to kiss it and make it sweeter."

—— end of excerpt ——

Coming Soon

The Rancher Takes a Bride

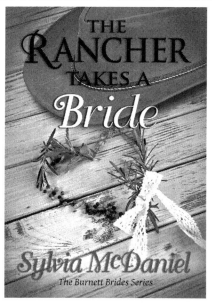

In Fort Worth, Texas, Rose Severin, runs a seance parlor where she speaks to the dead or at least she pretends to until she can earn enough money to get out of this cowboy town and become a famous actress like her mother. Travis Burnett is resolved to rid the western town of imposters like Rose. But Eugenia thinks the fiery Rose is just the woman for her obstinate son. She schemes to keep Rose at the family ranch where Travis soon realizes that the supposed spiritualist is more than just a pretty swindler.

The Outlaw Takes A Bride

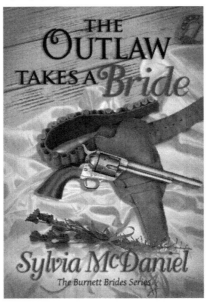

Everyone deserves a second chance. After the death of his best friend in the Battle of Atlanta, Tanner Burnett walked away from the civil war. Now, ten years later, he runs with the Sam Bass gang, trying to escape the memories of that horrible battle. But when a stagecoach robbery goes bad, he rescues injured Elizabeth Anderson, wanting only to get her to a doctor and rejoin his gang. But the injured beauty needs a nurse and Tanner is unprepared for the way Beth soothes his wounded heart and heals his spirit. Until he takes her to Fort Worth, Texas and learns she's his brother's mail order bride.

Books By Sylvia McDaniel

Western Historicals
A Hero's Heart

The Burnett Brides Series
The Rancher Takes a Bride
The Outlaw Takes a Bride
The Marshal Takes A Bride
The Christmas Bride

Boxed Set
The Burnett Brides

Lipstick and Lead
Desperate
Deadly
Dangerous – Coming Soon
Daring – Coming Soon

Southern Historical Romance
A Scarlet Bride

The Cuvier Women
Wronged
Betrayed
Bequiled

Boxed Set
The Cuvier Women

Sylvia McDaniel

Contemporary Romance
My Sister's Boyfriend
The Wanted Bride
The Relationship Coach

Boxed Set
Kisses, Laughter & Love

Christmas Romance
The Reluctant Santa

Short Sexy Reads
Racy Reunions Series
Paying For the Past
Cupid's Revenge – Coming Soon

Manufactured by Amazon.ca
Bolton, ON

37864031R00164